ILLUSIONS

Rewarding herself with a luxury cruise, Private Investigator Alexandra Best hadn't envisaged meeting Leanora, an elderly psychic who warned her of an impending death. Leanora herself is the victim of her own prophecy and when her daughter, Moira, begs Alex to investigate she is forced to reveal that someone has been stalking both mother and daughter. Taking on the case Alex discovers that Leanora was not the harmless, ethereal old woman she appeared to be but had planned elaborate blackmailing scams involving people in high places. When Moira is also murdered, the search for the culprit brings Alex to the brink of disaster...

ILLUSIONS

ILLUSIONS

by

Jean Saunders

Magna Large Print Books
Long Preston, North Yorkshire,
BD23 4ND, England.

British Library Cataloguing in Publication Data.

Saunders, Jean
    Illusions.

A catalogue record of this book is
available from the British Library

ISBN 0-7505-1812-X

First published in Great Britain 2000 by Robert Hale Ltd.

Published in Large Print 2002 by arrangement with
Robert Hale Limited

Magna Large Print is an imprint of Library Magna Books Ltd.

Printed and bound in Great Britain by
T.J. (International) Ltd., Cornwall, PL28 8RW

Chapter 1

Alex only noticed the woman properly when she was shown to a place at her breakfast table during the second week of the cruise. She had been aware of her before, but only as one of the faceless others on the luxury ship.

She was the kind of person you registered as a background accessory, like fading wallpaper or uninteresting paintings. She always wore beige or brown, and her hair was the sort referred to as a pepper-and-salt mixture. Whichever of the ship's lounges she visited, she usually sat in a corner like a silent observer, until people with apparently more social graces than Alex joined her out of sympathy.

Even now, sharing a breakfast table, the woman gave Alex no more than the merest hint of a half-smile as if to apologize for being alive at all.

Such subservience was irritating, whatever the reason for it. Alex found herself wondering what the devil had happened to girl-power – or in this instance, middle-aged woman power? God knew Alex herself hadn't particularly courted company on the cruise, but you had to be sociable. In any case, most of the other passengers were in couples, and definitely the wrong side of sixty and she certainly wasn't looking for a fling with any of the crew.

She was here to relax ... and to reward herself for successfully concluding a tricky case ... but she felt glamour personified compared with the little mouse of a woman seated opposite her now. And at nine o'clock on a sunny May morning her own bright red hair and designer black gear made her feel more uncomfortable than worldly-wise.

'Are you enjoying the cruise?' she felt obliged to ask, when the woman said nothing for several minutes.

'Oh yes. Thank you. It's very nice.'

'Good,' Alex said, desperately wishing someone else would join them, but the early onshore day trippers were preparing to leave as the ship eased into the port of Playa Blanca, and most of the others were obviously having a lie-in. She decided not to be uncharitable, although she prayed that because they were two women cruising alone, the dun one wouldn't feel the need to latch on to her at this late stage of the cruise.

'I'm Alexandra Best,' she said helpfully.

'Oh – Leanora Wolstenholme – Mrs,' she added, as if it was an afterthought.

Alex tried not to look surprised at the elegant-sounding name, knowing she had made an instant assessment and got it wrong. She'd have said the dun one was a spinster who had been saving up for years for this cruise – which certainly wasn't cheap – and was tagged with a far more lacklustre name.

She should have known better. In her job, things were rarely what they seemed, which had gone a long way towards making the whole concept of being a private investigator so attractive. She liked intrigue and puzzles and it gave her a heck of a buzz to succeed in solving them.

Oh vanity, thy name is woman, the idiotic misquote flashed through her mind... *And if it was, to hell with it.*

Surreptitiously, she studied her companion with a more practised eye, but nothing about her as she ordered her breakfast so diffidently, made her any more appealing than before. She was almost – well, creepy – in her nonentity. It had the strange effect of making Alex feel stifled.

'Please excuse me,' she said suddenly, leaving half of her toast and marmalade, which would be all to the good of her thighs, she thought nobly. After the mountains of food she had devoured on this holiday, she would need to fast for a month to recover anything like the shape she had before – and

9

that was nothing to write home about, she thought dismally, though it had never seemed to bother any of the opposite sex.

Child-bearing hips was the enthusiastic – and glutinous – term that came to mind ... yuk.

She left the dining-room and went up on deck, absorbing the scenery of Lanzarote. She could almost recite the guidebook's words. The north of the island had a dark, forbidding coastline, due to hundreds of volcanic eruptions in its history, where boiling lava had spewed out. It had not only smothered thirteen villages, but created an extra half mile of land in the ocean before the volcanic masses cooled, leaving part of the island with a strange, moonscape appearance.

Alex felt a delicious shiver at the legend, however true or embellished it was by the locals – or the tourist industry, more like. Loving the thought of the dark side of the island as much as the traditional villages and the man-made resorts. Everything had a darker side, even people. It was what made them interesting, unpredictable, and often frightening.

She brought her thoughts back to the island, wishing they were going to be here longer than one day. There was an organized all-day shore trip, but free time for those who wanted a more leisurely look around.

10

That was for her. She intended hiring a car and going into the interior, where the mountains reared upwards in varying shades of colour.

'Dreary, isn't it?' she heard a cigar-thickened male voice say, as she leaned on the ship's rail.

She took a fraction of a moment before she turned around, knowing who the owner of the voice would be.

This morning he wore a navy blazer with an important-looking badge on the breast pocket, and an immaculate white roll-neck sweater. His trousers were creased so sharply you could cut yourself on them, and his hair was dyed an even more improbable shade of black than usual. Alex wondered if he had it touched up daily in the ship's hairdressing salon. Unless it was a toupee, and Alex found herself mischievously hoping for a gust of wind to test it out.

'Do you think it's dreary, Major?' she said coolly now. 'I find it fascinating.'

She'd be willing to lay bets that he wasn't a genuine major, either ... she squirmed as his calculating eyes looked her over, clearly admiring her fringed, pike-straight red hair and the black sweater and tight-fitting trousers.

In her opinion the outfit was unprovocative, but it was her colouring that made all the difference, and as a fair-weather friend had once said, *'If you've got it, flaunt it, girl, and you've certainly got it, in or out of the clobber!'*

'Once you've travelled the world and seen the rain-forests of Brazil, you tend to find these little ports very ordinary,' the major went on grandly.

'Really. I wonder why you bother to come here, then,' Alex said, her best Sloaney accent sharpening, and hoping it would put him off. To her annoyance it always seemed to have the opposite effect, and he gave a deep chuckle, displaying discoloured teeth from too much tobacco over too many years.

'To meet interesting little ladies like you, my dear.'

She gave him a freezing glance. Talk about delusions of grandeur and self-importance! She was head and shoulders above him in height, and she looked down at him deliberately now.

'I'm sure there are far more suitable ladies on board for a gentleman of your years, Major. Now, if you'll excuse me–'

'Saw you got stuck with the weird one at breakfast this morning,' he said casually.

It wasn't the way he said it, but the words he used ... and since it was normally the other way around, Alex paused.

'Mrs Wolstenholme? Isn't that a little churlish of you?'

And oh boy, who was calling the kettle black *now*, when she had had similar thoughts herself!

But she'd hardly thought this old guy would have given the woman a second glance, or even a first one. A rich widow would have been more to his taste. Alex had seen his predatory glance around the dining-room before he pounced on the most likely ones to bore with his tales of faraway places.

'Wolstenholme?' he almost honked now. 'Is that what she calls herself?'

'Why shouldn't she, if it's her name?' And she had no intention of supplying him with the woman's first name either.

She felt momentarily defensive of Leanora, as if this gigolo was going to target her next – but that was the most unlikely thing of all. He always hovered around the ladies wearing the glitziest jewellery, especially in the small casino where the money flowed most freely. Leanora was obviously not one of those.

Alex hadn't realized just how observant she had been of this pompous oaf – but that went with the job, of course.

'Anyway, why did you call her the weird one?' she went on, unable to resist the question, while despising herself for letting herself be caught like this.

The sun was rising higher in the sky now,

and it was going to be a beautiful day. Even from here, the mountains near this side of the island were becoming bathed in all kinds of fantastic hues. She longed to be among them, isolated in her own hire car, and breathing in the atmosphere of new and unfamiliar surroundings.

'Calls herself a clairvoyant. Didn't you know?'

Alex felt her heart jump. No, she didn't know. And if she had been offered a million pounds to guess the dun woman's background, she would have failed miserably.

'A clairvoyant? Like a medium, do you mean, getting in touch with spirits and suchlike?'

'I suppose so,' the major sniggered. 'Though, the only spirits I'd care to be in touch with are the ones I put down me throat each night, wouldn't you say so, m' dear?'

Alex ignored this. 'I'm sure you're wrong about Mrs Wolstenholme. She's such a quiet little thing—'

'You ask the two old trouts on C Deck then. Pair of old whoozers if you ask me,' he said derisively. 'They consulted her, so-say, on a matter of some missing cash. I daresay her Red Indian guide from the other side supplied the answer. Load of old codswallop, if you ask me.'

As someone else caught his attention, he

went off chuckling, while Alex stared after him, mesmerized. How on earth did he get all this information? He was such an unlikely confidant, although she guessed there were always gullible women, flattered to hear of his adventures.

If the stuff about Mrs W was true, of course, and he wasn't just stringing her a line. She had no truck with anything in the least spooky, though her old sparring partner, DI Nick Frobisher, said that even the police sometimes consulted a medium in difficult cases – strictly unbeknown to the public, of course.

She gave up thinking about any of it as the ship was tied up at the port. Once the landing formalities and the bustle of disembarking were over, she walked briskly along to the nearest car hire place. There were plenty of them, and within half an hour she was in possession of an old Ford Fiesta, and a map that would take her from Playa Blanca into the hinterland of the island.

This was what she had concluded her last big case for, she thought blissfully. Although the intended winter cruise had been put on hold as a small clutch of minor investigations had come in, that she couldn't afford to pass. The fee from the big case had been a good one, but her growing reputation meant that she had to be available whenever new clients called for her services.

It was one of the things the self-help *Manual of Detection* had impressed on would-be private investigators, in the days when she had considered it her bible. Now that she was more streetwise in the ways of villains – and even the deviousness of some of her clients – she was tempted to write a small self-help manual of her own, to put the original author right on a few things.

But he was definitely right about one thing. Treat each case separately, and each client as an individual, for no two were ever the same. Every cheating husband or wife had their own reasons for doing what they did, and their partners had their own expectations for hiring her to find them out. Nothing was ever what it seemed. It was a phrase that Alex never forgot.

As she drove away from the pretty little town of Playa Blanca with a mental reminder to buy some souvenirs later, she found herself thinking about Leanora Wolstenholme, and all she had learned about her that morning. But not the obvious things. She knew them already.

It was that last bit that the major had confided that was so odd. And yet she didn't know why it should be, and she was probably confusing genuine clairvoyants with the fortune tellers at fairgrounds, all gypsy earrings and crystal balls.

She smiled faintly as a vision of an

erstwhile companion flashed into her mind.

'You don't want to have anything to do with that kind of oddball, Alex. It's all balls, anyway.'

Everything was, as far as Gary was concerned... For a moment she felt a tingle in her veins, and in various other places, remembering just how good they had been together for a while. It had been great while it lasted. But not for ever.

Thank God both of them had understood that, and once they had parted he had vanished like one of Leanora's forays into the ether. She shivered, but try as she might during her tour on that long, gloriously hot spring day exploring the darker side of the island, she couldn't get the nondescript woman with the autocratic name out of her mind.

Leanora Wolstenholme, Mrs. It was a strange way to say it, as if the husband was no more than an appendage, when anyone would expect her to be the hanger-on. The tagged-on little wifey to macho-man...

She was doing it again, Alex thought irritably. She was stereotyping the poor woman and being thoroughly sexist into the bargain. Unfortunately, with some people, you couldn't help it. She resolved to be charitable, while cheerfully reminding herself that since there were only two more days left of the cruise, it was unlikely they would meet again.

During the entertainment in the show lounge after dinner that evening, when the ship was once more at sea and heading majestically on its last lap towards Dover, she realized that someone had joined her at the table where several other couples were saying goodnight and moving away.

Alex glanced around, and met the eyes of her breakfast companion. But she wasn't quite so dull now, she thought faintly. Although still basically brown-hued, Mrs W was done up to the nines in a dated cocktail dress and feathery boa that might have done justice to a *Bonnie and Clyde* movie set.

'May I join you?' she said.

'Please do,' Alex said, hoping desperately that people wouldn't think they were travelling together, and ashamed of herself for doing so. Even so ... should she offer to buy her a drink ... or simply concentrate on the showgirls strutting their stuff...?

'I was hoping to have another word with you before the cruise was over,' Mrs Wolstenholme said.

'Were you?' Alex said in surprise, since the conversation at breakfast that morning had been practically nil.

She almost recoiled then as the woman put a skinny hand over hers. Christ, she wasn't a lesbian, was she? It wasn't unheard of on these cruises (or anywhere else), as

Nick Frobisher had pointed out lecherously, while offering to accompany her as her minder.

'I wanted to warn you.'

'Warn me?' Alex said, starting to feel like a parrot.

'You're a good person,' Mrs Wolstenholme observed, her voice even more monotone than Alex remembered. 'I see a golden aura around you, but it can't work miracles, so be on your guard. I see a death–'

'I think you'd better stop right there,' Alex almost snapped. 'I don't like that kind of talk–'

'Oh, please don't be offended. I don't mean to frighten you, and I'm quite sure it's not your death, my dear. But it will touch you in some way, so I felt that I had to alert you. But such visions, however obscure, do leave me very tired, and I'll say goodnight.'

She virtually glided away, leaving Alex speechless. But not with fear. She was enraged that even for a moment she had allowed herself to be caught up in the weirdness of the woman's prophesies. And coming right back down to earth in an instant. The old cow, she thought savagely, wondering how many other people she had scared with her creepy stories. And how many of them had consulted her further, and paid for the privilege? Even as she thought it, her breathing slowed. That was it, of course. You could never trust appearances, and Leanora was probably a con woman.

As such she probably had to be admired for her ingenuity, however grudgingly. Not that Nick would have said so. Nick would have run her in as soon as look at her.

For the first time in ages, she wished he was here. She could do with Latino rough good looks and his no-nonsense police jargon now, telling her she was a nut-case and she was in the wrong business. But she knew that. She had been told it before, but she still did it, because the idea of helping people and solving their mysteries and problems made her a kind of social worker of the best kind, she thought nobly. *Or a bleedin' saint,* as Gary Hollis might have said.

'Got rid of her then, have you?' she heard someone say, and she gave a heavy sigh.

'If you mean has Mrs Wolstenholme gone to bed, then yes,' she told the major pointedly. 'And I'm following her lead.'

'What? Had enough already? A young thing like you?' he leered. 'I thought we might have had a dance.'

'I don't think so,' Alex said. 'I really am too tired.'

'Pity. I used to be quite a mover in my day.'

I'll bet you were, Alex thought, as she went back to her cabin – and not only on the dance floor, you old lech. But she hadn't realized just how tired she was. She couldn't even be bothered to take a shower before falling into bed, and Leanora's flat voice was still disturbingly in her head, warning her to be careful, and that she saw a death.

Alex pulled the coverlet over her head and tried to push her right out of her mind, letting herself be soothed by the gentle throbbing of the ship's engines far below.

'It's not your death, my dear. But it will touch you in some way.' The bloody words kept running through her head and she couldn't get them out, and she resolved to keep as far away from the woman as possible for the rest of the cruise.

Fortunately, she didn't have to. The major, who seemed to know everything, reported that Mrs W had found a new friend, and the two women were seen with their heads close together like two nodding old hens every time Alex glimpsed them, until the ship finally docked at Dover.

Maybe the new friend should be warned, Alex thought, and then shrugged. It was none of her business, and in any case the cruise was almost over.

In the aftermath of a good holiday Alex felt good to be home, viewing her flat with new and appreciative eyes the way you always did when you had been away from some-

21

thing for a while. She had wanted to enjoy her two weeks without getting too attached to any group of people, and she had hopefully managed it without appearing too stand-offish.

Now, she relished being back in her London flat, and rediscovering the familiarity of it all. There was a mountain of mail to answer, and there would be more at her office. She could leave all that for now, but she could never ignore the flashing messages on her answering machine.

She switched it on while she wandered about the flat, dumping her luggage; kicking off her shoes and scattering her clothes, and slipping into her silky kimono in the luxury of being completely alone; making coffee, and drinking it black since there was no milk, and then thinking what the hell, the holiday wasn't over yet, and lacing it with vodka...

The first message on her machine took her by surprise. It was from an old friend coming to town and wondering if they could meet up. Alex sighed, wondering what on earth Rose Harding could possibly be coming to London for. It wasn't that she didn't want to see her again. She remembered her as a scatter-brained girl who lived on a neighbouring farm to Alex's parents.

Rose belonged to another life, and one that Alex had left behind years ago, in the days when she was Audrey Barnes, a Yorkshire lass with a broad Dales accent and no more than a childhood dream of becoming a somebody.

She certainly didn't despise her past, knowing that the past helped to shape the people they became. It was just that she was different now, having shed that part of her life as easily as if it was another skin. The persona of Alexandra Best, private investigator, suited her so much better, particularly since she had achieved it by her own efforts.

And she suspected from the cornfed note in Rose Harding's voice, that she was still the same as she had ever been. But she duly noted down the phone number, and made a mental promise to call her back when she had a moment.

There were a number of boring messages next, telling her that her dry cleaning was ready; and did she want replacement windows? And were there any children in the house, as a photographic firm was doing a fantastic offer for Easter...

A more familiar voice on the machine made her smile. It was rich and dark and sexy and it was Nick's.

'Welcome home, Alex. Good trip? Give me a call when you've had time to recover. I've got things to tell you.'

At the click that ended the telephone call,

Alex fumed. If that wasn't just like Nick, leaving her dangling with the hint of something to tell her that just might be exciting. And he knew damn well she had been born curious...

She was dialling his number on her mobile without even realizing it. He answered briskly, and she knew he was at his desk, and that she shouldn't have called in the middle of his busy day. But so what?

'Nick, it's me. Alex. I'm back.'

'Alex!' The voice became several shades warmer, and she could almost imagine him turning away from his colleagues, smiling into the receiver with that smouldering smile of his, fingers curling around the telephone cord, his long legs stretching out luxuriously in front of him...

God, she must have been more lacking in decent male company than she realized, Alex thought faintly...

'So how was it? Did it come up to expectations? How many conquests did you make?'

At the condescending question, her magnanimity towards him vanished. He was a male chauvinist of the first order, and she snapped back into the phone.

'I might have expected that from you! I didn't go on a cruise just to score–'

'Hard luck. All old codgers, were they?' he said lazily, reading her far too correctly,

24

damn him. 'Never mind. I'll book a table for tonight, since if I know you, you won't bother opening a freezer meal, let alone boil an egg. I'll pick you up around eight o'clock, OK?'

'You've got a bloody nerve—' she began, and then, knowing he was damn right, she laughed.

Besides, she wanted to know whatever it was he had to tell her, and she'd get it far more easily over a meal and a few drinks. And the diet could start tomorrow.

'OK,' she said, and hung up before her curiosity could get the better of her.

When she had sorted out the clothes to be taken to the launderette she switched on the answering machine again. There were a couple more messages, a second one from Nick telling her to call him as soon as she got home – which she wouldn't have done if she'd heard that imperious order...

He arrived promptly at eight o'clock, taking her in his beefy arms and exuding a scent of expensive after-shave that was manly and macho, as befitted a detective inspector, Alex thought, hiding a grin as she was pressed so tightly to his chest that she could hardly breathe.

'My God, I've missed you,' he said, holding her at arm's length when he'd had his fill of kissing and wanted to do his share of looking. 'There's truth in the old saying about absence making the heart grow fonder after all.'

'Pull the other one, Nick,' she said, swiftly reminding herself that he could be as ruthless or as gentle as he chose, whether he was interrogating a suspect or charming a woman. It was part of his skill as a policeman and a man, and he could do it at will.

It would be foolish to be taken in by him when he got that horny look in his eyes that said she was the only one he had ever wanted. She was tired and vulnerable. Even as she thought it, she wondered why, when a holiday was supposed to pep you up. But somehow it hadn't. Not this one.

'All right, so you're not in the mood for seduction,' he grinned back. 'Maybe you will be when you hear what I've got to tell you. Maybe you'll realize you wanted me after all.'

'What do you mean? Don't talk as if I'm losing you.'

'You are. And I didn't mean to blurt it out right away. I meant to ply you with drinks until you couldn't resist me, then bring you home and make wild, passionate love to you–'

'For God's sake, Nick! What's happened?' She twisted out of his arms, empty inside, and she didn't even know why yet.

'I'm being transferred,' he said abruptly.

26

'There's a likely promotion in the offing as well, and I want you to come with me, Alex. You can be part of it.'

'Transferred to where?' she said, unable to think of anything else he said.

She was right. She *was* losing him, and it was an unthinkable prospect. He was her friend, her old reliable, always there when she needed him, at the end of a phone for help and advice and never laughing at her crazy intuitions; well, not often – and preventing her from making a bloody fool of herself on more than one occasion.

'You'd better sit down. You look quite pale under that tan, and I didn't realize the news was going to have such an effect on you, darling,' she heard him say. 'If this means you're going to consider my offer, then I'd better come right out with it. Marry me, Alex, and come to Devon with me.'

He was pushing her down on the sofa before she knew what was happening. His arms were still around her, his lips still seductively close to her mouth as he spoke. He had always been a temptation, even though she had managed to resist him so far, and she closed her eyes for a moment, because in a crazy way it sometimes helped to see things more clearly...

Then she pushed him away.

'This promotion,' she said accusingly. 'I presume it would be more likely to happen

27

if you had a wife, would it?'

She dared him to contradict it, but she knew he wouldn't. They had always been honest with one another, at least on the personal front, and he gave a rueful laugh now.

'OK, so you've seen through me. But haven't I been asking you for ever to marry me–?'

'No. We never had that kind of relationship–'

'We never had any kind of relationship. You always held me off, when you knew how I felt about you – how I feel about you – and maybe I never said it in so many words–'

Alex sighed. 'Nick, I don't want to marry anybody right now. If I did, it would probably be you.'

'My God, that's enough to deflate any man's libido. Have you any idea how maddening that word "probably" is?'

She leaned forward and kissed him. 'Well, just be thankful for small mercies – no slight to your ego intended and take me out to dinner like you promised. Or is that off now? I still want to hear about this transfer to Devon, and exactly when I'm going to lose my best friend.'

And he had always been just that. She had few close friends. In her job it was difficult, so you learned to treasure your trusted best friends, and she would miss him like hell when he was no longer around.

He stood up and pulled her to her feet. 'All right, let's go. And I want to hear all about this cruise, and the people who were on it.'

She discovered that he was leaving in a month's time, and his replacement was moving in before then. By the time they got back to her flat that night, he had promised to introduce Alex to him, but she was aggressively against the whole idea.

'Why would I want to meet him? If he's anything like your pig of a station sergeant, he'll just despise me. Female and a private eye – can there be any two things more guaranteed to rub a copper's nose in it?' she said.

'You'll like this guy, but not too much, I hope,' Nick said, arrogant as ever. 'I knew him slightly some years back so I've no objection to him taking over my patch. His name's Scott Nelson. So now you know all about my plans, you can tell me what's been bugging you ever since you got home. I know there's something.'

'It's nothing.'

'Come on, Alex. I know you too well, remember? Did they show *Titanic* in the ship's cinema or something? Or did some-body come knocking on your cabin door in the middle of the night to spook you?'

She caught her breath. It was that one

word. If he hadn't used it, she might have passed it off. As it was, her hand shook over the coffee pot, and he stilled it with his own.

'What happened, sweetheart?'

'Nothing, and I'm just being stupid, but I suppose I might as well tell you. There was this woman – a clairvoyant by all accounts. I hardly spoke to her, but she gave me the creeps. And I had my suspicions that she might have been a con woman. There was no real reason for it, just an instinct. You know me and instincts! And I'm talking too fast, aren't I?' she finished abruptly.

'What made you think she might have been a con woman?' Nick said, ignoring everything else, and getting to the important bits.

It was part of his stock-in-trade. It was what made him a good copper. A suspect could ramble on for hours, and in the end, Nick would question him on the one point that might have got lost in anybody else's conversation.

'I really don't know,' Alex said more slowly. 'There was just something about her – the ability to merge into the background most of the time, and then becoming animated when she was in conversation with some elderly lady. Not with me, though. She hardly said a word to me, except once.'

'She must have been a good one then,' Nick said lazily.

'A good what?'

'Clairvoyant. She probably saw right through you, darling, and wouldn't have wanted anything to do with a private eye.'

'Now you're worrying me even more,' Alex snapped. 'I never asked her about herself, either, and it was somebody else who told me about her being a clairvoyant.'

'So perhaps this other person told her about you too. Look, forget her and tell me about the rest of the cruise. Or better yet, let's get horizontal instead. I really did miss you, Alex. I missed you like hell.'

He could be very persuasive, and when his voice deepened to a more seductive tone it was enough to make her toes tingle. She was lying half under him on the sofa and before she could gather her senses, his mouth was possessively on hers.

She kissed him back, breathing him in, tasting him. She liked him a lot. More than that. She loved him, in the way you loved your best friend, but not as a lover. He knew that. They both knew it, and after a moment or two she struggled out of his embrace, laughing to take the sting out of her words.

'For God's sake, Nick, I haven't got my breath back yet, and I need some sleep. Go home, and call me tomorrow.'

'And is that your final word?' he said, in his best quizmaster voice.

'*Believe* me it is!'

31

She was still smiling after he had gone, but she really was extraordinarily tired. She felt as if she had run a marathon, which was a laugh in itself, and she silently resolved to get more exercise. She needed to work out at the gym – or maybe just a run around the park, she amended.

She hadn't forgotten any of her karate skills, but a fat lot of good any of it would be if she had to chase after a suspect. It was time to think about work, and she could already feel the surge of anticipation at the thought of tackling a new case.

But when she finally tumbled into bed, she couldn't sleep. In the end she decided to give up and open some of her mail. So far she had managed to ignore it. There was the usual collection of junk mail, a few bills and enough cheques to counteract them, and several letters. One envelope had a Yorkshire postmark, and after a few moments she vaguely recognized the childish handwriting of Rose Harding.

She opened it quickly. She hadn't heard from her in years, and she would decide whether she wanted to pursue the acquaintance after she had read the letter – or to see if she could possibly get out of it. The mild guilt at the thought was magnified as she read the letter, written in one long, non-stop paragraph, the way Rose used to talk.

...You were always so sensible, Audrey – or do I have to call you Alexandra now? Anyway, I'd just like to talk to you, and if you'd come to the clinic with me, I'd be ever so grateful. Auntie's too nervous to come with me, but I need somebody to hold my hand, and I don't know anybody else in London. Oh, but you don't know, do you? After Dad left me all his money, I moved in with Auntie Ruth in York. Then I got this illness, and I can afford the best treatment, but I've already tried everything. I've been to America to see a top specialist, and tried crank diets, and crystal healing, and paid the earth for pills that are still on trial. I've had chemotherapy that made me sick, and I don't want any more, thank you very much. I even went to a psychic in York who was on a tour, but it didn't do any good. None of them did. These people think they know everything, don't they, but they can't cure the common cold, let alone cancer. Then I heard about this clinic in London, and it's just about my last hope. I'm told I've only got weeks rather than months, so I have to get on with it, don't I? I thought you'd have called me back by now, which is why I'm writing to you instead. I have to go to the clinic tomorrow.

Your old friend, Rose.

By the time she had finished reading the rambling letter, Alex was sitting bolt upright up in bed, rigid to her toes, and with tears of shock in her eyes. She felt terrible, knowing she had been trying to get out of meeting this girl at all. Rose had spoken on the answering machine on the day Alex's cruise began, and the letter was dated nine days ago.

There was no way Alex could sleep now. It was nearly midnight, but she had to find out what was happening. She dialled the telephone number at the top of Rose's letter, and after a considerable time, she heard the flat, rasping Yorkshire tones of an elderly woman. She remembered Rose's formidable Auntie Ruth, and for a moment she quailed.

'I'm sorry to bother you at such a late hour,' she stammered, thrown right back to her childhood days. 'But may I please speak to Rose?'

There was silence at the other end, and then the voice spoke harshly again.

'Who is this, please?'

'It's – Audrey – Audrey Barnes, Mrs Harding,' Alex gulped, furious to realize she was lapsing into her own natural dialect, but knowing it was the only way the woman would believe her. 'Rose wrote to me, but I've been away–'

'You don't sound like Audrey Barnes, and we've had enough cranks around here lately.'

'I assure you that I *am*,' Alex said desperately, considering the years she'd denied her own background. 'And what do you mean about cranks?'

'Oh, all that psychic healing nonsense she was getting into and suchlike. But 'tis all too late for that. Rose passed over last week, so you can't talk to 'er, anyway.'

The phone went dead, and Alex stared at it in disbelief. Until today she had forgotten Rose's existence, and now she was dead, and it was hitting her as hard as if she had just lost her best friend.

It was crazy ... but before she could stop herself she was dialling Mrs Harding's number again.

'I'm so sorry, Mrs Harding,' she babbled. 'But this psychic that Rose consulted. It wasn't someone called Leanora Wolstenholme, was it?'

The woman was suddenly bawling down the line at her.

'Whoever you are, stop pestering me. I told you, we've had enough cranks lately. I never heard of any such person as you mention, and the man at the hall was a toady fellow playing on silly girls' emotions. Now don't call me again, or I'll have the police on you.'

'I'm very sorry,' Alex mumbled, but the woman had already gone. And she was putting down the phone with shaking hands

35

and calling herself all kinds of a fool for even thinking there could have been any connection between poor Rose Harding and Leanora Wolstenholme, clairvoyant.

Chapter 2

Within a few days, Alex had managed to put it all into perspective. She had sent Rose's Auntie Ruth a letter of apology and condolence, and a large sheaf of flowers via Interflora for her to deal with as she chose.

She couldn't mention a funeral. It just seemed so awful to connect it with a girl of her own age. Twenty-six, and never been kissed – or anything else, Alex guessed.

Rose had never been attractive to men, and Alex always found it hypocritical to be charitable about anyone in that respect now that Rose was dead. But such circumstances only made you more aware of your own mortality, and of making the most of life while you had it.

Which was why she welcomed DI Nick Frobisher more eagerly than usual when he turned up at her office two weeks later. He was always so healthily alive and ready for a harmless flirtation which always did the old ego good. But he wasn't alone. Accompanying him was the most gorgeous hunk of male that Alex had seen in a long time. And all her senses told her the attraction was mutual.

'If you two would put your eyes back in your heads, I'll introduce you,' Nick said shortly. 'Alex, this is Scott Nelson, and if I had the bloody nerve to say so, I'd tell you to keep your hands off, Scott. But I know the response I'd get from our spiky Alex.'

'Ignore him,' Alex said. She put her hand in the stranger's, and felt instant electricity between them.

He was tall and lean, with vivid blue eyes, and although she had never particularly thought blond men attractive, this one was Robert Redford and Sean Bean all rolled into one. And she was hooked.

'Scott's shadowing me for the next few weeks until I leave for Plymouth,' she heard Nick say.

Lucky you, she thought, hoping she hadn't said it aloud.

'I've heard plenty about you from Nick, Alex,' he said, relaxed and easy. 'I know something of your work, and I'm looking forward to joining forces any time you need any help.'

Alex saw Nick grinning at her, expecting fireworks. If he had said it, she would have riled at once. *Effing nerve, offering to help her, when it was just as likely that she could help the police force.* Her investigations were frequently less obvious, and a damn sight more subtle than a flat-footed copper's... But that was then and this was now.

'I'll keep it in mind, Scott,' she murmured. 'Are you both rushing off, or can I offer you some coffee?'

She was slipping into domestic mode and she knew it. She had a million things to do, and she mentally swept them aside as easily as swatting a fly. But Nick wasn't prepared to let her get away with flirting with his oppo right under his nose.

'We're busy, and we don't have time for idle chit-chat,' he snapped, reducing her offer to that of a girlie coffee-morning. 'I just thought you'd like to know I sussed out your clairvoyant, and she seems OK. She operates in Worthing in one of those back-street seaside places, and there's no record of any shady dealings, so you can stop worrying about her.'

'I wasn't worrying,' Alex said quickly. 'But thanks, Nick. I appreciate it.'

And the last thing she wanted was for Scott to think she was scared of anything spooky. She had to keep her end up. At the thought, she went off at a tangent. Was he married, or attached, or seeing somebody, or available...? God, she hoped he wasn't gay. He was *far* too gorgeous to be wasted.

She resolved to do a little more digging about him when she saw Nick again. But once they had gone, professionalism took over. She got out the telephone book for the Worthing area, and scanned the listings of both the residential and business areas. Though why she should be bothering about Leanora at all, she couldn't think.

But there it was. Wolstenholme, Mrs E. in an ordinary-sounding street address. And with a different business address listed under Clairvoyants and Psychics. Well, well. It was *curiouser and curiouser*, as Alice said, because Alex certainly wouldn't have put the woman down as being that professional.

Thanks, Nick, for stirring it up again, she thought mildly, just when thoughts about her had eased off. But she was calmer now, and she pushed Leanora's dreary image out of her mind and got down to checking out the runaway husband case that had come her way. But it was one that definitely needed to be referred to the police and Interpol, she thought regretfully. Some things were just too complicated for her to handle, and she knew her limitations.

And it would give her a good reason to suggest to the client in question that she contacted DI Scott Nelson now that Nick had departed – and that Alex could probably prepare the way for her. She cheered up at once.

But she didn't know Scott well enough yet, and without Nick around, she was restless. The cruise had done that for her. Instead of leaving her feeling fresh and eager to return to work, it seemed to have done just the opposite.

Then there was Rose's death. Rose had called for help, and she hadn't been there for her. That had unsettled her too, and there was no interesting case to catch her imagination, just routine stuff, and sending out reports to clients.

She had finally finished her last roll of film and sent the whole batch of them to be developed, and she gave up thinking about work and went to collect them instead.

'My God,' she said, a while later. 'How the hell did you manage to get into so many of them?'

She had used six rolls of film during the cruise, with plenty of views, candid shots of life on board, and some of the cabaret. In far too many of them, the major was strutting about, and there were some of the small groups she had joined up with for lunch or quizzes, and there was always Leanora.

Alex hadn't been aware that the woman had been anywhere near her when she took her photos, and although she was usually just a background figure, it was creepy, spooky ... as if she intended to be remembered ... and if she didn't stop using those bloody words, she was going to get herself in a right old stew, Alex thought angrily.

She jumped when the telephone rang, and grabbed the receiver, glad of a diversion for her obsessive thoughts.

'Alexandra Best.'

The voice that answered was female and unfamiliar.

'Miss Best, you don't know me, but I wonder if I could come and see you. I don't come to London very often, but today would be convenient for me. Otherwise, if you could give me an early appointment–'

It was better than doing nothing. Alex mentally flipped through a non-existent list of dates, and spoke briskly.

'Actually, I do have some free time this afternoon, so if you could give me your name, and tell me what it's about?'

It helped to have some idea, in case she was able to get a fix on some facts and figures beforehand. A missing husband? A fraud? An inland revenue problem? A house break-in? There was no end to the problems people were prepared to ask a private eye about, rather than go to the police, and she had heard them all by now.

'It's about a murder,' the voice said. 'Well, sort of.'

Alex sat up straighter. *Sort of?* What kind of talk was that about a murder? In any case, there were procedures here.

'Have you contacted the police, Miss–'

'Oh yes, it's all in hand. But it's you I want

41

to speak to. Your name has cropped up, you see.'

By now, Alex could feel the slow trickle of sweat running down her back. Her nerves tingled and her voice was brittle.

'What do you mean, my name has cropped up?'

'Please don't think I'm prevaricating, but I really would prefer to explain later, Miss Best. What time can we say? About two o'clock at your office?'

Ruffled, Alex began to feel that the caller was dictating the terms, and it wasn't the way she liked to do business.

'I don't have a slot at two o'clock,' she said coolly. 'I can see you at 3.15, otherwise it will have to be—'

'3.15 is fine. And the name is Wolstenholme. Miss Moira Wolstenholme.'

The line went dead while Alex was still in the process of writing down the name on her jotter.

Her hand jerked and her pencil broke, and she swore loudly, knowing that if this was a scene in a movie, it would be the corniest of moments...

All the same ... *Wolstenholme* ... it was hardly the commonest of names. She dialled 1471 quickly, but the irritating recorded voice told her the caller had withheld their number.

She tried to slow down her spinning

thoughts, and collated what she knew as briefly as possible. There had been a murder. Somehow, in whatever circumstances she couldn't think, her own name had been mentioned. The woman who rang – presumably a relative of Leanora Wolstenholme – lived somewhere out of town. Worthing? Where Leanora lived?

Her flesh began to crawl again. She began recalling the silly snatches of conversation from Leanora herself, but she knew that she hadn't really forgotten any of it. It had simply been pushed to the back of her mind. Until now.

Be on your guard. I see a death...

I'm quite sure it's not your death, my dear. But it will touch you in some way...

She had never had any time for all that guff, but she made herself be open-minded for a moment, wondering just what it was that Leanora had seen – if anything. At the time she had scathingly thought it no more than the stock-in-trade of the clairvoyant to be mysterious, and to send a delicious little shiver to the client. She still thought it.

But now there was this Wolstenholme relative coming to see her, and her own name had been mentioned. Alex didn't like it. She didn't like it at all.

The phone rang again and she snatched it up, thankful to take her mind off this new development for a few minutes. It was Scott

Nelson. She had only seen him a few times with Nick since that first meeting, and he certainly hadn't rushed to make her acquaintance, after that initial *frisson* of awareness between them. Unless she had imagined it.

'I don't want to tread on any toes,' he said now, 'but would you care to come out to dinner with me one evening?'

Her heart leapt. If anything was guaranteed to bring her back to the land of the living, and to forget cranks and spooks, this was it.

'I'd love to,' she said, forgetting all about cool.

'Is tonight any good?'

'Tonight would be fine.' Forget the hair-washing and the launderette as well. Forget everything but the fact that he was the sexiest thing on two legs...

'I don't have your home address—'

She gave it quickly, deciding that for the first time since she'd heard about Nick's transfer to Plymouth, she didn't regret his leaving. And she was damned if she was going to feel guilty about seeing someone else either. It was none of Nick's business who she went out with, but he had always been proprietorial towards her, and it wouldn't have done his ego any good to know she was going out with his replacement.

She was already mentally going through her wardrobe and discarding most of it. If she had time to shop, she'd go up west and find something spectacular ... but two things stopped her. She didn't know what kind of place Scott would take her to – and she had a client due that afternoon at 3.15.

She saw the shadowy figure outside the glass section of her office door, and minutes later, the woman was inside. Alex greeted her, forcing a professional smile to her lips, and trying to hide her shock at her appearance.

She hadn't known what to expect. There had been no indication of age in the woman's voice. She could have been any-thing from sixteen to sixty. As it was, she looked like a well-preserved forty, loudly dressed, and bedecked in gold chains and silver rings. But the face, for all its mask of make-up, was a facsimile of Leanora's. The same narrow eyes, the same thin mouth, the same dull skin tone behind the heavy foundation, Alex guessed.

'Please sit down, Miss Wolstenholme,' she said. 'Would you like some coffee? And then perhaps you would tell me what this is all about.'

And she'd be damned if she was going to offer her any of her favourite chocolate biscuits, even though her own stomach was starting to rumble by now, due to a noble non-lunch for the sake of her thighs and tonight's promised dinner.

But trusting her instincts as always, she disliked this woman at first sight, and she waited for her to speak after she had accepted the proffered cup of coffee.

'You met my mother, I understand. Leanora Wolstenholme.'

'So I did,' Alex said, hiding her surprise that such a nondescript woman could ever have had a child at all. An unwelcome vision of the dreary female coupled up with some brute of a man flashed into her mind and thankfully out again.

'But you didn't say on the phone that she was your mother,' Alex went on hastily.

It would be ghastly if this clownish clone of Leanora was clairvoyant as well, and could see into her thoughts. 'And I'm not sure how you could have known anything about me. We spoke very little on the cruise.'

'My mother was in the habit of jotting down names and thoughts in a notebook. It was part of her life's work to be interested in people, of course—'

You could have fooled me, thought Alex.

'Your name was in it, as well as a lot of others. I found you in the Yellow Pages,' she said, almost accusingly.

'Really?' Alex said, feeling that this was getting more and more bizarre. 'Look, Miss Wolstenholme—'

'Oh, do call me Moira. It's such a cumbersome name, isn't it?' she said, with an attempt at a winsome smile.

'Very well. Moira. I trust your mother is well?'

'Oh no. I thought I had mentioned that.'

Alex stared at her. 'Mentioned what?'

Her heart was starting to thud, and she could almost have been clairvoyant herself, anticipating the next words, while trying to shut her mind to the possibility of them.

'Mother's dead. Murdered. A client found her in her office, slumped over the table on top of her tarot cards a week after her holiday. It was an awful shock for the poor man, of course. He thought she was in some kind of trance until his eyes got used to the dim lighting, And then he saw the knife stuck in her back.'

It wasn't so much the horror of what she was hearing, as the matter-of-fact way this woman was saying it. Her mother had been murdered, for God's sake, and here she was, telling it all as calmly as if she was reciting a shopping-list.

And all Alex could think of to say was the most appalling piece of insensitivity in the world.

'She couldn't have seen that coming, then, could she?'

Aghast, she bit her lips, desperately wishing she could take back the words, but

47

Moira smiled gently, treacly with under-standing.

'It's all right. We all say odd things at times, don't we? But that's just it. She *did* see it coming. She's known for ages that it would happen. That's why I'm not upset, because she had made all her plans for the funeral and everything, including the arrangements for when we would meet on the other side. I can see that you're a doubter, Miss Best, but death isn't an ending. It's a beginning, and we should all welcome it and embrace it–'

'Look here, I'm sorry,' Alex broke in, her voice cracking. 'But I think you've come to the wrong person. Maybe you need a priest or an exorcist. I can't do anything to help you – and I still don't know what you want, anyway.'

'I want you to find out who's stalking me, and to stop it before I'm next. It's not my time, you see, and there's still work to be done on this side before I join mother.'

Alex took a deep breath. She might doubt all this afterlife nonsense, (mentally crossing her fingers at the thought, just in case there *was* somebody up there listening) but she never doubted that Moira was a complete crackpot. But she obviously wasn't being asked to investigate a murder.

'Let me get this straight. I presume the police have got your mother's murder in hand, so that's not why you're here.'

'Oh no. They know who did it, and they've already got him in custody. The case is closed as far as they're concerned.'

'And you say you're being stalked?'

Bizarrely, into Alex's mind came the thought that if mother was still around, she could have been looking into her crystal ball by now and told Moira who was stalking her.

'I know it sounds strange,' Moira went on. 'I mean, who would stalk a woman like me? Unless it's for the money. Mother wasn't hard up, and it all came to me, of course. But then, you'd think a man might have enough finesse to do a little courting, even with someone like me, instead of trying to frighten me to death for some twisted reason of his own.'

The aggrieved note in her voice almost got to Alex then. It was somehow reminiscent of poor Rose Harding, who'd never had a man look twice at her either. But there the similarity ended. Rose had been a mouse of a farm girl, while the blowsy sight of this one was enough to scare off any man.

'I think you'd better tell me whatever you know about the person who's stalking you, Moira,' she said, more kindly. 'And if you could leave off the clairvoyant bits, I'd be obliged.'

'It's obvious that you're not a believer,

Miss Best. Mother mentioned that in her notebook.'

Alex was indignant at once. 'Just what *did* she put in this notebook?'

'I've brought it with me. You can borrow it, of course, since I suspect my stalker is mentioned in here too. It's a weird thing – and I promise I won't go on about it – but the closer you are to something, the less you can see it. Mother always said that too. She couldn't predict the time and manner of her own death, only that it would be violent, and soon.'

Mother seemed to have said a hell of a lot, thought Alex, considering she had said so little to anyone on the cruise. But maybe she had, and Alex simply hadn't been listening. She had also thought it amazing that such a dun little woman had travelled alone, but not any more. Not after seeing how she had asserted herself with would-be clients on the cruise.

'So who do *you* think the stalker is?' she asked Moira directly. 'Could it be someone you know? It frequently is.'

'No idea,' she said, shaking her head. 'I don't make enemies as far as I know. I'm a florist. Nothing harmful about that, is there? I do weddings and funerals, and floral arrangements for functions,' she added grandly.

'And you're being stalked,' Alex stated,

50

moving into professional gear. 'How? Is someone following you? Sending you hate mail? Telephoning you at odd hours of the day and night?'

'Oh, I've always had hate mail. People were a little afraid of mother, so they made me the target instead.'

'*Excuse* me? People were afraid of your mother? In what way?' For the life of her, Alex couldn't imagine anyone being afraid of Leanora ... and yet, hadn't *she* been, more than a little? She revised her thoughts at once.

Moira fixed her with a severe look. 'Mother was genuine, you know. She was definitely psychic. I never had her gift, but you don't have to see a seed growing under the earth to know that it will bear fruit in the course of time, do you? You know it, and you feel its power. Mother had that power.'

'I think we're getting off the track here,' Alex said firmly. 'What is it you think I can do for you?'

'Find the stalker and bring him to justice before I join mother in the Great Beyond. The last message I got from him was a bunch of dead lilies delivered to my shop accompanied with a black-edged card with my name on it the day after mother died. Is that proof enough of his intentions?'

'It may be, or it could be a cruel hoax,' Alex said. 'In any case, if you've been getting death threats, don't you think it's a matter for the police?'

Moira said nothing for a moment, and then she took a small notebook from her bag and laid it on Alex's desk.

'Mother felt it was a matter for you, Miss Best, otherwise why would she have wanted me to contact you? I'll leave her notebook with you and a cheque which should cover things for now, I think. They call it an upfront payment, don't they?' she said in an attempt to sound modern.

Alex tried not to let her eyes widen at the substantial size of the cheque. Mother had certainly been loaded.

'I have to go now,' Moira continued. 'There's a lot to do before mother's funeral. The floral tributes and so on.'

God, she was a cold fish all right. Her mother wasn't yet buried, and she was more worried on her own account than seeing the old biddy put decently underground. And if mother was now in the habit of talking to her from the Great Beyond, why couldn't she tell her the identity of the stalker?

'The cheque is more than adequate,' she said at last.

'Good. Mother liked you, and she thought you could help us.' She fished in her bag again. 'You might find the account in the local newspaper useful. You'll be contacting me then?'

She was gone before Alex could consult her diary and invent a dozen reasons never to see this woman again. If Leanora had been weird, Moira was downright creepy, and definitely the more dominant of the two women.

She left the notebook alone for now, and unfolded the local newspaper. The account of the clairvoyant's murder was front-page news, followed by the quick arrest of the man accused of the crime, and the eye-witness story from Leanora's client who had arrived to consult her, and instead of which, had discovered her body.

His first-hand story intrigued Alex most. The rest was routine stuff ... and she was instantly appalled at herself for glossing over the end of a woman's existence in those terms. Even a woman like Leanora had once loved and been loved, married and had a daughter. Alex shook her head slowly. Having met her, it was still hard to imagine her as a young lover, wife and mother.

Before doing anything else, she took another look at her holiday photos, studying the ones with background shots of Leanora. She hadn't ever been intentionally included, but in every one of them, her sharp eyes seemed to be looking directly into the camera, straight into Alex's eyes, deep and penetrating, asking for something, telling her something...

Quickly, Alex put the photos away and scanned the newspaper story again. Mentally thanking an enthusiastic local reporter with an ear for drama, Alex read the words of the eyewitness, repeated in full for a ghoulish public.

The man, one Vernon Cole, unemployed lorry driver, aged 52, had run out into the street in hysterics, shouting for somebody to send for the police and an ambulance. When he was questioned by the police, he had apparently babbled:

'I didn't know she was dead until I touched her, and then I let out a scream of fright. It was a hell of a shock to see that knife sticking out of her back and to see so much blood.

'It turned my guts, I can tell you. I never saw a dead body before, except my wife's, and she died naturally in bed. Nobody really liked Mrs Wolstenholme, mind, but she could definitely see things other people couldn't. After my wife passed over, she helped me to make contact, and I went back to her for comfort more than anything. It was always worth it.'

Alex had learned by experience to study sentences minutely. Separating them into words and phrases, and often finding more in them than speakers realized they had revealed.

In this case, it was the last phrase that

caught her attention. 'It was always worth it.'

'Always' meant that Vernon Cole had consulted Leanora more than once. 'Worth it' meant he had probably paid handsomely for the trouble. Went back to her 'for comfort', did he? And Leanora would clearly want to prolong the contact as long as he was paying upfront for the privilege.

Then there was that phrase 'so much blood'...

Didn't a single stabbing mean that the blood was contained until the knife was removed? So there had to have been more than one thrust of the knife, which indicated a frenzied attack. Referring back to the police report, Alex saw that she was right. One up for detection, girl.

But clearly, Leanora wasn't daft. Alex visualized the woman's *modus operandi* ... dangle the bait by inventing some significant phrase for the poor lost sap mourning his wife, and from then on, reel him in at frequent intervals in the hope of hearing more, at a hefty fee.

And she was turning into as big a bloody cynic as DI Nick Frobisher ever was, Alex thought. But by now, she knew some of the rottenness of human nature, as well as the finer bits. Unfortunately, it went with the job.

Nothing was what it seemed. Or sometimes it was exactly that. You had to take account of that too.

Anyway, as far as her new client went – and since she had pocketed the cheque, she had agreed to take her on, she realized – it wasn't Leanora's death that should be concerning her. So why did she think that it was? Why did she think that Moira's little charade in coming here with some cock-and-bull story of a stalker was just a ruse to get her to investigate her mother's death further?

She continued reading the entire newspaper account. The funeral had been delayed until the police and the coroner decided to release the body, and it was this coming Saturday. And Alex knew that whatever else she had on hand, she was going down to Worthing on Saturday to attend it.

She shuddered, but decided that the notebook could wait until tomorrow. Tonight she had other things to do. And if you didn't get your mind off the sometimes gruesome aspects of the job, you could go quietly insane.

She put the notebook in a drawer, locked up her office and went home to take a leisurely shower and decide what she was going to wear for her dinner date with Scott Nelson. She normally wore black from head to toe, since it made such a dramatic contrast with her flame-red hair and green eyes.

But after the events of the afternoon, the thought of wearing black was too funereal, and she needed to get her mind away from that. So after changing her mind a dozen times, she welcomed Scott at the door of her flat, wearing a slinky black top and a long emerald green skirt, with an elegant green choker around her neck.

'I hope I'm not too formal,' she said at once, as gauche as a schoolgirl on her first date.

'You look stunning,' he said gravely. 'But I knew you would. Nick said you were a snappy dresser, but my guess is that you look good in anything.'

'Careful,' Alex said, starting to laugh. 'I can get to like all this flattery.'

And thank God he hadn't added: *and out of it too...* She didn't want that yet. It was too soon, and she was amazed that she was even thinking self-restraint. But she didn't know him yet. There had been too many times when she had jumped into lust and then wanted out. This time could be different.

Besides, after their first meeting in Nick's company, he seemed more stand-offish than she had expected. Not unfriendly – after all, he had asked her out – but not over-easy with women, either.

'Have you found your way around town yet?' she asked, as they walked outside to his car. 'I thought we might have got together with Nick before he left to show you around.'

She tried not to show her resentment, but there had undoubtedly been a cooling off from Nick, after her refusal to marry him and become his token female accessory.

'I know London, actually,' Scott told her. 'My wife and I lived here for about a year before we went back up north.'

'Is she still there? Up north, I mean,' Alex said as casually as she could, wondering why the hell he had asked her out – building up her hopes, damn it – if there was a wife in the background all along.

And calling herself a bloody fool for assuming that one dinner date could be leading to forever – or anything.

'I don't know where she is. We're divorced. And before you ask, there are no kids, no mortgage, no other ties. OK?'

'Do I seem that conventional?' she said lightly.

'I'd like to think so. It's good to meet women who can still be feminine and not predatory these days.'

No jumping into bed right after the first date then.

She hoped she hadn't said it aloud, but from the way he was concentrating on the traffic, she knew she hadn't. At the time she didn't register the odd note of resentment in his voice either.

'I've made a booking at a nightclub. Is that all right with you, Alex? I thought some after-dinner entertainment might be nice.'

To avoid too much conversation, perhaps? And what the hell was wrong with her? Or him, for that matter. He was a great guy, and she had fancied him from the moment she saw him, but she was starting to read double meanings into everything he said – and they weren't to her liking.

Great guys with the combined looks of several hunky moviestars didn't always have great conversation or a sizzling seduction technique. By now something was telling her loud and strong that Scott Nelson was one of them. He was as pedantic as the stereotypical Mr Plod.

She also knew herself – and she was quick-witted enough to be easily bored. Over dinner, she knew she was right. He was great-looking, but there was nothing inside. He was like one of those empty shells you find at the beach. Boring. A nothing. Regretfully so.

As the meal went on she found herself looking around, studying other couples, and longing for the cabaret to begin so that they didn't have to continue this stilted attempt to be physically attracted any longer.

Well, maybe it was physical, but it certainly wasn't mental, and in Alex's book the two had to go together. She liked him ... but she no longer felt the kind of magnetism there had been between herself and Nick. It alarmed her, making her wonder, not for the first time, if she was frigid. Wanting the chase, but no longer wanting the capture when it was a certainty.

Except that in this case, she didn't think it was. Scott Nelson was never going to be more than a friend, a buddy, and despite her momentary misgivings about her own sexuality, Alex gradually felt a great sense of relief wash over her. So what if she was frigid – temporarily – and only as far as this one was concerned – there was nothing wrong in having a good mate, especially in the force.

She smiled at Scott more warmly, and saw his eyes widen in a kind of mild panic. So she had been right. He didn't want a relationship, just friendship.

'I always enjoyed a platonic friendship with Nick,' she said calmly. 'It's refreshing to be friends with someone of the opposite sex with no strings attached, don't you think?'

'I do indeed,' he said, while Alex wondered faintly if it was really her saying all these things.

Gary Hollis, her one-time lover, had referred to her as sexpot personified ... but Gary was in the past and she hadn't seen him since he'd taken up with a new love. And she didn't know why she should be thinking of him now, except that they had first met in a nightclub, sleazier than this one, when she'd thought him brash and dangerous and sexy in his leathers, and he'd taken her for a ride on his powerful Harley Davidson motorbike that was an extension of his own powerful, sexy personality.

Oh no, she wasn't losing it, she thought with a secret smile as the rush of adrenalin flashed through her senses, and the Italian waiter gave her an admiring look as he poured her another glass of wine. It was just that Scott Nelson wasn't the one to set her on fire after all.

'Do you know Worthing at all?' she asked him casually, having learned that he seemed to have gone just about everywhere during his time in the force.

'Slightly,' he said. 'Why do you want to know?'

'I'm going to a funeral there on Saturday. Nobody I knew well. An acquaintance. Sort of. I'll stay in the background.'

But he wasn't a copper for nothing. She should have known he'd pick up on her jerky sentences. Nick would have done so in a minute too, and she saw Scott's eyes narrow.

'It can be rough, going to a near-stranger's funeral. Awkward with the relatives and so on. If you want company I could drive you if you like.'

Her instinct was to say no. She was following up a lead, of sorts. Deciding whether or not she wanted to take on Moira's case or say bye-bye to what could be a fat fee for her services, since Moira was apparently the loaded one now.

'Don't you have other things to do? Other people to see?' she demurred. Another life?

He shook his head. 'A day at the coast would be very welcome, despite the circumstances.'

'What circumstances?'

'You did say you were going to a funeral?'

'Oh yes. Of course. But as I said, it's someone I only knew slightly. I might change my mind.'

He gave a small smile. 'But you won't, will you?'

'What makes you say that?'

'I'm no head shrink, but I'd say that when you decide to do something, you always see it through. Am I right?'

She laughed. 'Of course. It goes with the territory, doesn't it? Private eye or dedicated copper, you always see things through, don't you?'

He smiled back. His teeth were toothpaste white, and she wished she could still fancy him, but the feeling had vanished like dreams of a lottery win when your numbers didn't come up.

'Well, whatever it is that's really taking you down to Worthing, I promise I'll stay in the background as well, unless you invite me into your confidence.'

He raised his glass to her and she smiled back sweetly, remembering her vow to see hell freeze before she got a copper involved in her case – unless it was absolutely necessary.

Chapter 3

Long before Saturday, Alex had studied Leanora's notebook, and was staggered at the woman's astute sense of observation. She may have been an apparent nonentity on board the cruise ship, but she had a fine turn of phrase when it came to describing her fellow passengers.

But the notebook went much farther back than the past few weeks. It contained a mass of notes about Leanora's clients, acquaintances, relatives and friends, and if it ever got into the hands of some unscrupulous person who wanted to publish it, it could be scandalously hot, Alex realized. There was even the odd MP or two, seeking guidance on their respective relationships with call-girls and a junior minister's wife.

This notebook was a gold-mine, Alex thought, and she wondered if Moira knew exactly what she possessed. She could bring down a hell of a lot of people, if she chose. Leanora could have done it too, and presumably neither of them had that intention. But the more Alex read, the more she became intrigued by the pair of them.

She almost wished her old mate Gary was here. He'd be raring to go over this little mystery, egging her on to inform the newspapers for the highest sum ... which was why it was a bloody good job he *wasn't* around.

Client confidentiality was essential for her reputation, and so it must have been for Leanora. After all, if one of the influential people in this notebook thought she had betrayed them, they could have silenced her for ever...

'My God,' Alex whispered, her hand shaking slightly as she closed the book. 'Maybe that's exactly what did happen. Maybe it wasn't the guy they had arrested at all, but someone else entirely. Someone in higher places!'

She skimmed through Moira's newspaper again. It was a weekly, and as yet the police hadn't named the murder suspect, except to say that he was a local man, well-known for being a loner. The classic suspect ... as if that explained it all! And one woman's murder in a seaside town that seemed to have a cut-and-dried answer to the crime, wasn't newsworthy enough to attract the attention of the mass media.

Alex knew she had to find out more, and Nick might have missed something in the police files. She had the strongest hunch that Leanora's killer was still on the loose. She might be barking up the wrong proverbial now, but like a dog with a bone, she couldn't let it go.

'Can I speak to DI Nelson, please?' she asked the duty officer, recognizing his telephone voice. 'It's Alex Best.'

She could almost see the smirk on his face as he said he'd see if the DI was in, and to hold the line. They all knew of her friendship with Nick, and no doubt thought she had decided to try her luck with his successor now.

In their eyes she was the bimbo private eye, thinking she could do a copper's job – and some of them were the worst chauvinists on God's earth.

'Hello, Alex. What's up?' she heard Scott say. 'Don't tell me you've changed your mind about Saturday after all.'

'Of course not. But something's come up, and I'd like to discuss it with you. Do you have any free time before then?'

And this wasn't a pass, either, she thought, hoping her efficient manner would tell him so.

'Can you come into the station?' he said, clearly busy.

'I'd rather not. Could you come to my office? I'll be here all day.'

It was like a game of tennis, she fumed. Each of them was throwing the ball in the other's court, and challenging the other one to lose out.

'Is it a confidential matter?'

'Very.' And if he didn't bloody well play it her way, she was going to give up on him.

'I'll be there when I can, Alex, but I can't promise when,' he said at last, a different note in his voice that she couldn't quite fathom.

'That's good enough. Thanks.'

She hung up, wishing she'd never got him involved at all. And not really knowing why she had.

'So what do you want to know?' Scott said.

She knew that superior DI-compared-with-the-little-female-private-eye note in his voice. She had given up waiting for him at her office, and it was now past nine o'clock, and she had opened the door of her flat cautiously. She had showered after the heat of the day and wore only her red kimono, and she tied it more securely around her as

66

Scott Nelson eyed her with an arrogant male smirk on his face.

'Who says I wanted to know anything? Maybe I just fancied your company, but you've left it a bit late,' Alex said, while inwardly cringing at her own twee response. And just as instantly biting her lip, realizing how vulnerable she was. And of course it had been a mistake to open the door dressed as she was. But he was a copper, for God's sake, and if you couldn't trust coppers ... and whatever bloody fool ever put about *that* fairy tale wanted locking up, she thought savagely.

'Oh yes?' he said, a spark of interest flaring in his eyes now at her comment.

'I only said maybe,' she hedged, wondering what the hell was wrong with her, when she'd fancied him like mad at first sight. But not any more. There was something about him...

He moved across the room until he was close to her. Before she knew what was happening his arms had gripped hers tightly, and his voice had dropped to a trickly leer.

'What do you fancy? Is it a bit of rough? Is that why you invited me here? I know it turns on classy tarts like you. A bit of slap without the tickle–'

'I didn't invite you here. I said my office–'

He ignored her, and Alex felt a shock

67

ripple through her as his hands moved downwards and clenched her buttocks cruelly. He dug in his fingernails so sharply she knew they would leave marks and rip the silk of her kimono. She felt the piercing pain, sharp as needles as his nails probed her flesh, but somehow she managed to drag up a scrap of dignity, and not to wince or show any emotion but cold anger.

'If you don't get your effing hands off me this instant, you'll get my knee in your balls,' she said, her eyes clear and unblinking, and as hard as emeralds.

His own eyes widened. But not with fear or apprehension. There was gloating delight in his face.

'That's it, bitch, tease me,' he said, suddenly hoarse. 'It's what my old lady never did. She always gave in too easily, and I get off on a fight. Same as you. I can tell.'

One hand suddenly left her backside, and shot around to the front of her body, punching her in the belly and winding her until she staggered and fell on to her sofa. He was on her immediately, ripping her kimono aside and fumbling his hands up and down her body with no more finesse than an elephant.

He squeezed her breasts, tweaking the nipples until she gasped with the excruciating pain, feeling her and kneading her, and grinding against her as he tried to part her sex with greedy fingers.

But after the first shock of the assault, Alex recovered her senses, and with one almighty action, she rammed her fist into his groin and heard him howl with rage as he rolled off her and on to the floor, clutching himself. And even in those moments when she had tugged her kimono around herself and got to her feet, ignoring how every bit of her hurt, she had registered that no matter what he had done to her, or how he had violated her and exposed her body to him, there had been no sign of an erection. Nothing.

She knew him for what he was then. A good-looking strutter who couldn't get it up, no matter how much he tried, or whatever tactics he used. No wonder his wife had left him if he couldn't deliver the goods. Especially if he had had to resort to violence to get his kicks.

Her first furious reaction to report him to his boss faded at once. He wasn't worth it. He was pathetic, something to be pitied, especially when she saw how he was snivelling on the floor now.

'You've bloody ruined me for life, bitch,' he shouted.

She looked down at him, seeing the vivid colour in his face, and the humiliation in his eyes. He knew that she knew. She could taunt him, or betray him, and he knew that too. She could ruin him in more ways than one. She could strip him of his career ... for a moment she wondered if Nick Frobisher had ever known of his one-time colleague's penchant for sexual violence, and doubted it. Nick would never have allowed her to get into this situation without warning her.

'Get up, Scott. You look ridiculous,' she said at last. 'I'll make some coffee and get a bag of frozen peas from the freezer to put on that lump of dough in your trousers. And then we'll talk. Savvy?'

She didn't wait for a reply as she stalked off to the kitchen, wondering just why she was prepared to take on the role of mother-confessor to this little pisser. But maybe if she did, it would stop him trying it on with a weaker, more vulnerable woman. As she registered her own thoughts, she felt her hands shake over the kettle, because she knew of old when dealing with weirdos just how dangerous the situation could have been.

They would do anything to hide their humiliation at being found out for what they were. And she wasn't that strong, damn it. She may have skills at her disposal that other women didn't, and she knew that one good karate chop could have silenced the bastard for good, but she was still a woman after all.

'I'm very sorry, Alex,' she suddenly heard Scott say humbly. He was right behind her, still clutching himself, and she whirled around, spilling water from the kettle, and seeing his abject face. 'Look, if you want to beat me, I'll understand. I know I deserve to be punished.'

'*Christ*, Scott. I'm not into that,' she said, disgusted that he should think she could be a party to his needs. 'Get back and sit down, for God's sake. You don't need punishment. You need help. Have you sought counselling for your problem?'

His eyes flashed more aggressively for a moment. 'Bloody counsellors do more harm than good. My wife went to one, and all it did was make her up and leave me.'

'I doubt that it was the counsellor that did that, Scott,' Alex said carefully. 'It was your own behaviour that was at fault, wasn't it?'

And if trained counsellors had failed, who the hell did she think she was, trying to tackle this guy's huge problem with a few choice words, a cup of coffee and a bag of frozen peas? She opened the freezer quickly, and thrust the bag into his hands.

'Take these and do the business in the other room until I bring in the coffee,' she ordered.

And once he had left her, she slipped into the bedroom and into a high-necked sweater and jeans, trying to ignore her shaking hands and the darkening bruises on her body as she did so. She was the one who

71

needed frozen peas, she thought, but not yet. Not until she had got the bastard out of her flat.

But before she had spooned a good dollop of strong coffee into two mugs and composed herself, she heard the front door slam, and when she went into the sitting-room, he had gone.

And now she really did have second thoughts about what to do about him. If he had gone blundering off into the night, ready to pick up some poor innocent kid to vent his spleen on, whatever the hell that was, she would feel responsible.

She began to feel physically sick. She abandoned coffee and had a hefty swig of brandy instead before she went into the bathroom, forcing down the urge to throw up. And while she was gingerly applying witch hazel to the ugly bruises appearing on her body and flinching as she dabbed the weals on her buttocks with Savlon, her wild imagination was already reading the morning newspaper headlines outlining a girl's savaged body dumped in a ditch...

She found it almost impossible to sleep that night. Her brain and her stomach were still churning, and it hurt far too much to lie on her back. She wondered how she would ever sit down again, let alone drive any distance in her car.

But one thing was for sure: the trip to Worthing was definitely off. At least, as far as Scott Nelson accompanying her was concerned.

If she never had to see him again, it would be too soon, and anyway, she was pretty sure he'd be feeling the same way. Rejected weirdos never went back to the scene of their humiliation. Or so she hoped and believed.

In the middle of the following afternoon there were two callers at her office. She looked up with dislike as she saw two of Scott Nelson's colleagues. She had never cared for Sergeant Thomas, who saw her as no more than an irritating flea who scratched his nick's surface from time to time. She didn't know his companion, a red-necked constable, fresh out from Hendon by the look of him, and eager to make a hit.

'What can I do for you, Sergeant?' she said amicably, sure that this wasn't a social call. It never was. And even more sure by the fat-cat way he smiled at her, and sat down uninvited on the other side of her desk before saying a word.

'Would you like a seat, Constable?' she said pointedly.

'Nay – no – you're all right, Ma'am – Miss–' he said, his voice as broad as her own Yorkshire tones had once been, before she had refined and rounded them, and she smiled at him more warmly because of it.

'So?' she said directly. 'To what do I owe this – now what shall I call it? What's the opposite of pleasure?'

She heard the constable smother a snigger, and his superior gave him a freezing look.

'Read the lady your notes, McAdams,' he snapped.

More red-faced than ever, the boy was all fingers and thumbs as he flipped open his regulation notebook.

He was hardly out of short trousers, Alex thought, unaccountably feeling all of her twenty-six years.

'At 2.15 pm yesterday, you telephoned the station and asked to speak to DI Scott Nelson, and you were told that he wasn't in,' he repeated, parrot-like.

'So I did, Constable,' Alex said gently.

But her heart lurched at the mention of Scott's name. Surely the rat wasn't trying to do her for assault, was he? If so, she could show these two a thing or two in the way of bruises, if she felt like it. Which she certainly didn't...

'And then DI Scott Nelson called you back, and at your insistence he arranged to meet you as soon as he was free,' the voice droned on in a monotone.

'All right, what's going on?' Alex said.

'What's all this about my insistence? If DI Nelson has got something to say about me, why isn't he here to say it himself?'

She looked directly at the sergeant, and instinctively sat up straighter even though it hurt like hell to put pressure on her backside, and the idea of turning the other cheek held no charm. There was no comfortable cheek she could turn.

'What would DI Nelson have to say about you, Miss Best?' he said silkily, and she knew she'd fallen into the trap, sweet as honey.

It was the easiest trap a copper could set. Dangle the bait and just wait for the suspect to grab it. But what suspect, for God's sake?

'I really have no idea,' she said coolly. 'But I refuse to discuss my movements with you. What I do in my free time is my own business, and if DI Nelson logged our private telephone conversation I shall have words to say to him.'

The sergeant raised his hand slightly as the constable made as if to speak.

'It was hardly private, Miss Best. The whole unit heard DI Nelson's responses to your invitation.'

Invitation? The implication was obvious, and Alex's temper flared at once. In view of last night, it was ludicrous, but she wasn't giving this oaf the lascivious pleasure of knowing it.

'I don't know why you're here, but I would like you to leave, and I assure you DI Nelson will confirm that our discussion was on a purely business matter,' she snapped.

But it wasn't, of course. They had never got far enough for her to try to get him to winkle out any inside info about one Leanora Wolstenholme, so-called medium, psychic or whatever ... and she knew that the sergeant's unblinking eyes would have registered the flicker in hers.

'I'm afraid DI Nelson is in no position to confirm anything,' he said smoothly. 'DI Nelson was found in his garage this morning, having died through carbon monoxide poisoning by means of exhaust fumes, and leaving a note simply saying "I'm sorry". Since you were the last known person he had contact with, I am naturally wondering if you can throw any light on the matter?'

As the impersonal voice went on, virtually making a mockery of a man's death, Alex couldn't think straight. For one thing, the pounding of her heart almost drowned out the police sergeant's words. And then professionalism took over again. Just what the hell was he suggesting?

'Are you telling me DI Nelson's dead?' she stammered.

'That's usually the case in these circumstances,' he drawled sarcastically.

God, he was an insensitive bastard,

thought Alex. Even though there had been nothing going on between herself and Scott Nelson, Thomas didn't know that. For all he knew, they might have been having a torrid love affair, and he'd been witless enough to throw the words at her so brutally.

But of course, it wouldn't have been witless at all, her whirlwind thoughts raced on. His words would have been calculated to the nth degree, catching her on the hop, making her say things she didn't intend. Making her blurt out whatever indiscretions his nasty little mind had cooked up ... and she knew well enough to take things slowly, and not to rush into anything.

'I'm shocked to hear the news, of course, but I can't help you,' she said, choked.

'I can't agree with that, Miss Best. In fact, I require you to come down to the station for fingerprinting–'

'*What?*'

'There are fingermarks all over certain areas of DI Nelson's – er – person,' he said, in a clumsy attempt to be delicate, which only exaggerated the ridiculousness of the words. Alex knew full well that the only contact she had made on Scott were on her attempts to fend him off, and that full-blooded fist ram on his genitals. *And* he'd been fully clothed.

They couldn't pin anything on her for it. And it had to be suicide, anyway. Scott wasn't known well enough here yet for anyone to have a grudge.

Her juddering nerves settled a little as she saw the little pulse beating at the corner of Thomas's mouth. She knew then that the old bugger was trying it on. Trying to ferret out some sleazy connection between herself and his DI, just for the hell of it. Life in a nick wasn't always at fever-pitch. There were dull, routine times as well as all-hands-on-deck murder hunts to get the adrenalin going at full stretch. It might be unsavoury to the general public, but that was what policing was all about. Just as an army needed a war to keep it pepped up, a police force needed crime. There were also times when a good shot of healthy sleaze was just what was needed to spice things up a bit. And there was nothing like internal sleaze.

'Sergeant,' she said, a pitying note in her voice. 'I'm terribly sorry to disappoint you, but DI Nelson and myself were no more than acquaintances. He called at my flat last night because he had been too busy to see me here at my office, but it was only on a routine matter, I assure you–'

'And that was?'

Sod the man. He may be world-weary in some respects, but like any astute copper he was like a dog with a bone when he sensed something. They all were. It was the nature of the species.

'DI Nelson was going to drive me to Worthing on Saturday, to a funeral. I thought he might have had some inside information about a lady I met on holiday recently. She's just died. A violent death. I shouldn't have been asking, I know, and it was entirely unofficial. I'm not involved in the case. In fact there isn't any case to answer, since I gather that they've got someone in custody for it.'

She was stumbling, trying to fumble her way out of the unspoken accusation that she had intended probing police files. And probably by way of sex, if she interpreted the sneering look in Thomas's eyes correctly.

'You were trying to find out facts from a police officer while not being involved in the case, Miss Best? It hardly rings true, does it? So just why were you and DI Nelson going to Worthing together?'

She didn't like the way he said that word 'together'. She glared at him. 'I told you. I wanted to attend a funeral. DI Nelson was just driving me.'

'Don't you have a car?' he said, knowing that she did.

'Look, this has nothing to do with DI Nelson's death, so can we please get on with what you came here for? I'm upset to hear about it, and I'd like to be on my own.'

She couldn't say the words without a

shiver running through her. It all seemed so unreal, so macabre. Last night he was with her in her flat, molesting her, hurting her, almost weeping in his frustration, and then simply vanishing without explanation.

And now he was dead, presumably by his own hand. She might have been able to help him, but she never got the chance. She was as impotent as he ever was.

Thoughts of Rose Harding rushed into her mind. She hadn't been able to help her either. She had been too late. And regardless of what this beady-eyed copper was thinking, she resolved that it wasn't going to happen a third time. Whatever Moira Wolstenholme wanted her to do, she would do it. Right now, all three cries for help had merged into one.

'All right, Miss Best,' Thomas said, getting to his feet, and indicating to his constable to snap his notebook shut. Alex hadn't even realized that he had been taking notes all this time, and she should have done.

'I think we can forget the fingerprinting for now, and in any case, we've probably got them on record somewhere,' Thomas went on. 'We don't seriously think you had anything to do with Nelson's death, but we needed to hear your story. In any case, the note was addressed to his wife, not you.'

'You devious *bastard!*' Alex burst out before she could stop herself. 'You just

80

wanted to see me squirm, didn't you?'

He grinned. 'Takes one to know one,' he said. 'But I'd watch that tongue of yours in future. It could get you into trouble–'

'In – to – trouble–' the constable repeated slowly, having opened his notebook again.

Thomas scowled at him. 'He's still green behind the gills,' he commented to Alex. 'But he'll learn. And you'll be needed for the inquest, of course. We'll be in touch.'

He swept out of Alex's office, the young man scuttling behind him like an apology, the lingering whiff of his underarms indicating his nervousness.

And then Alex wilted, finding it hard not to give way to weeping for the waste of a man's life. Whatever Scott Nelson had been like in recent times, he had once had a wife who loved him, and hopes for the future, like everyone else. And now he was dead.

She shivered as if the day had suddenly gone cold. She was registering the fact that there had been three deaths in such a short space of time, and all of them touching her in some way. One natural, one murder, one suicide ... and she had a job not to make it sound like a ghastly music-hall farce.

Swiftly, she made her thoughts change direction from the ghoulish to the practical. The nick was now short of a DI. Maybe they'd bring Nick Frobisher back from Plymouth. Good old tried and trusted Nick.

The police system didn't necessarily work that way, but if there was nobody else available it could happen as a temporary measure.

Alex almost wished she had Leanora's crystal ball to tell her it was going to be so, and she drew in her breath at the thought. But she *needed* Nick now. She needed someone wholesome and substantial beside her ... and she was turning into a shivering idiot, instead of a so-say professional PI able to deal with all eventualities. Hah!

Her heartbeats slowed down. But pride wouldn't let her call him and blab out all her anxieties. Even so, she needed to talk to someone. Without thinking she reached for the telephone and began dialling Moira Wolstenholme's number ... as if to reassure herself that somebody she knew was still very much alive.

'Moira Wolstenholme,' she heard the strident voice reply after a moment, just as if her mother hadn't so recently died. Or *passed over*, as these people said, as if to deny the finality of it all.

'Oh Moira, it's Alex Best here,' she said, hearing herself twitter, and trying to still her hammering heart. But people like Leanora and her daughter made her nervous, and she couldn't deny that either. 'I was just wondering if you would feel offended if I attended your mother's funeral. I don't want to impose on your grief–'

'Of course you must be there. Mother expects it.'

'I beg your pardon?'

There was something that sounded like amusement in the voice at the other end. 'Mother wants you to be there, Miss Best. She told me so last night.'

'Did she?' Stupefied, Alex stared at the dancing sunlight on her office door and wondered if she was going quietly mad, or if it was just the rest of the world around her.

'You mustn't be alarmed to hear me say so,' Moira went on kindly. 'But we shall both look forward to seeing you on Saturday. Do you know Worthing at all?'

'No–'

'Then why don't you stay a few days and take a look around? We need to talk more. anyway, and there's plenty of room here at the house–'

'Oh, no,' Alex said, praying she didn't sound as panicky as she felt. 'If my commitments permit me to stay longer, I'll find my own accommodation, but thank you for the offer.'

Amusement was definitely in the other voice now, laced with a small measure of steel.

'Well, you know best, but I'm sure you'll recall your commitment to mother and me. We *are* retaining you, remember.'

This was clearly her way of saying goodbye, and Alex put down the phone as quickly as if it was red hot. Damn the pair of them with their spooky innuendoes, she thought furiously. Putting the fear of God into people – and she couldn't even remembering saying definitely that she would look into their affairs. But she did still have Leanora's notebook in her drawer, and she admitted that holding on to it meant a commitment of a sort.

She must be losing her grip, she thought now. She liked riddles and puzzles. She trusted in intuition and hunches, but she didn't like anything of a psychic nature that was frankly akin to cuckoo in the case of these two old birds.

She grimaced at her own feeble joke. But it seemed as if she was being drawn into their affairs whether she wanted to or not. She simply didn't seem able to resist, and whatever had happened to good old will-power?

She almost jumped out of her skin when the phone shrilled out again, grabbing it and gabbling out her name, and then holding the receiver away from her ear as if she expected to hear Leanora's voice reaching out to her out of the ether.

'Is that you, Alex? You sound very unlike yourself so I gather you must have heard the news by now.'

'*Nick!*' she said, with a burst of thankfulness. 'Oh Nick, am I glad to hear your voice.'

'Well, that's the best reaction I've had in months. Pity I'm not there right now to cash in on it. But from the sound of you, you're in need of a shoulder, am I right?'

'Damn right,' she mumbled. 'And the news you mentioned. It's about Scott Nelson, I take it? They got on to you fast enough, didn't they?'

'News travels fast on the police jungle drums. So how is it with you? I heard the story that you were probably the last one to see him.'

'You're not reading anything into that, are you?' she said, defensive at once.

'Christ no! You're not a suspect, and it was clearly a suicide. But jealousy was always my middle name as far as you're concerned, sweetheart, so you can't blame a bloke for wondering how far you and he had got involved. I know a spark when I see one.'

'Well, if you did, it very quickly went out,' she said swiftly. She hesitated, knowing how quickly he jumped on a hint of anything, however insignificant, but then rushed on. 'Nick, how much did you know about Scott? His private life, I mean. I know he was divorced–'

'Yeah. And it was rumoured that he knocked his wife about, but he denied it so positively that nobody really believed it.'

'Believe it, Nick. *Believe* it.'

There was a mulling silence at the other end, and then he spoke more quietly. And he was at once her best friend, her confidant, the good old reliable she missed so much.

'What happened, sweetheart?' he said, his voice gentle. 'He didn't hurt you, did he?'

And then the professional caring note dropped and he was wild with rage. 'If the bastard tried to rape you, I'll–'

'You'll what? Kill him? It's too late for that, isn't it? He's done the job for you,' she said, misery swamping her, together with an inner personal rage that hadn't got to her until now.

And knowing savagely, that she would have had those same murderous feelings if he *had* raped her. It wasn't only villains who were capable of such feelings, nor the intent to carry it through, if push came to shove. And Scott Nelson had been capable of pushing any woman to the limit. He could have pushed *her*...

'Are you telling me that's what happened?' Nick's voice penetrated. 'Did he rape you? If so, you've got to report it. Alex. You know that.'

'He didn't. He didn't even try. It wasn't like that. What the hell would be the point, anyway? He's dead.'

And she wasn't going to betray the poor bastard's inadequacy now that he couldn't answer for his actions, either. It was over, and all she wanted was to forget it.

'Is that the truth?'

'When have I ever lied to you, Nick?'

'Plenty of times when it suited you, my sweet—'

'Oh well in the course of a score, yes. But I'm not lying now. I'm not hurt in the way you mean, but I'm shocked that he's dead, *and* by the way Thomas told me.'

'I'll bet. He's an unfeeling bastard. Anyway, I've got news for you. I'm coming back next week for a while, until they can find a suitable replacement.'

'My God, maybe I'm psychic after all,' she burst out, her heart swelling with relief at his words far too much to consider what she was saying.

'Does that mean you'll be glad to see me?' he said, his voice as rich and sexy as ever now.

'You have no idea how much,' she said fervently. 'I'm going away for the weekend, but when I get back wc must get together, Nick.'

'Darling, there was never any doubt of that.'

'And no strings,' she reminded him.

He laughed. 'Oh, I'm not really into the marriage thing any more than you are, Alex. I'm counting my lucky stars that you refused me. Imagine what a hell of a life we'd have had together. On second thoughts—'

'Goodbye, Nick,' she said, still smiling as

she put down the phone before he could expand on it.

But the smile soon faded, because the events of last night and that afternoon were fast catching up on her. The silence of her office was making her feel claustrophobic and she had to get out of it. She needed to be home, with the security of her own four walls around her, putting the latch on the door and the chain across, and letting nobody else invade her space.

Her breath caught on a little sob as she remembered how easily she had let Scott Nelson in last night. But he had been a friend. A colleague. A buddy. And she should have learned by now, that you trusted no one until you were absolutely sure of them. It was one of the first and most basic things you learned at the hard school of private investigating. And what a rotten world it was, to have to accept such a thing.

Chapter 4

There was never a good day for a funeral. In Leanora's case, it was drizzly and misty, and as unlike early May as it was possible to be. Except in England, where nothing was reliable, Alex thought gloomily, fighting her way down the A24 and into the outskirts of Worthing and the cemetery where Leanora's remains were to be dispatched.

She bit her lip as the irreverent thought bounced into her head. But it had always been so, as far as she was concerned. It was as good a way as any for avoiding too much thought about the gruesomeness of the inevitable for all of them, rich or poor, famous or infamous.

Her thoughts skidded sideways again, wondering if he or she – the killer – would be present at the burial. It was a well-known fact that they often were. Dutifully solemn, or bereaved, or grieving, or openly weeping. It was very likely that plenty of Leanora's clients would be there too, and if nothing else, it would be an interesting study of people, and she refused to feel shame at her own cynicism.

Moira wanted her mother's killer caught, for God's sake ... and then she had to pull her thoughts up short, remembering that it wasn't why Moira had contacted her. He was already in police custody, charged with the crime – and Alex had already called his solicitor while she was here, and been frigidly assured that it was an open and shut case.

She eased her car into the church car-park and got out, flipping open her umbrella in annoyance. Rain certainly added to the misery of the day. And then she gaped at the sight of the people moving towards the church.

They were nearly all dressed in garish colours and chattering like magpies. It was more as if they were going to a party than a funeral, and she felt ludicrously out of place in her normal black attire. For a moment she hung back, wondering if she could be in the right place, and then she saw Moira swooping down on her from the church doorway, a study in scarlet, Alex thought irreverently again.

'I'm so glad you came, Miss Best,' she twittered. 'And I know mother's thrilled too. But do come inside out of the rain. It's nearly time for her entrance.'

Good God, she spoke as if it was a theatrical first-night, Alex thought, dazed. But she soon saw that that was how it was intended to be. That dun-coloured little woman on the cruise had somehow effected this bizarre congregation to turn up like birds of paradise ... but it wouldn't have been Leanora who did that. It would have been Moira – on mother's instructions, of course.

Alex swallowed, reminding herself that the rest of them were the batty ones, not her. From the look of them she was the only sane one around. And with the regulation elm coffin stained in midnight blue and

90

stencilled with a glittering moon and stars, she knew she was right. The sooner she got out of here, the better.

'Beautiful, isn't it?' someone whispered behind her, as she tried not to imagine what lay inside the box. What kind of get-up would Leanora have chosen for her funeral garb?

'Lovely,' she muttered, turning slightly at hearing a voice that was half-sincere, half-mocking. And then she got an enormous shock, seeing a face she remembered.

'Talk to you at the bun-fight later,' said the major. 'The performance is about to begin.'

'What are you doing here?' Alex demanded when the farcical occasion was over, and the chattering magpies were all trying to outdo one another at the Wolstenholme manor.

'I could ask the same of you,' he said. 'Last I saw of you, you were trying to avoid the old bird.'

'And you were being very enigmatic and suggesting that she wasn't who she said she was,' she remembered at once. 'I hope you're eating your words now, seeing her home and her daughter. And you still haven't answered my question.'

One of the blue-rinsed ladies floated towards them, a vision in yellow chiffon and chunky gold jewellery, and pounced on Alex.

'Tell me your star sign, my dear. I see such an aura about you that I'm sure you must be a Virgo. Am I right?'

'Mrs Wolstenholme said she could see an aura about me too,' Alex prevaricated. 'I begin to think I must be trailing some kind of ectoplasm around with me—'

The woman shrieked with laughter and clapped her hands as excitedly as a child with a new toy.

'Oh, what fun you are. I knew my feelings were right about you, my dear. Do tell if you've made contact with dear Leanora since she passed over.'

'Certainly not,' Alex snapped. 'I don't believe in that kind of thing.'

'Careful, Miss Best,' she heard the major chuckle. 'You'll have a dozen heart attacks to your credit if you start mocking the believers.'

She moved quickly away from the woman who was frowning angrily now. She lost the major in the crowd, and then she found Moira by her side.

'Don't take any notice of Doreen, Miss Best. She can't help it, no matter what the occasion. We did mother proud though, don't you think?'

'Very. But I really think I must be going now—'

Moira nodded. 'Come and see me tomorrow. We'll talk then. And we both thank you for your time.'

Alex escaped from the house before she could hear any more nonsense about mother being on hand – or in the ether to thank her. There was a strong scent of incense in the house that made her claustrophobic, and now that the rain had eased, there was a wonderful freshness in the air outside. The kind that was absent in London, but smelled refreshingly of the nearness of salt and sea and wide open spaces.

'May we have words?' she heard the major say beside her as she unlocked her car door with fingers that shook more than she wanted them to. She whirled around on him.

'Do you always creep up on people?' she said, and then she bit her lip, because he was almost nauseatingly normal after the clowns at Leanora's funeral. 'I'm sorry. This day has upset me. It isn't how I expected it to be. It's not how I'd want people to behave if it were me–'

'Neither would I. Look, why don't we have some tea? I don't drive, I'm afraid. I came down by train–'

'Oh, get in,' she said ungraciously. 'I'm sorry. I don't usually speak to people like that. I'm not myself–'

'Who is?' he commented.

'And when we get to a café, you can

explain that remark,' Alex said determinedly. 'And you can tell me just what you
know about Mrs Wolstenholme that I don't.'

'And you the detective!' he said with a
mocking smile.

She felt her mouth drop open, because to
her knowledge she had never told him what
she did. Nobody on the cruise ship had
known it, which made it all the more weird
that he was here. It was almost as if he was
following her – which was ridiculous, of
course. *Come into my parlour, said the spider to
the fly*... but in this case, which was she?

At the hesitation in her face he gave an
approving nod, and lost the chaffing note in
his voice. And there was a sudden keenness
in his eyes that was a world away from the
bragging oaf on the cruise ship.

'Full marks for spotting my deliberate
mistake, girl, so I had better come clean.
The name is Major Harry Deveraux, army
retired, and now an investigating officer
with the Special Branch. And just to put you
in the picture, we've had our eye on Mrs
Wolstenholme for some time.'

'Good Lord,' was all Alex could say.

She resisted the urge to feel cheated, even
though during her last encounter with the
lady and her observations, she had sensed
there was more behind Leanora's dreary
exterior than first appeared. She should feel
pleased about her intuition, but she knew of

old that if the police – and especially Special Branch – were involved, she would be out. There was no place in highscale investigations for a one-woman operation.

'Tea?' the major reminded her. 'My treat, of course.'

'I should bloody well think so,' she said grudgingly, and then she smiled. 'Sorry. Tea would be lovely. I couldn't face any more small-talk back there.'

'No more could I. And I found out what I wanted to know.'

'And what was that?' she said casually, as she started up the engine and swished the windscreen wipers across the window to clear away the last traces of rain.

The major laughed. 'Unsubtle, my dear Miss Best. But we'll compare notes over tea.'

And you'll tell me just how much you want me to know, and no more, you old bugger, thought Alex. Well, two could play at that game. She tried the shock treatment.

'Are you convinced they've got the real killer?'

'Aren't you?' he said, too quickly.

'I asked first.'

'Is that why you're here?'

'I'm here because Moira invited me on her own account. We – uh – happened to meet socially, and then I discovered her connection with Leonora–'

'And that has whiskers on it, Miss Best – or may I call you Alex?' the major said easily. 'And the name's Harry. We don't need to be so formal, do we?'

She glared at him. She knew that technique. Taking her off guard, pretending an easy friendship, and then tossing in an artless question to get at the truth. She'd known DI Nick Frobisher far too long not to recognize it. But she believed in the direct approach.

'So why are you here if not because there's some doubt about Leanora's murderer?'

'I didn't say that. You're the one who seemed to question the identity of the murderer.'

She wasn't sure that she had, except by implication. But these clever devils instantly seized on the slightest bit of ambiguity in a remark.

'Watch out for the one-way system when you get nearer the sea-front,' the major said suddenly. 'There's some parking in Montague Street and we can walk to Marine Parade from there. We can take a look at Madame Leanora's premises in one of the side-streets on the way if you haven't seen it already.'

It was a job for Alex to stop her jaw from dropping again. He obviously knew the town and where Leanora operated. Damn the man. She began to feel cheated again.

This was *her* case, and already she felt it slipping away from her.

'I haven't, and I'm not sure I want to,' she muttered, knowing that of course she damn well did. It was on the plans. But in her own time. And not with him.

He laughed out loud, reverting at once to the buffoon she had met on the cruise.

''Course you do, sweetheart. Pretty little thing like you must be just dying to know what fate's got in store for you!'

'Well, Leanora's not there to tell me, is she? And I thought I already knew my fate – until you popped up again, like the proverbial bad penny.'

And if this was no way to speak to what was it? – an investigating officer in Special Branch – then she didn't care. She thought he was a bit over the hill for that job, after a full army career, but presumably he was good at what he did. But she hadn't asked for his company, and didn't see the need to be any more forthcoming than she chose to be.

'All right, cards on the table over tea,' he said, more soberly. 'And no pun intended. Let's leave all that to the sharks and charlatans that prey on gullible folk.'

Alex followed his instructions then and negotiated the narrow streets until she. reached the car park at the wider Montague Street. She got out of the car, breathing in the clean salt air, the streets washed and freshened after the recent rain, a watery sun beginning to brighten the sky.

'Moira was very convincing about her mother,' she said as they walked. 'She swore she was a genuine clairvoyant.'

'No doubt, as far as the trade goes.' He gave it no more status than a street vendor on a Saturday morning stall.

'You're not a believer then?'

He snorted. 'It doesn't go with the job.'

'You can never quite dismiss it though, can you? I mean, there are people who see things that others don't–'

'And I thought you had brains as well as beauty,' he scoffed, his eyes boldly lingering over her figure, the old lech. She didn't rise to the bait.

'I do. But I'm willing to give genuine people the benefit of the doubt,' she said, nettled.

And she was even more annoyed at sounding so defensive, because she seemed to be siding with those loonies at the funeral, rather than going along with her feet-on-the-ground instincts. But that was the danger. They swept you along with their beliefs, until you were engulfed in them before you knew it. That was where they scored over the vulnerable.

'Anyway, you can't deny that the police occasionally consult mediums,' she added triumphantly. 'So there must be something in it.'

'Especially when they're making a nice little income in certain sidelines,' Harry said, motioning her to turn down a side-street now.

'How? Selling crystals and charms and all that rot?'

She realized he had stopped walking, and that they were outside a small shop premises with the name Madame Leanora over the door. An elegant sign boldly advertised clairvoyance and discreet readings, with tarot cards a speciality. The darkened glass on the shop window displayed nothing at all. The whole façade was presumably meant to create an aura of mystery, but to Alex it was gloomy and a bit unnerving, and she heartily wished she'd never met the woman.

'Don't you want to see inside?' Harry asked softly, his voice quietly goading her, challenging her.

'What? We can't – I mean it's closed. We can't just break into the premises, and if I wanted to see inside, I'm sure Moira would arrange it–' she hedged.

And now that she was here, she didn't really want to go inside at all. Not – one – tiny – cotton-picking bit...

She heard the echo of her one-time lover's voice in her head. *Are you sure you're in the right business, Alex?*

No, Gary, she wasn't. Not this kind of business, anyway. She could deal with clients who retained her to investigate income-tax fraud. She was prepared to do a stakeout surveillance for as long as required for a straying husband or wife. She was capable of tracking down missing funds or teenagers on the run – though she didn't care for that much.

Straightforward crimes of the minor variety were one thing – but this was something else. This was venturing into areas she didn't like and didn't want. And damn it, she was only hired to find out who was stalking Moira – and had apparently been stalking Leanora too. She had almost lost sight of the reason Moira had contacted her, and she wasn't damn well going to be side-tracked any longer.

'I wasn't suggesting that we break in, sweetie,' the major said calmly now. 'It's all legit, naturally. Official business and all that. Moira gave me a key.'

Well, presumably this had been done beforehand, since Alex wasn't aware that he had even been speaking to Moira at the funeral. But then, with so many people around, it wouldn't have surprised her if half of them had been complete strangers. Filled with morbid curiosity perhaps, to see this spectacle for a woman whom many

100

people would have feared. Anyone who dabbled in the occult or the afterlife was greeted with suspicion bordering on fear by most folk.

But she was probably demeaning all the genuine mediums and clairvoyants, and she had no real reason to think that Leanora wasn't one of them. Nor did she have any option but to go inside Leanora's premises right now unless she wanted to look like a bloody nitwit who didn't deserve the title of private eye at all. She took a deep breath. Wasn't this what she was here for? And hadn't she been born curious?

'So what are we waiting for?' she said.

'That's my girl,' Harry crowed, squeezing her arm and making her cringe at such chauvinistic praise.

She still found it hard to get used to the fact that he was not what she had thought he was. A bragging bore, sizing up the most likely females on the cruise, and chatting up every one of them whenever he got them cornered. Definitely not of the sober, elderly Special Branch ilk.

And she should have asked to see his identification. It was the first thing to get clarified if ever there was any doubt. But why should there be? She had taken him on face value, simply because his attitude had changed, and he now seemed to be *exactly* who he said he was.

Bad move, Alex, she told herself, seeking anything to take her mind off the jitters she felt as they went inside the dim interior of Madame Leanora's premises.

'Christ Almighty, did somebody die in here?' she heard her companion say tightly, and her heart leapt.

'You know somebody did,' she stuttered. 'Leanora did.'

'Sorry, girl. I was forgetting. It's this bloody incense or joss-sticks or whatever the hell it is!' he snapped. 'I've seen most things, but I never could stand all this hocus-pocus. Turns my guts. Where's the bloody light switch?'

He seemed to have reverted again, Alex thought. He was a chameleon, and he seemed almost as jittery as she was now. She registered the fact briefly, and then felt a flood of relief as the light came on, and the room was bathed in a red glow. And at once it became a normal room – if normal was the word to use for such an exotic interior.

'My God, you'd never have associated the old girl on the ship with all this crap, would you?' the major said.

Alex was hardly listening. She was thankful for having a photographic memory as she took in the atmosphere. It was the kind of place beloved by movies, where they exaggerated the set-up for maximum effect. But now it seemed that clairvoyants – this one at least – really did decorate their premises in the most exotic way imaginable.

Deep red drapes everywhere added to the suffocatingly aromatic ambience. The small circular table was covered in a black, bobble-edged chenille cloth that seemed of another era. A crystal ball had pride of place in its centre, and the shelves were stacked with crystals and baubles, books of magic, about ESP, the tarot, and the occult.

It seemed almost impossible to identify that dun-coloured woman Alex had met with all this ... but then she remembered her evening attire ... the feathered boa and dated cocktail dress, and the keen-eyed gaze she had locked onto Alex when she had warned her of a death ... and she knew that in this stifling atmosphere anyone could believe anything...

'What are we supposed to be looking for?' she said in a cracked voice, seeing the major poking around on the shelves, opening book covers and flicking open a pack of tarot cards and scattering them on the floor with apparent disdain.

Alex picked them up resentfully, replacing them in their cardboard box with a shudder as she glimpsed the cards depicting the Hangman and the Fool. Such things had always unnerved her. How the hell could anyone prophesy anything from a pack of cards that some said were works of the devil and akin to satanism?

'Anything that will give us an inkling into her dealings,' he said briskly in answer to her question.

'Just what were these dealings you're so interested in? Cards on the table, remember, Major?'

She tried to be jocular, but for the life of her, she couldn't call him Harry. He'd been the bombastic major on the cruise ship.

She hadn't liked him then, and she didn't like him now. Nothing had changed that.

'Blackmail, Miss Best.'

And what had happened to Alex? It seemed as if he too, had decided to keep their relationship on a more formal footing. Thank God.

'Blackmail? That sweet little old lady?'

He laughed. 'Now who's kidding who? You never thought of her as a sweet little old lady any more than I did!'

'I certainly never thought of her as a blackmailer!'

'People are rarely what they seem. You should know that in your business. In our business.'

She spoke as lightly as possible, considering that her heart was starting to beat sickeningly fast.

'How odd. That's just what I'm always telling myself. So tell me, which one of your personas really applies to you, Major? Are you the wicked flirt I met on the cruise, or the man from Special Branch? I should have asked to see your ID. Remiss of me, wasn't it? And you should have reminded me!'

She felt a chill run through her even as she said the jerky words. Nick Frobisher would have flashed his card at her at once. So would Scott Nelson. So would any real copper.

She heard him give a low laugh. 'Are you saying that you're prepared to believe in this old biddy's arty-farty stuff, and yet you're doubting my credentials?'

'I'd like to see your ID before I answer that,' Alex said steadily. 'And then I'd like to get out of here and have some tea like you promised me,' she added, to allay his suspicions.

Just in case he *wasn't* who he said he was.

And preferably in some nice, normal, seaside teashop, where the only aromas were of freshly baked cakes and steaming tea and coffee, and the plaintive cry of the seagulls would overcome the pounding of her heart.

'Of course,' the major said smoothly, his hand moving towards his inside pocket.

For a moment, Alex froze. Was he about to pull out a gun and murder her here and now? Or more likely a knife, since this was the place for a stabbing, she thought wildly, remembering Leanora's fate. And did your whole life really flash before your eyes in such a moment? Hers hadn't – yet.

In those few seconds she was completely disorientated, and then she heard a loud hammering, and hardly knew whether it was her thudding heart or the blessed sound of someone coming to rescue her.

'Is everything all right in there?' she heard a male voice say uncertainly, and she twisted around to face the young copper standing in the doorway. He was silhouetted, dark against the sunlight now that the rain clouds had cleared, but her relief was so great that if he had been the Grim Reaper himself, she could have kissed him.

The major pushed past her, almost knocking the young copper over, and brushing himself down as if to be rid of the remnants of the dusty interior.

'Everything's fine here, Constable. My ID card – Special Branch,' he said, thrusting it under the startled young man's eyes. 'Miss Best and I have permission to be here today, and were about to lock the place up again. But you're to be commended for your alertness. Full marks.'

'Thank you, Sir,' the copper, little more than a boy, stuttered. He all but saluted, Alex thought, still dazed at how quickly the major had taken charge of the situation. And whatever he had shown the constable, it had clearly satisfied him. So she had probably been wrong about him after all, she thought hopefully.

She spoke quickly as the constable walked away.

'Look, I'm sorry–'

'Never mind that. But I'll have to forgo tea after all, or I'll miss my train. It was interesting to meet you again.'

Without another word, he strode off, lost in the crowds that had appeared like magic after the morning rain.

Alex had no idea where the railway station was, but she didn't care. Whoever he was, she wouldn't care if she never saw him again. They had just attended a funeral, however bizarre, and merely saying that it was interesting to meet her again without any reference to the occasion, was just about the most insensitive thing anyone could say.

Once outside, she took a few deep breaths to rid herself of the cloying atmosphere inside Madame Leanora's, and her general resentment of the major, and went to find a teashop. Something hot and strong was needed. And the sexy, *normal* image of one Gary Hollis slid unwittingly into her mind.

She could do with his no-nonsense chatter now, and his earthy style of seduction. Anything to take her mind off the weird and mystical, *and* although Gary wouldn't have been flattered by being put in that mould, she knew damn well he'd have complied. Willingly. Enthusiastically.

The crowds were becoming thicker now.

Someone bumped into her and apologized briefly, but her mind was still on other things. Wondering with a stab of longing if she would ever see Gary again, while knowing that it was probably only time and distance that made thoughts of him so wanton.

But they had been so good together. Good to the point of spectacular ... and the stirring inside her was more than somewhat as she entered the little tearoom with its olde-worlde bell clanging over the door, and the chintzy curtains and red-checked tables there to greet her.

'What'll it be?' said a bored waitress.

'Tea and a cream doughnut, please,' Alex said, and to hell with her thighs.

She felt in her jacket pocket where she kept her purse with small change, and froze. It wasn't there. She fumbled rapidly through her handbag, and it wasn't there, either. She remembered somebody bumping against her in the crowded street, and knew what must have happened. She felt so bloody stupid, and so vulnerable, and so close to tears.

Before the waitress could come back with her order, she got out of there, fast. It wasn't the right thing to do, and maybe if the girl had been better-mannered, she wouldn't have run out on her. But she had other things to think about right then, trying to remember what had been in her purse.

Not much, thankfully. It was just the one where she kept a few notes and ready change, and she wasn't in the habit of keeping her credit cards in it. They were safely in the inner compartment of her bag, together with the rest of her money, her ID and driving licence. The thief wouldn't have got much for his trouble, but the experience shook her all the same.

And he wasn't going to damn well get away with it, she fumed, as anger took over. She may not have lost much, but there might well be some dear old lady carrying all her life savings around with her, against all establishment advice, and she might not have been so lucky.

'Can you tell me where the police station is?' she asked the nearest passer-by.

'Corner of High Street and Union Place,' she was told.

She walked it, if only to try and clear her head. In the back of her mind was the uneasy thought that one or two of her business cards might have been in her little purse. She couldn't remember whether or not she had put any of them in it. If so, then the thief would know her name and address. She tried to reason that if he was a local and maybe a kid, he probably wouldn't bother with an address in London.

Worthing was more upmarket than many seaside places she could mention, she thought resentfully. (A *haaaandbag?* came soaring into her mind.) But somehow you never expected petty theft to happen here –and what an idiotic thought *that* was.

All the same, you didn't go out on a sunny afternoon expecting some bastard to dip his fingers into your pocket, did you? Regretfully, she knew that that these days such things happened anywhere.

She reported the theft without any real expectation of ever seeing the purse again, and when she detailed its contents she played down the reason she was making such a fuss, more intent on reporting that there was a thief about.

It was an inane remark if ever she heard one, she thought stupidly, especially in a busy town like Worthing. Every big town or seaside venue was fair game for pickpockets.

But the theft was duly registered in the day book, and the duty officer's eyes flicked over her with interest as she gave him her occupation crisply, and told him where she was staying in the town.

'Caught any criminals lately?' he said, in what was meant to be a jokey manner, and she froze him with a glare.

Much later, he reported that one look from those green eyes could probably freeze an Eskimo, but he wouldn't mind getting his hands around those luscious curves.

And then there was nothing else for Alex to do but take a general look around the town, although it had lost much of its charm for her now. Thankfully, there were no seaside stalls or kiss-me-quick hats to be seen, but neither was there anything much to do. She almost wished she'd accepted Moira's offer to stay at the Wolstenholme house while she was here, but rejected the thought at once. For all she knew, right now Moira and her weird cronies might be holding a seance, just to find out if mother had enjoyed her day.

But after a night at the well-appointed guest house she had chosen, (all en-suite, newly refurbished, television and telephones in all rooms, lifts to all floors, early morning calls on request) she ate a far heartier break-fast than usual, telling herself that when in Rome etc etc ... and then drove back to the house that now belonged solely to Moira.

'How nice and early you are,' Moira said delightedly. 'Do come and join us, Alex. None of us got up very early this morning, and we were just having coffee.'

'We?' Alex said faintly, having expected this meeting between herself and Moira to be private.

And *necessary*, she thought quickly. For pity's sake, this meeting was for the inten-tion of discussing the stalker who had been pestering herself and her mother, not for some social occasion. That *had* been the purpose of contacting her.

She followed Moira into the lounge, heavy with ornate furniture and ornaments of a definitely occult variety that Alex hadn't noticed in the mêlée of yesterday. She preferred not to study them too closely, and found herself facing half a dozen people whom she vaguely recognized from being at the funeral. From the look of them, they still wore the same weird garb as before, and Alex felt the beginnings of panic. Or maybe *trapped* was the more favoured word.

'Have I come at the wrong time?' she said quickly. 'I can easily come back again—'

'Not at all. We were expecting you.'

Who was? Mother et al?

But after all, there was nothing untoward in the gathering except pale and sleep-deprived faces to explain the morning after the night before. And from what Alex quickly deduced, the gallons of strong black coffee were to counteract a jolly night of exchanging memories and anecdotes about Leanora, which were presumably intended to send her happily to whatever destination awaited her in the Great Beyond.

Christ, she thought, *I'm even starting to think in their terms now. And it had better stop right now!*

The coffee drinking was evidently a ritual that wouldn't be hurried, but at last the all-night visitors had departed, and Moira

112

turned to Alex with a little contented sigh.

'Mother would have loved their company. Well, she did, of course,' she added quickly, after what Alex considered the first sane comment since she had known the woman. 'And what did you think of her special day? Not quite as you expected?'

'Not exactly,' she murmured. 'But tell me something. Did she always go on holiday alone? I'd have thought she would have wanted your company.'

'Oh no. Mother always came into her own when she travelled alone. The vibes were strongest when I wasn't there to confuse things,' she said with a beaming smile.

Alex almost hated her. She wasn't normal, sitting there with that bright, fatuous look on her face, as if expecting Alex to say how lovely the funeral had been, and how refreshing it was to see all those garish outfits, and not a tear in sight. It definitely wasn't bloody normal.

She put down her final cup of coffee before the bitter, stinging taste of it burned her throat beyond help. For the first time, she wondered if it contained anything other than coffee. And if it did, it was too late now...

'So now we'll talk,' Moira went on. 'I presume you'll want to see mother's premises, and I suggest we go there this morning. I need to pick up a few things anyway.'

She stopped abruptly, seeing the look on

113

Alex's face.

'It doesn't alarm you, does it? I assure you, there's nothing to be afraid of, Miss Best–'

'It's not that. It's just that the major–'

'The major?' Moira frowned. 'What major is that? I don't know any major.'

A slow trickle of fear ran through Alex.

'Major Harry Deveraux. He was here yesterday. In the church. At the burial. At the house,' she said, feeling desperately as if she was going into Cluedo-mode. 'He said you had given him a key to Madame Leanora's premises.'

'I certainly did no such thing,' Moira said indignantly. 'I don't know anyone of that name.'

'But he was a guest – or so I assumed. He was on the cruise where I first met your mother. I thought he was an old bore then, but yesterday he seemed different. *Was* different. He said he was an investigator with Special Branch, and he seemed to know all about me, and about your mother–'

Her voice trailed away. The major had never said anything about knowing Leanora on the cruise, except to query her name. Or had that simply been a ruse to engage Alex in conversation? Thinking back, she knew it had worked.

'And he said I gave him a key to mother's premises?' Moira's voice penetrated her thoughts.

'Yes. We went there. He was looking for something. Whatever it was, he didn't find it, and then he went on a train back to wherever he had come from. As far as I know.'

'This needs thinking about,' Moira said. 'Do you suppose he could be our stalker? Following mother on her cruise, and then turning up here? It makes sense, doesn't it?'

Maybe it did, but the eager and almost feverishly excited way that Moira was seizing on the obvious solution made Alex even more certain that he was not the stalker. Whoever it was, he was still out there.

But Major Harry Deveraux, if that was his name, had something to do with these two women that she didn't yet know about. And whatever it was, she was going to make it her business to find out.

Chapter 5

Alex didn't leave Moira's house until late that afternoon, after being persuaded to stop for lunch. During that time she had learned virtually nothing new, except that when she showed Moira her holiday photographs, Moira emphatically denied ever having seen the major before.

And apparently he had cannily avoided any contact with her at yesterday's funeral. Alex tried to put the uneasy thoughts out of her mind as she returned to the sane comfort of the Worthing guest house.

Mrs Dooley, the landlady – if that was what you called such a stiffly coiffed lady who clearly wore her best clothes night and day – ran a clinically clean establishment where no speck of dust would dare to be seen.

It was just what Alex needed after the stuffy atmosphere of Moira's house. Large though that was, it still had the effect of closing in on you, partly because of the heavy furniture and the blank eyes in the many animal figurines and statues that seemed to be forever watching.

Before she left, Alex had been surprised to glimpse a swimming-pool in the back garden. While they had all been confined to the house in the misty rain, she hadn't noticed it before, and she couldn't resist an unlikely picture of those two strange old biddies doing their daily lengths in whatever weird swimming-cozzies they might choose to wear.

She jumped at the sound of her mobile phone, and the irritating musical melody jangled her nerves.

'Alex, where the hell have you been? I've been trying to get you all day,' the well-remembered voice snapped.

'Sorry, Nick,' she muttered, not sure why she was apologizing, but at least he was somebody normal. Reasonably. 'I've had my mobile switched off. Business reasons.'

'Oh yes. So what's happening?'

'Nothing much. Where are you?' she countered.

'Where do you think? I was hoping for a night out. Now I'll have to phone my other girl.'

She heard the teasing in his voice, and without warning her heart warmed towards him. God, she wished he was here right now. If he was, she'd have no qualms in falling into his arms and into his bed. She needed the contact of somebody warm and loving and – yes, normal. In every physical respect Nick was certainly that. And she knew the danger of feeling that way when she was jittery and vulnerable.

'Make the most of her then,' she whipped back. 'Is that all you were calling me about?'

'I thought that was enough,' he said, aggrieved. 'But actually, no. You're needed at Scott Nelson's internal inquiry on Thursday as you were the last person to see him alive. I thought I'd warn you before you got the official call.'

She tried to ignore the leap of her heart.

'So soon? And don't make it sound as if there was anything sinister about his death.

117

There wasn't – was there?'

'Sorry, darling. I didn't mean that at all. It was obviously suicide, but I gather his ex is intending to be there as well, so be prepared.'

'Oh? Do you think she'll want to paint me as the wicked other woman?'

'You tell me. Could she?'

He either had to be joking, or trying to find out if there had been anything between herself and Scott Nelson, but for the moment Alex didn't see it that way.

'If he was divorced, he was a free agent, so don't try to lay that one on me, Nick–'

'I'm more interested in whether or not he tried to lay one on you, darling.'

'You've got a bloody nerve!'

And then she relented. 'But, for your information, no, he didn't. I've already told you that, haven't I?'

'I just like to hear it. Especially in person.'

She had a sudden suspicion. 'Where exactly are you?'

'Take a look out of your window. There's a small park across the road.'

'I don't believe this!'

But she walked quickly to the window and saw the park and the pond beyond, sparkling blue in the sunlight. And the bench where he was waving to her, mobile phone at his ear.

'How did you know where I was?' she demanded.

'Saw the report on your stolen purse at the local nick and made a note of the address. Nelson would have been staying there too, of course, after bragging about his conquest with the luscious lady dick. You got off lightly, I'd say.'

She heard the grim note in his voice. It was Scott's suicide that had prevented him coming here, and Nick was as bloody insensitive as ever, but she knew how lucky she had been to escape what could have been pretty ugly. She'd had a small taste of it already.

'I'm coming down. Stay right there,' she said.

She switched off her mobile before running down the two flights of stairs, ignoring the lift. She ignored the screech of a car's tyres as well as she ran across to the small park and was clutched tightly in Nick Frobisher's arms. But after one kiss she began pummelling his chest as the events of the past few days suddenly overcame her.

'Why didn't you warn me about Scott?' she almost sobbed. 'You should have told me—'

'It was only ever hearsay, Alex, and nobody narks on a colleague without evidence. You know that.'

'I know—'

'So what's this case you're on? You're not just here for your health, are you?'

He spoke so calmly, so soothingly, wanting to help. To be her best buddy ... and wanting to cash in on whatever scam she'd got wind of. And she knew him too well.

'My business, Nick. And my client's. You know that. So why are *you* in Worthing?' she asked pointedly. 'You didn't drive all this way just to let me know about the inquiry.'

'Couple of days off,' he said casually. 'I like the seaside – reminds me of my youth–'

'Come off it. You never take days off without a good reason. Are you following me?'

'Is there any reason why I should be?'

She felt like screaming. He was playing with her, and they were getting nowhere. Then he handed her something that looked very familiar.

'My purse,' she exclaimed. 'Where did you get it?'

Good God, it wasn't him brushing into her in a crowded street and scaring the living daylights out of her, was it? If it was, she'd kill him...

'Some do-gooder handed it in at the local nick soon after you left it. Empty, of course. Careless of you, Alex.'

She resented the sneer. 'There was nothing in it of any value,' she told him, ignoring the thought of a stray address card or two. 'Just small change. It was only the thought of some petty thief being on the loose that made me report it. I wish I hadn't now, then you couldn't have tracked me down,' she

120

added truculently.

He laughed easily, his arm sliding around her waist. His Latino good looks were streets ahead of anything that wimp, Nelson had had to offer, and she quickly squashed the thought.

'Too late, babe. I've booked in at the same hostelry as yourself, so let's go and persuade the dragon lady to give us some tea, and then we'll talk.'

She fumed as Nick steered her through the busy late afternoon traffic. But she was on her toes now. The fact that he'd called in at the local nick told her he probably wasn't just here for his health. He was after something, and as yet she didn't know what it was. But she wanted something too, and he was her means of getting it. She needed to find out just what major whoever-he-was, was playing at.

She smiled at Nick more sweetly, ignoring the answering flicker in his eyes, and in ten minutes time they had the front lounge of the guest house to themselves, and were being served with afternoon tea and cakes by the gushing landlady.

And Alex had to admit that if he could melt that iceberg, he could charm anybody.

'So come clean, Nick.'

'Ladies first,' he said smoothly.

'Bollocks. There's supposed to be no difference between the sexes in our job, so

I'm not saying a word until you do.'

He gave a sigh. 'Sometimes, Alex, you should stop seeing things that aren't there. If you want the God-honest truth, I was worried about you.'

Alex stared at him, all other thoughts flying out of her head at the concern in his eyes.

'Why?' she asked bluntly.

'Why do you think?' he said roughly. 'You've had two bloody awful experiences lately. I don't know how far Nelson had got with you, and I'm not asking – but coming on top of that there was his suicide, and for all I knew you might have snapped. You're not infallible, darling. It happens to the best of us.'

'Oh.' She didn't know what else to say. It wasn't what she had expected at all.

'So why did you really come here if it wasn't for a bit of nookie with Nelson?' he went on casually.

'Cut that out!' she said, glaring at him. 'I came to attend somebody's funeral, if you must know. Someone I met on the cruise. And yes, I *have* been feeling the strain lately. This woman was the oddest person. The clairvoyant woman I told you about. She could unnerve anybody. She told me she saw a death, but it wasn't mine – or hers. You'd think she'd have seen *that*, wouldn't you? Then I heard from an old friend I hadn't seen in years, and shortly afterwards she died. Then Scott Nelson committed suicide, and Leanora herself was murdered. A lot of coincidences, wouldn't you say?'

'It certainly seems like two deaths too many to me,' Nick agreed as she babbled on. 'But why attend her funeral? Knowing you I can't imagine you kept in contact with a weirdo.'

'It seemed like the decent thing to do.'

'Really?' He oozed scepticism now. 'And just how did you come to hear about it?'

'Her daughter contacted me. And stop giving me the third degree, Nick. I don't like it.'

She took a great gulp of tea, and winced as it burned her throat. But it gave her a moment to gather her wits. As she put her cup down, she gazed out of the lounge window, and spoke more thoughtfully.

'I think the daughter felt she wanted to talk to anyone who had recently met her mother on the cruise. People are like that. It gives them a kind of comfort—'

'Pull the other one, Alex. I know about the murder, so what did the daughter really want?' he said coolly.

She met his eyes then, copper-cold and steady, above the rim of his own cup. Thinnest bone china, Alex registered. The cup, not the man. There was nothing thin-skinned about Nick.

She brought her wayward thoughts back to his question.

'I don't have to tell you that,' she said at last.

'No, you don't,' he said agreeably. 'So what shall we do tonight? Go on a pub crawl and get quietly drunk?'

She should have been prepared for his quick change of mood. It was the standard way of taking a suspect off guard. But she wasn't a suspect, damn it, and she was quick-witted too, and after the trauma of meeting up with Leanora's acquaintances, she latched on to his suggestion with relief. Besides, anything was better than having him probe her every move, and finding out just why Moira had called her. She put up a token resistance all the same.

'Since when did you coppers get *quietly* drunk on a pub crawl? I've been there, remember?'

'Well, I promise not to make a noise when I go sneaking into your room after hours, babe.'

She laughed. 'Get lost, Nick!'

All the same, she couldn't resist the picture of the buxom Mrs Dooley, snooping about the guest house in the wee small hours in a voluminous nightgown, her rigid hair spiked with rollers, hoping to catch any shenanigans among her house-guests. It was such a ridiculous image, smacking of boarding-school/house-mistress stuff, but it was a hell of a turn-on.

'Well, Alex?' she heard Nick say softly. 'Do we go out and paint this town red tonight, or what?'

'Why not? Why bloody not? I could do with a few laughs,' she said recklessly.

They walked, of course. It wouldn't do to be hauled over by some earnest-faced young copper for drunk driving. She could imagine the hoo-hah at the local nick when their identities were discovered. *And* the field-day the local rag might have.

So they walked, which was good fun in itself, discovering the local pubs, some stuffy, others raucous with karaoke singing, and finally stepping out into the chill of the night air with Nick Frobisher's arm wrapped tightly around her waist, and her own clinging to him. Holding each other up, virtually, and the incongruity of it didn't escape her.

It was a good thing the gen pub couldn't see them now, she thought, abbreviating everything in her head because she wasn't capable of stringing long words together right now...

'We'd better creep into the guest ho so we don't shock the natives,' she stuttered.

'Guest ho? Whassaguest ho?' Nick said solemnly.

He was far more sober than she was, she registered. But he had drunk as much, or more, than she had. He was clearly able to hold it better. Or else he had a bigger gut capac – capas – whatever.

Bully for him, she thought, automatically tightening her stomach muscles for a moment before she let them go in uncaring abandon. So what? It wasn't as if she was going to *sleep* with him. He wasn't going to know the extent of her thighs...

Alex choked again as the image of a seaside postcard came into her mind, her own head superimposed on the vast buttocks of a squat fat lady.

He chuckled with her, even though he wasn't following her thoughts, and then a sudden downpour of rain sent them racing towards the guest house, arms still melding them together like Siamese twins, until Nick managed to fumble the outdoor key in the lock, and they crept upstairs to their rooms like two conspirators.

'I've got a bottle of vodka in my room. Your drink, I believe, ma'am. One for the road?' he whispered.

'What road?' she giggled.

'I'll bring it in two shakes,' he said, almost pushing her inside her room.

She was still giggling when he returned, a bottle in his hand. She hadn't moved away from the door, which seemed to be holding her up, and he had to push it open. She stumbled and would have fallen if he hadn't caught her.

'Time for beddy-byes, I think,' she heard him say, and before she could ask him if he thought this kind of infantile talk attracted the opposite sex, he had scooped her up and lay her on the bed, and was proceeding to undress her.

'This wasn't part of the plan, Nick,' she mumbled.

And she should be drying her damp hair...

'I know. Trust me. I'm a–'

'You're a rat,' she said, and then, unable to resist the erotic touch of his hands on her bare flesh, she wound her arms around his neck and pulled him on top of her. 'But a very nice rat, I must admit. One of the nicest I know–'

'Did anyone ever tell you you talk too much?' he said, his mouth so close to hers she could feel the roughness of his evening stubble on her skin. She could breathe his breath. She could feel him hardening against her softness, and she needed to be loved, to be safe and wanted and loved ... and she knew he had wanted her for so long...

She awoke with what the boys at the nick would call the mother and father of a hangover. The room smelled stale, and for a few moments she couldn't remember where she was. It wasn't the bedroom at her flat, that was for sure.

There was a kind of screaming in her head that she finally identified as the noise of seagulls, which definitely wasn't part of the London scene. There was strong sunlight streaming in through a gap in the curtains and she winced as she turned away from it too quickly.

Her eyes focussed on the bottle of vodka beside her bed. Unopened. And she couldn't imagine what it was doing there...

Memory of the night before rushed at her so fast that she gasped with the shock and fury of it. She ran her hands down her body, knowing she would be naked, but still hoping against hope that she wasn't, and that it was all a bad dream.

She hadn't actually let that love-rat Frobisher screw her ... *had* she? Once that happened, she would be vulnerable and he would know it. She groaned, sitting up carefully, then immediately pulling the duvet back over her when she glimpsed the love-bites on her breasts. Oh God.

She leaned over, hugging the mound of her knees, her red hair spilling like fire over the duvet, as she unwillingly recalled what had happened.

Picturing herself giving in so wantonly to DI Nick Frobisher. No, not *giving in,* she admitted with brutal honesty. Not that old virginal chestnut. Taking all that he had to offer ... demanding it ... and getting it...

She heard a gentle tapping on her door, followed by the landlady's voice. She grabbed her kimono and slid it around her shoulders, quickly pushing the vodka bottle under the bed, knowing Mrs Dooley would definitely not approve.

'Please come in,' she called as normally as she could, considering how her heart was pounding. Ridiculously, she wondered if she was about to be ordered out of the house as a scarlet woman.

Mrs Dooley walked into the room with a tray of tea and toast, despite the fact that there were tea-making facilities in the room. This wasn't normal treatment from a guest ho landlady, was it?

'I'm sorry to hear you're not feeling well, Miss Best. Your friend has had to go back London urgently but he said he'd be in touch and he knew you would understand.'

Oh, she understood all right, Alex thought. It was just as she always thought. Nick was a charmer of the first water if he could persuade that old harridan to bring her tea and toast in bed. But apart from that he was a gutter-rat. The worst kind.

She knew she had to keep up the anger as long as possible, simply to ward off the blow to her ego. Keeping at bay the knowledge that she felt used and stupid. She had let this happen after all her efforts to keep things between them on a professional basis and not allowing personal feelings to intrude, other than having him as her best friend. Which he was, but which certainly didn't include *having* him...

She pushed down the maddening little burst of memory that said it had been good though. Bloody good. Stupendously good. The best.

But since Mrs Dooley seemed inclined to linger and chat, she decided it might be useful to get her version of the poor lady who had recently been murdered in the town. And Mrs Dooley proved to be very talkative indeed.

She was still pondering over what she had learned after the landlady left her, and then spilled half of the over-sweet tea on the duvet as her mobile phone shrilled out. She almost fell out of bed, grabbing the phone quickly and spitting out her name.

'Did I wake you?'

She stared into space for all of ten seconds while that obnoxious phrase 'running the gamut of her emotions' raged through her mind. Seeing the man behind the voice. Feeling the man. Being warmed and caressed and loved by the man ... drowning in him and becoming part of him.

And just as quickly hating him and

despising herself for letting him make her feel so vulnerable – and alive.

'You've got a hell of a nerve,' she snapped.

'I know,' said Nick. 'It's part of my charm.'

For the first time since she had known him, she sensed a faint note of uncertainty in his voice. Disembodied voices on the phone did that. Revealed things about a person they weren't aware of. She hardened her heart. Nothing could make Nick Frobisher uncertain. Certainly not the thought of seducing her in a Worthing guest house. She'd just be one more notch on his proverbial belt.

'What do you want?' she snapped again.

'Just to check that you're all right, darling. You went out like a light last night, and I knew you'd have a hell of a head this morning. Sorry about that. Maybe the pub crawl wasn't such a good idea after all.'

'That wasn't the only thing,' she muttered. None of it was a good idea. It changed things between them, and that was something she hadn't had time to contemplate yet.

'What? I can't hear you, babe. All hell has broken loose here. There was a vicious racial attack in the early hours. The owner of one of those twenty-four-seven shops is in intensive care, and it's dodgy whether or not he'll make it.'

'And that's why they called you back?' she

said sceptically, her selfish anger over-coming the swift wave of sympathy she felt for the shopkeeper. Racial attacks were the dregs, and it was one thing they were completely agreed on.

But was it a genuine call back to the station to head up the enquiry, or was it just because you couldn't face me this morning? her thoughts ran on.

'It's my patch, Alex. And you know what I think of these bastards. But I'll look up that major bloke for you when I've got a spare moment. Give me a call when you get back to town.'

She cut him off without answering. All right, so it had been her intention to ask him to do a bit of checking on the major's cre-dentials, but she honestly couldn't remem-ber getting around to it. Presumably she must have done, but much of last night was just too hazy in her memory. And that made her angry, because God knew what else she might have told him that was none of his business.

She groaned, knowing she had been even more stupid than she realized. During the pub crawl Nick had undoubtedly winkled out of her far more than she had intended.

But then she began to think more logically. What did it matter? She needed to know if the major was all that he said he was, and Nick had been her quickest means of finding out whether or not he was on police files as a con man, or if he was exactly who he said he was.

She finished her tea and toast and began to feel slightly human again. A quick shower helped to clear her head marginally more, and although she was more fragile than usual and the dark circles under her eyes weren't exactly flattering, she answered the next call on her mobile less aggressively.

'Miss Best – Alex – oh dear, I do hope you haven't gone back to London yet. I need to see you urgently. Can you call round to the house again this morning?' came Moira Wolstenholme's agitated voice.

'I'm still here, Moira. What's wrong?'

'I'd rather tell you in person. Well, *show* you. It's sick, it really is. These people don't know what they're doing. They don't know what they're playing with. It's not a game. If mother were here now–'

'I'll be with you in half an hour,' Alex said, as the words became more disjointed. 'Keep calm, Moira. Whatever it is, I'm sure we can sort it out.'

She certainly wasn't sure. She wasn't God, but she had to keep up the façade of being ultra-professional, which seemed the most unlikely thing in the world this morning.

She felt far less like Alexandra Best, sophisticated private eye, and far more like Audrey Barnes, country-girl from the wilds of Yorkshire, watching too much television and dreaming of living in London where the streets were paved with gold. More like crap, she thought grimly.

But she wasn't doing anybody any good by wallowing away in this bedroom. She had a client to see who needed her help, and even though she wished she'd never set eyes on either of the Wolstenholme women, she was still intrigued by the thought of dun-coloured Leanora turning out to be something of a Mystic Meg, and inciting some unknown person to murder her.

Fending off Mrs Dooley's fussing, now that she had apparently decided to treat her like an honoured guest, Alex slid thankfully behind the wheel of her car and found her way back to Moira's house. In sunlight it looked even larger and far more imposing than it had the first time she'd seen it, shrouded in misty rain on the day of a funeral.

Well, come on, they were the worst of circumstances, Alex told herself, fighting back the irritating apprehension she still felt at having anything to do with the Wolstenholme women at all. She knew she shouldn't feel this way. PIs were meant to be able to cope with all situations.

But she'd never had to contend with this type before, and she doubted if even Mr all-seeing all-knowing DI Frobisher would feel as comfortable with a pair of psychics as with a common-or-garden murderer. She caught her thoughts up short, appalled at herself.

What had happened to sensitivity? Where was the tender-hearted little Audrey Barnes who had once wept into the night over a stray hedgehog that had got caught and strangled itself in a fence on the moors?

She hardly noticed she had stopped the engine of the car and was sitting there motionless, lost in a kind of time-warped misery, until she saw Moira come hurrying out of the front door.

'I've been watching for you, Alex. Do come in, please. The kettle's just boiling.'

So this was just a morning tea-party after all, was it? Alex thought indignantly. Moira certainly didn't seem flustered now. Well, if she thought she could treat Alex as her personal slave, to come running whenever she called, she could think again. Except that she was paying her a fat fee for the privilege. At the thought Alex bit back the stinging comment she had been about to make and followed the woman into the house.

'What do you think of that?' Moira asked, her voice a mixture of triumph and excitement bordering on hysteria, as she pointed to the dining-room table. 'Take a look while I bring in the tea.'

Alex looked. A large piece of paper was spread out, covered in the kind of magazine cut-out letters many anonymous letter-writers used to disguise their identity. She sighed. There was nothing new in this.

'It must have been delivered by hand sometime during the night,' came Moira's voice from the kitchen.

She came in with a tray of tea and biscuits and dumped it near the offending missive.

'I'm not bothered by insults, Alex, I've heard them all before. But this is new. What worries me is how they say they came about this information. It worries mother too. These people don't know what they're doing.'

Alex tried to ignore the reference to mother's part in the proceedings. She read the haphazard message aloud, keeping her face and voice as impassive as she could.

'Co-operate, Miss W. or your days are numbered. We need something from you, slag, and the ouija board reveals that another bitch has it. Get it back from Miss B, or else.'

Alex felt her face flood with colour as she got the full impact. She was so dizzy for a moment that she felt the room spin. Her senses instinctively backed away from anything to do with ouija boards or any of that occult nonsense, but she knew that whatever else the message meant, Miss B had to be her. And the sender of this garbage had meant her to know it. Which meant she was involved in a far more sinister way than she had had any intention of being.

'Are you all right, Alex? Drink this.'

In those moments she hadn't been aware of Moira leaving the room, but now she felt a glass being thrust against her lips. She drank automatically, and felt the sting of the brandy slide down her throat.

'I'm quite all right,' she said huskily. 'But you don't believe this tripe, do you?'

She bit her lips as she spoke, knowing she was probably offending her, because presumably Moira did. It would be all part and parcel of mystic Leanora's stock-in-trade that Moira had been weaned on.

'No, I don't,' Moira said vehemently. 'Mother believes in the ouija's powers when it's expertly handled, of course, though when she was on this side she never deigned to use it herself. The charlatans and fairground fortune-tellers who did so gave genuine psychics a bad image.'

Alex decided they were getting away from the main purpose of this meeting. And she had no wish to hear more of Mother Wolstenhome's theories. She wished she need never hear anything of her again. But now she was involved. Personally. And she didn't like it.

'So you think this came from your stalker?' she said now.

'Oh yes. It's his trademark. It's similar to all the others, except for this reference to the ouija board.'

And to me, thought Alex.

'Then we must track him down,' she said, pushing all other anxieties aside. 'What about his previous letters? If he always uses the same newspapers and magazines, we can at least identify the kind of person he is. Forget about class for the moment, and accept that a *Guardian* reader wouldn't be in the same social scale as a *Sun* reader for instance–'

Moira shook her head. 'He's too clever for that. Sometimes he uses complete words, and I've recognized some of them as the names of women's magazines, and from fishing magazines as well as various other newspapers.'

'So he's playing with you. Teasing you.'

'That's not what I'd call it,' Moira said resentfully. 'He's scaring me, that's what he's doing. And what's this thing that he wants, that you have? *If* it's you.'

'It's me all right. And I'd say it's your mother's notebook where she kept details of all her clients. That's what he wants, Moira. You gave it to me, remember?'

'But how did he know that?'

They looked at one another. Alex had told no-one about the notebook, and it was hardly likely that Moira herself would have done so. Unless it was at the funeral shindig, when everyone had got more than a bit merry and some had stayed on overnight, swapping anecdotes and comparing notes about the dear departed Leanora. Had she mentioned it to the major, she thought suddenly? But now wasn't the time to confide in Moira about such a possibility.

'I think I should go back to town and check that everything's still where I left it,' Alex said. 'But it's also time you told me what could be in that notebook that someone else would not only be so keen to find, but desperate enough to commit murder for it.'

'Mother didn't confide everything in me—'

'But you knew who some of her clients were, didn't you? And this house, Moira – who paid for it?'

'What does that have to do with it?' she said.

'Your mother was hardly in the big-time, was she?' Alex went on relentlessly. 'She wasn't a household name like those who do the travel circuit and draw huge crowds. One of my friends attended one of those lectures in York, so I know what I'm talking about. Nobody had ever heard of your mother, as far as I know. So how could she afford all this?'

'Not that it's any of your business, but my father left her well provided for,' Moira said sullenly.

Alex shook her head. 'I don't think so. I've been hearing some very interesting things about your background and the tragic local murder. Your father was a local bus driver, wasn't he? And he died years ago, long before you and your mother moved into this flashy place. That's why she still dressed the way she did when I met her on the cruise ship. In her heart she was still the same little housewife she had always been, scrimping and saving, and it suited her to watch and listen, and then amaze people by her psychic powers.'

As Moira glowered, Alex went on swiftly. 'I'm not saying she didn't have any powers, but she knew how to use them all right. So how did she come by all this wealth?'

Moira crumpled suddenly. 'It wasn't my idea, or even mother's idea. Someone suggested how they could make some money, and don't ask me who it was, because I don't know. It wasn't harming anyone.'

'It harmed her in the end though, didn't it?' said Alex, without any idea what Moira was talking about, but knowing enough to pretend that she did. It was how Nick operated.

But she could see by Moira's tightening

140

lips that she wasn't going to get anything more out of her, and she was more than anxious to get back to London now. She needed to check that Leanora's notebook was safely where she had left it, and to feel assured that nobody was trying to get at her. She didn't want to be anybody's mysterious Miss B. She'd rather revert to being Audrey Barnes any day.

She listened to her own chattering thoughts, and gritted her teeth. This *wasn't* how a private eye was supposed to react. She smiled at the other woman encouragingly.

'Don't worry, Moira, we'll sort out this stalker one way or another. Most of them are harmless, and take a sadistic kind of pleasure in hiding behind these puerile messages. May I take this one with me – and any others?'

'I don't have any others. I burned them.'

'That's a pity,' Alex said, silently fuming, 'but never mind. I'll see if I can get anything out of this one.'

She didn't know what, but she had to sound confident and authoritative. It was what Moira was paying her for.

Moira rammed it back into the large envelope and handed it over silently. 'And you'll be in touch?' she said at last.

'As soon as possible. And if you get any more like this, let me know at once and don't destroy them.'

She had the feeling that Moira was as anxious to be rid of her as she was to get out of there. For all its size, and the sunlight streaming through the windows, the house was as oppressive as ever, and she was sure she could feel Leanora's presence hovering over them.

She shuddered. She felt so jittery that London and normality would be like a breath of fresh air, and she had no intention of staying in tonight. She'd call a friend and go out to a club, maybe even the *Rainbow Club* where she'd first met Gary Hollis. It was sleazy by any standards, but a bit of good old honest sleaze might be just what she needed.

To hell with it, she might even give Gary a call, she thought recklessly. She hadn't seen him in months, and tearing through the night on his Harley with the scent of his leathers in her nostrils was enough to get the adrenalin going in her veins. Which was quite something, considering the state of her nerves right now.

But once she got back to town after endless jams and hold-ups in the traffic, she knew she had to go to her office before she did anything else. Just to check that all was well.

She unlocked the door and went in, and then she simply stopped dead, her heart pounding with sickening speed, and her stomach contents curdling at the chaos she found there.

Chapter 6

Every drawer in the place had been pulled out and overturned. The desk lamp was broken and papers were scattered everywhere. For a few seconds Alex simply couldn't take it in. She felt personally despoiled and violated, as if she was exposed to the world. And then rage took over at the utter carnage in front of her. She flung her bag into the midst of the shambles, righted her chair and sat down on it shakily, breathing hard for control.

Like a horse gathering up steam, her father used to joke. And at the thought of his teasing voice her eyes stung, and she dashed the weakness away, knowing how close she was to tears. But she wouldn't damn well cry. It wasn't her style.

She had to think logically. Somebody had got in here, knowing she was away. *Or maybe not*. It could be simply a coincidence. *And pigs might fly*. But you had to consider all the options. It could have been a straight-forward burglary ... but the only things on show worth stealing were her computer and other office equipment, and they appeared to be untouched.

And it could have been somebody looking for something in Miss B's possession, the thought screamed at her. The thought had been there all the time, but she had deliberately put the most likely possibility out of her mind, knowing that she couldn't ignore it for ever.

She swallowed. What had begun as a bit of harmless curiosity on her part because she couldn't resist looking into what made a clairvoyant tick, had turned far uglier.

Leanora's murder was a matter for the police and really none of her concern, since the killer was already in custody. But now she was involved, whether she wanted to be or not. And just how far she was involved, she still had no way of knowing.

She gave a shudder. All her instincts urged her to tidy up her office and restore it to its usual, well, not exactly pristine state, but a comfortable shambles that belonged to her alone. Opposing that was the certain knowledge that she should inform the police, not touching anything until it had all been gone over for fingerprints.

But that would entail explanations, especially if Nick got to hear of it, which he surely would. And she couldn't guarantee not to blab more than she should to him.

More than she wanted to, anyway. She still had a case that involved client confidentiality.

Already, she knew she wasn't going to report this break-in. The superintendent of the building had greeted her quite cheerily when she arrived, so he couldn't have been aware of anything amiss or he would have told her. Being a stickler for procedure, he would also have reported it already. And that fact alone told her two things.

One, that the burglar was a professional who had got into the building without alerting anyone. And if he was that efficient it would seem futile to bother changing the locks. And two, although he might have left no trace for outsiders, he had definitely wanted to let her know of his presence by leaving the gigantic amount of chaos for her to find.

A chill ran through her that had nothing to do with the office's recent lack of use. He had wanted her to know he'd been searching for something. But he hadn't found it.

Before leaving for Worthing, she'd locked it away in her small hidden wall safe. She flicked open the controls. The notebook was still there, and she rammed it into her bag and hugged it to her for a moment. Then she set about systematically tidying her office with robotic precision.

By the time she left, having checked the

answering machine messages and also that nothing had been done to her computer – no cryptic messages or wiped disks – she left the office and went home. She entered the flat with her nerves brittle-sharp, but nothing had been disturbed there.

She began to breathe a little more easily. So maybe it hadn't been the stalker searching for Leanora's notebook after all. Maybe it really had been a coincidence. Maybe it had been the sneak-thief who had made off with her purse and found one of her old business cards inside, with only the address of her office on it, and had taken a chance on finding something worth taking. *Then why not the computer?* a nagging little voice asked, but she refused to listen.

It was far easier on the nerves, she decided, to be as lulled into a sense of relief, as it had been to fly into a panic. And no real harm had been done. She still had the important item, and once she had taken a shower and washed her hair to remove the grime of travelling, she was going to curl up with a hefty drink at her side, study Leanora's notes more thoroughly, and put any relevant details on the laptop that she kept safely at home.

The phone was ringing as she came out of the bathroom, her hair turbanned in a thick towel.

'Alexandra Best,' she said automatically.

There was no answering voice, and she felt a swift curl of fear knot her stomach.

'Who is this, please?' she said, as coolly as she could.

The line went dead, and she immediately dialled 1471. She didn't wait for the number, and simply pressed 3 to get the caller back. After several rings, someone picked up the phone and she heard a low chuckle.

'They say curiosity killed the cat, don't they? Mind it doesn't kill you, Miss Best.'

She slammed down the phone, staring at it as if the face behind the voice would suddenly materialize in front of her. It wouldn't, of course, and that kind of thinking was more in Leanora's line than *hers*.

She frowned. She didn't know the voice. But she could describe it – just. She knew Moira had had calls from her stalker, and she quickly dialled her number.

'Moira, it's Alex Best,' she said abruptly cutting across the niceties in the other woman's reply. 'Look, there's something I need to know. Can you describe the voice of the man who's called you before? The stalker, I mean.'

'I suppose so,' Moira answered. 'I always referred to it as a man, mind you, although it was so muffled, and sort of *dark*, if you know what I mean, that it could have been a woman. It was definitely educated though, and it didn't have any regional accent. Why? Have you discovered something?'

'Well, hardly. I've only been back in London for a couple of hours. But I'm working on a theory,' she said vaguely, 'and I just wanted to get all the information I could.'

'I see. Well, actually, I was going to call you. There was something in the local paper this evening. Trevor Unwin's killed himself.'

'Who?'

'Mother's killer. They've named him now, and he's been found dead in his cell. Apparently he had terminal cancer, and they think he'd been storing up his pain-killers and sleeping tablets, so he won't even be brought to justice. It's rotten luck, isn't it?'

Good God, is that the only way she can describe it – as rotten luck? thought Alex.

'It hardly matters in one sense, of course,' Moira went on matter-of-factly, 'because if he's on the other side now, mother will be able to deal with him.'

'That's one way of looking at it, I suppose,' Alex said in a strangled voice, just managing to resist mentioning the hope that they had both been dispatched in the same direction.

She was *definitely* going whacko now, she thought, as whacko as they were.

'Well, thanks for letting me know, Moira,'

148

she said, when they ran out of conversation. 'I'll be in touch.'

She finished drying her hair, wondering what significance, if any, this could have on the case. So the loner had killed himself. It wasn't unheard of, especially if he had been facing a life sentence for murder, as he surely would have been. Though just how long would that life have been if he had terminal cancer? Did he even know?

Had he consulted Leanora at some time? And had she been the one to tell him his days were numbered, and this had triggered him into the frenzied attack on her? Or had someone paid him to do the deed? And if so, what did he have to gain by it if he was truly alone in the world?

But was he? The unanswered questions surged in Alex's head now. Even a loner had to have some acquaintances. Family. People who knew him. Nobody could be totally alone and living on their uppers. The Social Services saw to that. And as far as she could tell from the newspaper report, nobody seemed to have bothered too much about his motive for murdering Leanora. He had so obviously been guilty of the crime.

A picture of the way that insipid little woman had been hacked about was suddenly so vivid, so very red in Alex's mind, that she shuddered uncontrollably for a few minutes, until she realized the phone was ringing again.

She snatched it up. It might be Nick. Or Gary – though that was extremely unlikely, unless he was possessed of some of Leanora's sixth sense, and knew how badly she needed to talk to somebody normal.

It was the girl who lived one floor down. The model-cum-out of work actress.

'Oh Alex, the postman asked me to take in a packet for you while you were away. Shall I bring it up?'

'Of course – come and have some coffee, Charmaine – or something stronger. I'll be glad of some company.'

'Oh – thanks, but I can't stay long. I'm meeting someone later. There might be a job in the offing.'

'Great,' Alex said mechanically. 'See you soon then.'

She didn't blame the girl for her lack of enthusiasm. She didn't exactly invite confidences from her neighbours. She wasn't deliberately stand-offish, but she considered that the less people knew about what she did and how she went about it, the better.

Unfortunately, it also shut out friendship, and if she wasn't careful she could turn into as much of a loner as one Trevor Unwin, she thought with another shudder.

Consequently, she ushered Charmaine into her flat with a wider smile than usual. She had dressed in jeans and T-shirt after

150

her shower, and her hair had been combed to a pike-straight sheen now. As always, Charmaine commented on the fact after declining coffee on the grounds that it was fattening, and opting for something in a glass.

'God, I wish I had hair like that. Mine's a ball of fluff if I don't straighten it out with tongs before every shoot.'

She made it sound as if she was on a modelling assignment every day of the year, which Alex knew she certainly was not.

'At least you're a natural blonde,' she said generously.

'Oh sure,' Charmaine grinned. 'Everywhere, too,' she added with a wink.

Alex laughed, handing her a glass of wine and pouring her own favourite tipple. The stick-thin model-cum-whatever perched on the edge of a chair now, and already made her feel gargantuan, so what were a few more ounces on her thighs?

'So where's this packet you took in for me?'

'Oh Lord, my brains! I nearly forgot.' She fished it out of the so-called model's bag she always carried. Alex wondered if she took the thing to bed, since it was never out of her sight. She handed over the brown paper packet with the printed label addressed to Miss A. Best.

It didn't look like anything much. Probably publicity material or junk mail, and it could be left until later.

'So what's this new job that might be in the offing?' she asked, when small talk flagged. Charmaine wasn't a great conversationalist, and that was putting it mildly.

'It may be a TV ad,' she said with more animation. 'I can't say too much about it yet, but this agent I'm meeting is keen to get me on the small screen.'

'Be careful, Charmaine,' Alex felt obliged to say. 'You know what I mean.'

'Oh, don't worry about me. I've been around!'

And she was all of nineteen, which made Alex feel like Methuselah at twenty-six. And Charmaine was already glancing at the watch on her slender wrist, clearly wondering how long she had to stay, when she was itching to be somewhere else.

'Well, thanks for taking in the packet, and I hope it all goes well for you,' Alex said, winding up the meeting neatly, and ignoring the obvious relief in the other girl's eyes.

Minutes later she was alone and slitting open the sellotaped packet with minimal curiosity. And then her heart leapt. Instantly she remembered something Moira had said.

He sent me some dead flowers once...

And now he'd sent them to Alex. They were wrapped in plastic to stop the liquid from the stems seeping out through the post

... wasn't it illegal to send substances that leaked through the post? ... they had once been lilies, and the leaves had already mouldered and were a disgusting mess inside the plastic. There was no card, no message, but there didn't need to be.

It was him, of course. The stalker, the vandal, the probable hitman, once-removed. She threw the lot into the bin, then took a few deep breaths and pulled it out again.

This was no way for a PI to behave. There might be clues in the wrapping, the label, the postmark ... but it was so smudged that she couldn't read it.

It was odd though, that two women should have been sent dead flowers. Even odder when Moira herself was a florist. The crazy suspicion entered her head that maybe it was Moira herself doing this. Perhaps she had gone completely off her rocker by now, and...

'Stop it,' she said out loud. 'You're the one going crazy now, and this is just some lunatic trying to scare you.'

It had to be *him*, though. Mr X. And Alex had to prove that she was made of stronger stuff than he thought.

The phone rang again, and she flinched, sure it would be him, checking that she had received his little gift. But contrary to what he might think, her fear was receding now, to be replaced with a cold anger. And even if she *was* still bloody scared, he was never going to know it.

'Alexandra Best,' she snapped into the phone.

'I'm sorry to bother you, Miss Best, and I do hope I've got the right person,' said a male voice she had never heard before. It certainly wasn't the muffled, sadistic voice of her earlier caller, and she tried to get her own voice in gear.

'Well, I'm not sure I can tell you that until I know what it's all about. Who is this, please?'

'You won't know my name. It's Graham Johnson, and Miss Wolstenholme gave me your number.'

'Moira?' Alex said.

He did say MISS Wolstenholme? This wasn't Leanora trying to make contact from the Great Beyond then?

'I believe that's her name. I called her just now, since some of our people want to visit her to pass on our condolences about her mother. Then it came up about Trevor, and I mentioned I might have a little problem of my own there, and she said I might care to get in touch with you.'

For a moment the name Trevor meant nothing. And the conversation was so garbled she thought she must be dealing with another nutter. And then Alex remembered.

154

'Do you mean Trevor Unwin? The man who stabbed Miss Wolstenholme's mother?'

'That's the one,' Graham Johnson said.

He cleared his throat. 'I'm sorry if I sounded disjointed just now. It's all so confusing, you see, and so unexpected. It might mean nothing – I mean, its probably not a police matter – but you never know–'

As he paused uncertainly, Alex spoke swiftly. 'Mr Johnson, do you – did you know Trevor Unwin?'

'Oh yes. Well, as much as anybody did. He came to the home from time to time.'

'What home is this, Mr Johnson?' Alex said carefully.

The phrase like watching paint dry, was filling her head, but she was already dragging a pad towards her and taking down everything the man said. It might mean something or nothing – but you couldn't afford to miss out on the slightest sliver of information. And her own curiosity about Trevor Unwin had already been aroused. The caller spoke more firmly, a hint of pomposity in his voice now.

'I'm sorry. I'm not making much sense, am I? I'm the manager of a rest home for the elderly, and Mrs Bessie Unwin has been with us for many years. Trevor is – was – her son.'

'I see.' Alex felt a small sense of triumph. She knew it. Even a loner wasn't completely alone in the world.

'I don't really want to discuss it over the phone, Miss Best, but something – well – rather strange has happened. I'm afraid I never go to London. I'm so occupied here with my people, you see.'

'I understand, Mr Johnson, and it's no problem. I'm happy to come to you. So where is this home, please?'

'It's the Happy Days Retirement Home in Beckingham, a small out-of-the-way village ten miles north of Worthing – it's quite pretty and very rural, set in several acres–'

She hauled him into the present as his voice wandered on to a mini sales spiel. She didn't need to know that. First of all she needed to know about anyone who might remember a regular traveller...

'So I presume that Trevor Unwin visited his mother there. How did he get there, Mr Johnson? Did he travel by bus or train, or drive a car?'

'Good Lord, no. He used to ride his bicycle.'

Alex thought rapidly. This was going nowhere fast, and as his voice stopped abruptly, she knew he was unprepared to go into any more detail over the phone.

'Mr Johnson, I've only just got back to London, and I have to be at a meeting on Thursday, but I can be with you on Friday. I'd very much like to hear whatever it is you

156

have to tell me, and to meet Mrs Unwin too.'

'You won't get much out of her, I'm afraid. She rarely speaks to anyone, and when she does, it's mostly gibberish. Alzheimer's, you know.'

'But the other people in the home must have met her son, and spoken with him? And so did you, and your staff?'

He sounded so unhappy, virtually apologizing for having contacted her at all, that she could have been tempted to give up there and then. But she knew she wouldn't. Not with this slenderest of leads, even though she had no idea where it would take her. She hung up with the firm promise of meeting him on Friday afternoon. He sounded such a fusspot that what he had to say might not be of the slightest use, but trying to get some insight into Trevor Unwin's character seemed a good place to start.

The *only* place, she admitted, since so far her investigations had got nowhere. And she knew she was still confusing Leanora's murder with the reason Moira had contacted her – to find out who the stalker was. But Alex just knew they had to be connected.

Presumably the police were satisfied regarding their killer. They had got their man, and now he had topped himself, saving the tax-payer the expense of keeping him in custody for ever more. End of story.

And she was getting as callous as Nick himself, she thought, appalled at herself. A man was dead, for God's sake, and had been tormented enough to save up his painkillers and sleeping pills and do away with himself.

She called the guest house in Worthing next, and booked in for the following weekend, with the possible option of a longer stay. Let Mrs Dooley think she was enchanted with her cooking or whatever. It was a useful base, and she clearly needed to see Moira again and compare notes.

But her earlier lethargy had gone, and so had much of her jitters over the dead flowers. She had to forget it, and even if she didn't know what it was all about yet, Graham Johnson had sounded mysterious and cagey. And he obviously hadn't confided in Moira, except to make her curious too.

She spent the rest of the evening decoding much of Leanora's muddled information from her notebook and putting names and dates onto her laptop computer. At first sight it had seemed quite meticulous, but now Alex realized that it was anything but tidily done, as if Leanora had merely inserted information as and when it had occurred to her.

Some of the names were somewhat

familiar, but most of them were not, but once she had printed out her own list, it would give her the chance to go through the *Who's Who* and other directories in her office, and see just what kind of influential people, and others, had consulted Leanora.

She was still amazed that anyone had, but she was sure many of them had to be monied people. There had to be a profitable way for the Wolstenholmes to live the way they had. Regarding the stalker and his threats, the word blackmail had loomed in her mind, but was still an avenue to be explored.

There was always the thought, though, that if the two of them had worked out some elaborate blackmailing scam through Leanora's gullible clientele, big money could be involved. And the more any blackmailing scam went on, with the perpetrators becoming ever more greedy, and demanding more and more payments for their silence, the more chancey it became for one or other of them to be silenced for good. Or both.

Alex wasn't looking forward to Thursday. Internal police hearings were always closed shop affairs, and they never welcomed outsiders, particularly of the female private eye variety.

Ex-wives who might produce tears and

tantrums were also a necessary evil, but the former Mrs Scott Nelson was a woman who said very little, and was older than Alex had expected. Though the kind of dance Scott might have put her through in the past had probably aged her considerably.

Alex gave her own version of events coolly and concisely, in her expensive sloaney voice that gave authority to the words, while her brittle glare at some of the station constables dared them to read anything into the fact that she had been apparently 'entertaining' Scott Nelson at her flat on the evening before his death.

'DI Nelson came to see me on a private matter, and only stayed a short while,' she said crisply. 'It was not a social call, and after he had told me what I wanted to know, he left. There was no indication that he was depressed enough to commit suicide. But since I am not qualified in that direction, that is all I am able to tell you.'

'Were you and DI Nelson in the habit of meeting at your flat, Miss Best?' she was asked next.

'No, we were not. He was an acquaintance, no more.'

'According to the medical evidence, DI Nelson had a number of scratches on his face, and considerable bruising to his genitals. Can you explain how this came about if your meeting was not on a *social* level?'

160

Alex froze the questioner with a look. 'It was definitely not *social* in the way you're implying, sir. DI Nelson may have had certain expectations of the evening, but I certainly did not. There was an unfortunate scuffle, and I do admit to pushing him away in a way that left him in no doubt that I did not welcome his attentions.'

She spoke stiffly, as if she was in the witness box, in terms that she was sure he would understand. She hated him. And she also hated the way the ex-wife stared at her so unblinkingly, as if she could read everything that she wasn't saying. As if she could guess very well how her husband would have behaved, whether Alex had repulsed him or not.

But she would surely know. She *must* have known what her husband was like ... she had divorced him, for God's sake. Alex gave her a sympathetic half-smile as the wife turned her head away when the inquiry finally dragged to an end.

She prayed that she wasn't going to be accosted by the wife later. Or was she a widow now? Was an ex-wife a widow? Or screamed at and pummelled and accused of being a whore. It happened. You never could tell with abused or rejected wives, and she must have suffered in the past. She must have loved her husband once, and maybe still did.

161

That thought was confirmed when Nick told her over a desperately-needed cup of tea in the canteen that the wife had demanded to have Scott returned to her once the inquest was over and the body was finally released for burial.

'Good God. I thought she'd have been glad to see the last of him, knowing about his abuse and his womanizing.'

'It's not unusual in these cases,' he said, shrugging. 'She'll have the satisfaction of having the last say as far as he's concerned. He'll belong totally to her then, and nobody else can touch him.'

Alex grimaced. 'I think that's gruesome.'

'Forget it, Alex,' he advised, seeing her pale face. 'You weren't that upset by it all, were you? Don't tell me you fell for him after all,' he added, unable to hide his resentment.

'I didn't. I just think what a lucky escape I had.'

'Thank God for that. I wouldn't want to see you wasting yourself on memories of that has-been,' he said. 'I'd rather your memories were of much sweeter times.'

He squeezed her hand, his eyes flickering with a smile, and she knew he was thinking of that night in Worthing. She couldn't smile back. She remembered it all too well – or most of it, anyway – but a repeat performance would complicate things, which was why she had no intention of telling him she was going back there tomorrow.

'Not now, Nick, please,' she muttered.

'OK,' he said, with one of his mercurial changes of mood. 'Finish your tea and come into my office. I've got some information for you.'

'Oh?' she said, thankful that he apparently accepted her comment as reaction to the ordeal of the morning.

'It's about your Major Harry Deveraux.'

Her attention was instantly caught. Where she had been pale before, she felt her face flood with warmth. She had almost forgotten about the major with her new interest in Trevor Unwin. But perhaps at last she was about to know that the major was all that he said – or not – and that would leave the prospect of his involvement with the Wolstenholme women wide open.

'Lead on,' she said quickly.

Once in his office he closed the door so that they wouldn't be overheard, and then produced a one-page print-out of information. Alex was disappointed, having hoped for a great wad of documents.

'Is that it?' she said.

'Your man is either a bloody clever con artist or he has the luck of the devil. But two things I can tell you for certain. He was in the army, although he never rose above the rank of captain. And he never worked for Special Branch. Whatever ID he flashed about, it wasn't genuine. My guess is he's probably got a dozen of them, and passports too, to cover every eventuality. I've met the sort, and they get away with it far more often than you might think.'

'I know that,' Alex said. 'But if that's the case, then what was he doing at Leanora's funeral, and why did he want to snoop around her premises afterwards? They never spoke to one another during the cruise as far as I could tell, and they must have seen one another. I know he saw *her*, because he commented on it to me.'

It didn't follow that Leanora would have noticed him, of course. Among five hundred or so passengers, you couldn't see everyone. But the major and Leanora had been on the same dinner sitting, like herself, and he had probably been observing her all that time. He'd also been chatting up the wealthier women, she remembered, and had made a point of chatting to *her*.

Had he known, even then, who she was, and what she did? The thought suddenly chilled her. He may not have been a genuine Special Branch investigator, but he knew his way around all right.

'I compared a couple of those holiday snaps you loaned me with our mugshots,' Nick went on.

'I never loaned you any holiday snaps!' she said at once.

164

Nick spoke coolly, unfazed as usual. 'Sorry darling, slip of the tongue. I borrowed them from your room at Worthing. Thought it might be useful.'

'You've got a hell of a nerve—'

'Do you want my help or not?' he asked, silencing her. 'Anyway, he doesn't turn up anywhere on our files, unless he's also a master of disguises. Are you sure you're not making too much of this guy, Alex?'

'No, I'm not,' she said, resentful of the way he was quizzing her now. 'What would you think, when he somehow got hold of a key to Leanora's premises that her daughter didn't know about, and gave false credentials to me and the young copper who questioned us? I wasn't born yesterday.'

'So is there anything else you want to tell me?'

'Like what?'

'Like why you're so bloody jittery over him. Has he threatened you in any way? Or contacted you since?'

She tried not to flinch, but he was looking at her steadily, and she couldn't stop the pulse beating at the side of her neck. He'd know she was damn scared of something, but he knew nothing about any stalker who might not be terrorizing Moira, but was putting the fear of God in her!

She was tempted to tell him everything, but if she did it would no longer be her case.

'*No*,' she said, 'and if I'm jittery, it's because I don't like being pulled in here and made to feel like a slut with your bloody constables sniggering behind their helmets and getting a hard-on at the thought of my fisting Scott Nelson in the balls. Is that enough to be going on with?'

He leaned back in his chair, his hands linked behind his head, and grinned at her.

'I love it when you talk dirty in that posh voice–'

'And that line has got whiskers on. So can I go now?'

'Nobody's keeping you, darling. How about dinner later? You look like you need cheering up. Italian or Chinese?'

She felt like telling him to stop patronising her as the little woman, and just what he could do with his Italian or Chinese. Instead she heard herself agreeing. Why not? If she treated it as a good exercise in keeping her mouth shut and veering away from any subject he didn't have to know, then she might as well let him pay for the privilege. But she added the proviso that they kept strictly away from anything to do with police work or PI work, just to put it on record.

Once he had agreed, she stepped outside the police station, breathing in the London traffic fumes as if they were nectar, and walked forcefully towards her car, aware that several pairs of eyes in the uniformed

166

section were probably watching her progress from the top floor windows and making lewd comments. If it wasn't so bloody undignified, she'd turn and give them a two-finger salute, she thought, or even a one-finger one...

'Can I speak to you for a minute?' she heard a voice say as she thankfully turned the corner into the road where she had parked her car.

'Oh – yes, of course – Mrs Nelson,' she said, caught off guard by the woman's unexpected appearance.

Was this it then? You never knew about rejected wives. Was she going to produce a knife and get her own revenge on the woman she assumed was her husband's latest paramour, or simply hurl insults at her for all the world to hear?

'I wanted to say I'm sorry,' the woman went on humbly.

'Sorry?' Alex said.

'Yes. I'm sorry if Scott offended you in any way. He couldn't help himself, you see. I know you must think this is very odd, but I'd really like to know how he was on that last evening. Although we had been divorced for a couple of years, I still worried about him.'

'Did you?' Alex said, starting to feel like an echo.

Mrs Nelson gave a half-smile. 'You're

surprised, Miss Best. But I was a lot older than Scott, and I knew what he was like when I married him, and it didn't matter. He wanted a mother-figure, and I – well, I suppose I wanted someone to look after. We suited one another, and I knew all about his little indiscretions. And despite all they said about him, he never hit me, you know. I was his mummy.'

Alex felt herself mentally backing away. She heard plenty of bizarre things from clients, many of them unsavoury and some of them downright sick, but she didn't like the way this conversation was going.

'I'm so sorry,' she said gently.

'Yes, well, I just wanted you to know that I don't bear you any grudge, Miss Best. When Scott needed his freedom, I gave it to him. I even pretended it was on account of his bullying, but my Scott never hurt me, and he still kept in touch. I would have done anything for him, like most of his other ladies.'

She gave an almost beatific smile before she hurried away along the street, leaving Alex stunned for a moment.

Stunned, and feeling normal, and healthy, and glad beyond measure that a normal, healthy man was taking her out for dinner that evening, and she could put all thoughts of weirdos, psychics, stalkers, and every other damn crackpot, out of her mind for a few blissful hours.

Chapter 7

Before Alex left London she looked up the Happy Days Retirement Home at Beckingham in the *Yellow Pages*. There was an impressive and wordy advertisement describing it as a retirement home for gentlefolk, and of particular interest to those who sought a more refined establishment for the care of their elderly loved ones. She wondered which of those categories Bessie Unwin came into.

She didn't intend getting to Beckingham too early in the day. She stopped for lunch at an olde-worlde pub that was over-priced to pay for its tourist-attracting decor, and arrived at Happy Days in mid-afternoon.

Alex's first impression of Graham Johnson was that he resembled a middle-aged cherub. He was nearly as wide as he was tall, and he had a shiny moon-face with a smile that split it in two. He had a busy-busy walk that was clearly meant to imply efficiency, and although she realized that she towered above him, the warmth of his handshake dispelled any thought that it might embarrass him. And he was clearly more at ease talking to people in the flesh – the ample flesh – than he was on the phone.

'I'm pleased to meet you, Miss Best, and you come highly recommended, of course. Now what'll it be? Tea or coffee?' he said, when they were seated in his south-facing office.

From the spacious window, the lawns stretched away into the distance and some of the elderly people were strolling about the fragrant grounds, with watchful attendants nearby.

There seemed to be as many attendants as patients, Alex thought, though presumably some of them would be house-bound. Even bed-bound, which was something to make her shiver and resolve to take more exercise.

'Coffee would be lovely,' she replied now, wondering what it would cost to place a relative here for an endless number of months or years. It certainly didn't look cheap, and presumably was intended to provide a final home for those who could afford it.

Which made the connection between Trevor Unwin, loner, murderer, visiting here by bicycle – and his long-term Alzheimer's mother – all the more intriguing.

'So what do you think of our little establishment?' Johnson said conversationally, when a young girl in a blue helper's overall had brought in coffee and biscuits on a tray and disappeared again.

'Very impressive,' Alex said. 'I'm sure the people here are very comfortable.'

'Oh, more than that. We give them the very best of care, and we live up to our title,' he beamed. 'We aim to relieve relatives of every small anxiety—'

'And this applies to those with a severe medical problem, such as Mrs Unwin, does it?' she broke in, before he could launch into more self-praise of his 'little establishment'.

'Of course! Her doctor is one of our regular visiting GPs, and we have living-in, fully trained, medical staff. Nothing is too much trouble—'

Alex flipped open her notebook, after asking if he minded if she took notes. She could have taped the interview, but a notebook was useful in two respects. As well as reminding her of the important aspects of the entire conversation, while her eyes were lowered she could keep her expression as bland as she needed to. And sometimes it was advisable not to express her personal feelings...

'You mentioned that you had taken some of your people to pay their condolences to Miss Wolstenholme, Mr Johnson,' Alex reminded him, realizing that she would have to focus his thoughts on the reason she was here, or she would never get to know what it actually was.

'Ah yes,' he answered, his smile slipping. The sudden frown between his eyebrows altered his face completely, Alex thought in amazement.

Seconds before, it had been round and cherubic. Now, with those dark eyebrows winging upwards at either side of his temple, it was almost satanic. How weird.

'What was the reason for the visit? Did they know Miss Wolstenholme?' she asked, sipping the scalding coffee.

'No, but several of them had consulted her mother on a number of occasions. Perhaps I forgot to tell you that.'

'Perhaps you did,' she agreed, his words confirming her suspicions about Leanora and her well-heeled clientele. 'And after you had seen Miss Wolstenholme you called me because you were worried about something concerning Trevor Unwin.'

Good God, at this rate it was going to take forever to get anything out of him, she fumed.

'That's the oddest thing, Miss Best,' he said, leaning forward conspiratorially now. 'I felt I had to tell someone about the circumstances, and when Miss Wolstenholme mentioned that she had a private investigator helping her on a little private matter, I thought you were the one I should contact. It always pays to have a professional who's been personally recommended in these circumstances, doesn't it?'

'Absolutely right, Mr Johnson,' she said, trying not to wince as he visibly preened himself on his own daring at employing a private investigator at all.

And although she would hardly describe the stalking threats as a *little* matter, that was no concern of his, and she had no intention of enlightening him on why Moira was employing her.

'So what is it that's worrying you, Mr Johnson?'

'I mentioned that Trevor Unwin had a terminal illness, didn't I? Cancer. He only had a few months to live, and he knew that. Apparently he had always been a saver, proper little Scrooge by all accounts, and when he was invalided out of the army some years ago, he put all his savings and his pension into his mother's care here. An admirable thing for a devoted son to do, wouldn't you say?'

Alex murmured that she would. Especially when it put the coffers straight into Graham Johnson's pudgy hands.

'Which made it all the more unbelievable that he should have made that dreadful attack on the poor defenceless lady in Worthing,' Johnson continued. 'He was a strange one, of course. Kept himself to himself – well, you know the type but we all liked him well enough. It was obvious that he lived very frugally, but eventually the money was going to run out, and I know he was worried about what would happen to Bessie after he passed on. That was what made it so unexpected.'

'What was that?'

'Well, he called it his little windfall. More like a lottery win, if you ask me, though if it was that, he wasn't telling. And he was never a gambler anyway, not even a pound for one line, though some of our ladies do like to have a little flutter and have formed a little syndicate. Nothing serious, you under-stand—'

'So what can you tell me about Trevor's little windfall?' Alex said, biting her lip as she realized she was falling into little-Johnson-mode ... and at this rate, she'd be checking into Mrs Dooley's guest ho after dark.

Johnson leaned forward, elbows on his desk, his fingers laced together. His piggy eyes sparkled with the fussy pleasure of imparting gossip, and his breath emanated across the desk, reminding anyone within breathing distance that he had had curry for lunch.

Alex sat well back in her chair, and waited. But something was stirring in her mind now. And her sixth sense told her it could be something big.

'That's just it. Nobody knows where it

came from. But some weeks ago when he visited his mother, he brought a large amount of money with him and said there would be a similar amount to come later. It was to cover her expenses as long as possible, and if she passed on before it was used up, it was to be used for the benefit of the home. Also, if I thought it advisable to do so, I should invest it so that there would be interest to draw on. Well, I ask you! He wasn't the type to know about investments and interests and suchlike. He was a simple man, not a city whizz-kid!'

'And the second amount of money, Mr Johnson,' Alex said carefully as he paused for breath. 'Did he deliver that too?'

'Oh yes, all in fifty pound notes, like the first lot. If I didn't know better, I'd have said he robbed a bank, but I tell you, Miss Best, he didn't have the gumption for that. So what do you make of it? Should I inform somebody, do you think? I mean now that he's gone to his grave, I suppose it's all legal for me to do as he asked? There was no will, I understand, and the money is still sitting in my safe.'

'How much money are we talking about, Mr Johnson?'

'Twenty-five thousand pounds each time. I mean, where did a simpleton like that – and may God forgive me for speaking ill of the dead – but where would he have got

175

such a huge amount of money? I don't imagine he could have accumulated that much from an army pension, do you?'

'I wonder if you can remember the exact date that Trevor brought you each of the payments?' Alex said, ignoring the question, while she wrote down the figures and tried not to show her growing excitement.

'Of course,' he said. 'My records are all in order, and I have it in my ledger.'

He opened a large book and ran his finger down several pages until he found the entries.

'Is this important, by the way?' he asked, glancing up.

'It may just help to find out whether or not he did indeed have a lottery win, or maybe a large insurance policy matured,' she said. 'I agree it sounds improbable, but in my job you learn to examine everything, however unlikely.'

'So what do you think I should do about the money?' he said anxiously.

His longing to keep it for Bessie Unwin and his little establishment was so obvious that Alex could have puked. She tried not to dislike him so much.

'Do you have anything in writing from Trevor regarding the gift for his mother's care?' she asked.

'Oh yes. I requested that he stated exactly what he intended. There were also invoices

176

and proper receipts. It's all here in Bessie's file.'

He went to a wall cabinet and brought out the file, and Alex certainly couldn't fault his attention to detail. Bessie Unwin had clearly been here for some time if the wad of notes inside the folder was anything to go by. No wonder Trevor needed money for her upkeep. She checked the authorization letter from Trevor, and the two delivery dates of the money confirmed her suspicions.

'Well, I would say that as far as Mrs Unwin is concerned, she had a very caring son,' she said, pushing aside the memory of her disgust at the graphic newspaper report detailing the murder of Leanora.

Superficially, the two things didn't add up. On the one hand, there was the caring, devoted son; and on the other, a frenzied murderer. But if the motive was strong enough ... and if a man already doomed to die could be persuaded by a slick con man that there was one sure way in which he could give his mother comfort for the rest of her days. A way that ensured that the hit man himself never got involved.

'Mr Johnson, I would say that as far as the transactions between yourself and Trevor Unwin are concerned, everything here is above board,' she told him. 'I see no reason why you can't do exactly as he wanted, and there is no need to inform anyone else.

Presumably your books are regularly inspected by the Inland Revenue and the VAT inspector–'

'Oh, my Lord, yes! We have to be very scrupulous in all our dealings–'

'And you have Trevor's letter and the invoices and receipts to prove that as far as you are aware the sudden influx of money into your accounts was come by legitimately,' she said, knowing it was against all her instincts to believe it. 'There would be no reflection on you, Mr Johnson. I would suggest that you take some financial advice and invest the money to provide a regular income for Mrs Unwin's care.'

He beamed at her. 'You've been an enormous help, Miss Best, and of course you must give me your fee for this consultation.'

'Naturally,' she said drily, having no intention of doing otherwise. 'And before I go, I'd like to have a few words with Mrs Unwin, and also to speak with one or two of the ladies who consulted Mrs Wolstenholme. I did know her slightly, as it happens, and it always helps to share memories with other people.'

And *that* was talking tongue-in-cheek if anything was. The only memories of Leanora she had were freaky ones, but Graham Johnson clearly believed her, and pressed her hand in a pseudo-comforting manner.

She made a huge effort not to snatch her hand away from his. Slimy little man, she thought, with his mind more likely on just how he was going to manipulate Trevor's little windfall than anything else right now.

Graham Johnson took her along to the day lounge, which was full of inmates in various stages of head-on-chest dozing, or struggling with craft work or jigsaw puzzles, or just gazing out of the windows, reliving the past.

Bessie Unwin greeted Alex with a delighted smile and called her Dolly. Johnson explained that she was in a world of her own now, and that Dolly was her sister, long deceased.

'Humour her,' he advised. 'No matter what you reply to her questions, she'll repeat them over and over, and she'll probably fall asleep in the middle of it, I'm afraid.'

Alex knew he must be right, but she hated the way he spoke so glibly about the elderly woman with the thin grey hair and the constantly twisting fingers.

'How are you today, Dolly?' she mumbled to Alex.

She hesitated, not quite knowing how to reply, and felt Johnson's fingers pressing her shoulder. She twisted away from him, and he shrugged and left them to it.

'I'm – much better today, thank you, Bessie–'

'So how are you today, Dolly?'

She tried again. 'I think I've got over my cold–'

'How are you today, Dolly?'

'How are *you* Bessie?' she said, trying a different tack.

'How are you today, Dolly?'

A female voice nearby spoke sympathetically. 'Give up, dear. It will go on like this for ages until she gets tired. She can't help it.'

Alex saw an elegantly dressed woman with blue-rinsed hair leaning on a zimmer frame. Bessie's voice brightened as she registered the newcomer.

'How are you today, Dolly?' she said, looking past Alex at the other woman.

'You see?' the woman said. 'I'm Mrs Partridge, by the way. Are you a welfare visitor?'

'Not exactly,' Alex said in a strangled voice, thinking how bloody awful it was to have to spend your final days like this. But already Bessie had lost interest in them both and was fiddling with her skirt and muttering Dolly's name incessantly.

'Don't be alarmed. She'll have forgotten all about her sister when she's had a little doze,' Mrs Partridge said. 'Her son was the only one who got any sense out of her, and that wasn't much.'

'What was he like?' Alex said, thankful for the lead.

'He was a good boy to his mother, but we all know what he did, of course. Terrible, wasn't it? And Madame Leanora was such a nice lady.'

'You knew her then?' Alex said, with the feeling that she had struck gold.

'Oh, I was one of her regulars. Several of us saw her once a month, when Mr Johnson took us on our mini-bus trip to Worthing. She prophesied that I'd be able to walk without this old frame one of these days, and I believe her. Well, you have to have hope, or you wonder what it's all for, don't you?'

From the look of her frail body Alex doubted that Leanora's prophesy would come true, but faith and hope did strange things, even if they didn't always produce miracles.

'I'm sure it was one of the highlights of your trip, Mrs Partridge, but it must have cost you ladies a fair amount,' she said carefully.

'Money doesn't compare with health, dear. You'll find that out when you get old. Look around you in this place. We all know where we'll end up, but if Madame Leanora could give us hope and a bit of entertainment into the bargain, then it was worth every penny.'

And I'll bet you all parted with a good deal more than pennies, Alex thought.

By the time she left she had spoken to several more of Madame Leanora's ex-clients, and none of them had a bad word to say about her. It seemed they had all adored her, and only one of them was sour-faced about the visit to Moira.

'I didn't like the daughter,' the woman said with a scowl. 'Stuck-up piece, I thought. I asked if she was psychic too and if she would take over her mother's business, and she told me nobody could take her mother's place and that the premises were only on lease and it was already in the estate agent's hands.'

'I'm sure she didn't mean to offend you,' Alex said.

'She wanted us out of there,' the woman said darkly. 'I fancy she thought we were invading her privacy, when we only wanted to show our respect.'

Alex murmured something appropriate and turned with relief when Graham Johnson said he would see her in his office as soon as she was ready. The whole place was depressing her. Light and airy though it was, it still had an air of decay about it that was unavoidable, she supposed. Not that anyone seemed unhappy here, she admitted. Far from it. And it was obvious that they all got the very best of care.

But she needed to get out of there, and once she was in possession of her fee and had obediently signed the receipt for the Happy Days records, she escaped, feeling as if she had just been released from prison.

'How very nice to see you again, Miss Best,' Mrs Dooley trilled when she arrived at the guest house. 'You'll have heard all about our latest scandal, of course? I really don't know what Worthing's coming to, what with murders and suicides. It always used to be such a *nice* town.'

Alex could hear the underlying excitement in the landlady's voice, despite the indignity. Scandal or celebrity status always brought business to a town.

'I'm sure it still is a nice town, Mrs Dooley. One bad apple doesn't spoil the bunch, does it?' Alex said, wincing at the cliché, but sure that Mrs Dooley would appreciate it.

'You're a wise young woman, Miss Best, and so very pretty too. Is your nice young man coming to join you this time?'

'Nice' was clearly her favourite word, thought Alex, as she composed her face. And she was clearly the flavour of the month for booking in for a second time.

'He's not actually my young man, Mrs Dooley, just a friend, and a sort of colleague.'

183

'Oh well, you've plenty of time for all that, I daresay. Just don't leave it too late, will you, dear?'

'I won't,' she said, not sure if she should feel insulted at the implication that at twenty-six she was practically over the hill already. But not compared with the folk she had just seen, she remembered soberly.

She had been given the same room in the guest house as before, which was comfortingly familiar and *that* was an ageist thought too, she realized. She took a few deep breaths at the window overlooking the park, resolving to jog around it first thing in the morning. There and then she did a few aerobic exercises, just for the sheer joy of being young and healthy and still in control of her mind and body.

Once she had done the minimal amount of unpacking, she looked through her day's notes. Apart from the shock of learning how much money had been involved in the transaction between Trevor Unwin and his unknown benefactor, one thing stuck out from Graham Johnson's rambling conversation.

Trevor had been in the army. And so had Captain alias Major Harry Deveraux. There had to be a link. Her first instinct that maybe the major *was* involved in the stalking, or even the killing, was too strong now to be ignored.

She kept remembering little things about

him that hadn't seemed important before. He had been dressed immaculately at the funeral, in a dark, unobtrusive suit that wouldn't attract attention ... and leather gloves. Gloves that had never been taken off, all the while he was poking around at Madame Leanora's. Leaving no fingerprints...

She decided to phone Nick for a little more information, knowing she had to tread carefully.

'DI Frobisher,' she heard him reply efficiently.

However scratchy their relationship was at times, she had always been reassured by the sound of his voice. It was strong and rich. It could be as hard as necessary when dealing with crims, and yet there were other times when it could become as tender as ... with a little shock at where her thoughts were going, Alex caught herself up short. This was no time for erotic memories.

'Nick, I'm sorry if you're busy—'

'Never too busy for you, sweetheart,' he said at once.

But she knew that he was often *far* too busy to take calls when he was up to his neck in police work. So she must have caught him at a good time for once.

'I've heard from my friend in Worthing again, and the man who murdered her mother has topped himself. All the extra publicity has disturbed her all over again, as you can imagine,' she invented. 'But she thinks he may have been in the same regiment as that major or captain I mentioned to you. Don't ask me why she wants to know – something to do with her mother, I think – but I said I'd try to find out. Is there any way of checking?'

God, it all sounded so feeble, and she hadn't thought things through before she called him. He'd surely know there was something in the wind ... and had she really referred to Moira as her friend?

'I'll see what I can do,' Nick said casually. Too casually. She knew that. 'Are you home this evening?'

'No. Maybe. I'm not sure yet. Call me on my mobile, Nick, as soon as. OK?'

'It may not be that quick, but whenever,' he said, just as vaguely. 'Take care, Alex.'

She could almost see him smiling as he put down the phone. She could almost see that smug *I-know-something-you-don't* and that *I-know-you're-up-to-something* smile ... and she tried to ignore it. She could probably have gone through channels and found out the information about Trevor herself, but it would have taken time. And Nick could do it far quicker. She had to hope he'd swallowed her story.

Over dinner that evening the landlady bustled about supervizing her dining staff, and paused at Alex's table.

186

'Your young man telephoned earlier, Miss Best, to see if you had arrived safely. Perhaps he'll be joining you for the weekend after all.'

Alex felt her hands go rigid in the midst of putting a portion of broccoli on to her plate. So he'd sussed her out ... but despite Mrs Dooley's coy remarks she doubted that he'd come all the way down here just to give her a message. He'd rather play the cat and mouse game that was one of his stock-in-trades.

She admitted that every new revelation in this case was making her nervous. She was already of the opinion that there were higher stakes at risk than she had believed at first, and wondering even more fervently whether or not it would be prudent to inform the police of her findings and hand everything over to them.

There came a time when you had to weigh things up sensibly, and accept that there were some things you just couldn't handle alone. But she wouldn't do any of it without consulting Moira and getting her opinion. Moira was paying her fee and should be calling the shots.

And she was in danger of talking out of the side of her mouth like a regular Hollywood gangster if she wasn't careful, she thought, almost choking over her steam-hot roast potatoes.

'Everything all right, dear?' Mrs Dooley said anxiously.

'Fine, thank you,' Alex gasped, her eyes watering as she grabbed her glass of wine and nearly sank the lot in one swallow to counteract the ruination of her throat. How the hell did you get roast potatoes that hot? she wondered.

She was embarrassed to have made an exhibition of herself in front of the other guests, and it didn't help to hear the two small boys at the corner table being shushed up by their harassed parents. She made a mental note that if she ever had children, she'd insist on self-catering holidays...

Her mobile was ringing when she returned to her room. She should really take an evening stroll to ward off the effects of Mrs Dooley's hefty portions of food, but it could wait.

The voice spoke as soon as she answered.

'I thought you'd like to know that Captain Harry Deveraux died ten years ago,' Nick said.

'What?' Alex said, her heart jolting, and forgetting all about accusing him of tailing her. 'He can't have done, unless I've been seeing ghosts–'

'Whoever you've been seeing, his name isn't Harry Deveraux, Major or Captain! So where does that leave you?'

'I don't know,' she said slowly. 'I'll have to

think about it. What about the other name I mentioned, Nick? Any luck on that one?'

She tried to be casual, though it was hard to keep her excitement contained. Why would anyone masquerade as someone who was dead? Nobody did that without a reason, and it had to be suspect. Either that or they were simply obsessed with delusions of grandeur, and remembering the way he had ponced about on the cruise ship, that certainly fitted Harry whoever he was.

'Your murderer was a private in an infantry unit,' Nick told her, 'and get this. There was a Sergeant Harold Dawes in the same unit who was dishonourably discharged for falsifying army records very successfully over a period of months. He was a dab hand at forgery, it seems.'

'So?' Alex said expectantly when he paused for effect. 'Am I supposed to infer something from that?'

'You should, darling,' he said drily. 'I'd have thought the powers of deduction of one Alexandra Best, alias Audrey Barnes, might have got the significance of the initials.'

She was there before he had finished speaking, but she didn't intend letting him guess how her heart was pounding.

'Thanks. Nick. The two of them probably don't have any connection, but at least I can let Moira Wolstenholme know.'

There was silence at the other end, and

then he was curt.

'When are you going to come clean with me, Alex?'

'When I can,' she said simply. 'You know all about client confidentiality—'

'I know when something's really bugging you, and I'm always there if you need me. You know that too.'

'I do,' she said solemnly. 'And if ever the going gets rough, you'll be the first one I call.'

She crossed her fingers as she spoke, knowing that pride and self-esteem wasn't going to let her admit anything of the sort unless it was absolutely vital.

She hung up and switched off her mobile for a while. She needed time to think. Nick had put an entirely new question in her mind now. If this Harold Dawes was in the same army unit as Trevor Unwin, the two men would almost certainly have known one another.

And if Harold Dawes had been masquerading as Harry Deveraux, turning up in his obnoxious guise on the same cruise ship as Leanora Wolstenholme – who was later stabbed to death by Trevor Unwin – then she had to be on to something at last.

She didn't know *what*. It was a far cry from being hired to find out the identity of a stalker, but she just knew there had to be a strong connection. And then there was the money. Did Harry/Harold have that kind of money to pay off Trevor for doing his dirty work? Somehow Alex doubted it. An army sergeant's pay couldn't be so good that he'd throw away money as if it was paper – and for no special reason that she could think of.

She was fairly certain that none of the Harry/Harold names were in Leanora's notebook, so presumably he couldn't have been one of her clients. So if he hadn't forked out the pay-off to Trevor Unwin for killing her, who had?

The words MISTER BIG? loomed up in her mind, and she felt herself groan. It was all so gangsterish. And it was so very feasible too. Leanora – Madame Leanora – had had some amazingly influential clients who would have consulted her and given her far more information than they realized.

And if one of them was being seriously blackmailed by the Wolstenholmes, then he could have paid an acquaintance – a known con man – to find a guinea-pig with nothing to lose. Trevor Unwin with a cancer death sentence already hanging over him – to kill Leanora and pocket a handsome fee for his aged mother's comfort.

The rush of possibilities was so great that it was hard for Alex to think logically and not to let her imagination streak away with her. Such a Mister Big, whose name she couldn't get out of her head now, had to be stinking rich to pay both men for their silence. Because she was damn sure the middle-man would want a handsome payment for his services as well. Whoever Mister Big was, he had to be a top dog somewhere.

And he had been stalking Leanora and Moira for some time, trying to frighten them off, which apparently hadn't worked, since the threats were continuing. And not only to them.

Alex felt a chill like ice run down her back. These people had dealt coldly and clinically with Leanora. They were continuing to threaten Moira, and now they knew she was involved. The burglary at her office, the packet with the dead lilies, and the guttural phone call told her that.

Why the hell hadn't she taken down that phone number? It was one of the first things she should have done, if she hadn't been so bloody unnerved by it all. Some private eye she was...

She felt suddenly stifled, if not over-whelmed with nerves, and she had to get out of doors. She left her mobile switched off and walked around the park opposite the guest house for half an hour, breathing deeply and trying to make sense of what she knew so far. It had seemed so simple at first.

Someone was sending Moira hate mail and making the occasional obscene phone call. It wasn't surprising if Leanora had been in the habit of scaring the daylight out of people, despite her dreary appearance on the cruise ship. But that had to have been an illusion too, Alex realized. In her psychic garb in the cloying atmosphere of her business premises, she'd no doubt have held the whip-hand over any gullible person who entered it. She was a far tougher nut than she appeared, and probably wouldn't have been fazed by anonymous threats.

Moira was an easier target. Especially if the stalker was half inclined to believe everything he had learned from Madame L. Taunting Moira would be a way of getting rid of his own nerves, and proving he was still in control. But was that all there was to it? Or was there a far more sinister meaning behind all the threats?

Alex knew she had to confront Moira. If she had a duty to do her best for her clients, then so should they be honest with her. She knew that they frequently weren't, but she had to find out if the two women really had been up to no good, and if blackmail had been involved.

It was going to be a bloody sensitive confrontation. If she was wrong, she would be thrown out on her ear, and she could say goodbye to any further fees from this case. But did it matter?

With a shudder, Alex knew it was developing into one of the most unsavoury cases she had handled. Or could be, if her suspicions were right. She had always trusted her instincts, and she had a gut instinct about this one. It was growing stronger all the time, and she didn't need any of Leanora's psychic powers to tell her when something was seriously bad.

And right from the start, she had known Harry Deveraux was bad news. She had despised him on the cruise, and she had mistrusted him when he'd turned up at Leanora's funeral.

But she couldn't put off seeing Moira for ever, and she left the park and went across to her car. She slid inside it and gripped the steering-wheel for a few minutes. She wasn't looking forward to the next half hour one little bit, and there was something more than a gut feeling inside her now.

There was a gnawing, uneasy sensation, the kind you got before you went to the dentist, knowing damn well it was going to effing well *hurt*, no matter what they said! Only this feeling was ten times worse. A hundred times worse.

'Damn it, Leanora, get out of my head, can't you?' she muttered, almost without thinking.

And then she felt her skin crawl at even fantasizing for one second, that she could be influenced by a psychic – especially a dead one.

She crunched her gears and the car shot forward, narrowly missing a van coming around the corner. She mouthed an apology at the obscenity she saw coming from the driver's lips and just managed to resist returning his two-fingered salute.

Instead, she somehow got her jittering nerves together and drove away as steadily as possible.

The sun was setting low in the sky now, and throwing a golden sheen over the waters of the Channel as she climbed the hills towards Moira's house. The advent of a lovely summer sunset had the effect of making the whole town look serene and beautiful, which was more than the way Alex was feeling.

Because how the hell did you challenge a recently bereaved daughter to ask if she and her mother had been operating a black-mailing scam?

Chapter 8

Despite all her intentions, Alex found it impossible to go straight to the house. She had to get her thoughts in order, knowing she must be as tactful as possible or she would get nowhere. And what if she was wrong? What then? Moira was hardly going to be best pleased to know that she and her mother were being suspected of a serious crime.

She drove around for a while, her mind muddled with indecision. Before she realized it, she had headed out of Worthing and was well on to the Brighton road. It was a while before it dawned on her that something her father used to say kept intruding into her thoughts. *If there was a problem to be solved, it was far better to confront it head-on.* He had been so strong, mentally and physically – and she had never felt more feeble or insecure about what she was doing right now. And she knew he wouldn't have been proud of her dithering.

Unconsciously she straightened her shoulders, reminding herself that wasn't the way Nick Frobisher would be handling things either, and that thought was enough to send her back the way she had come.

By now it was dark, and once at the Wolstenholme house, she turned off her engine and sat in her car, staring at the place for a few minutes before she walked purposefully across the gravel to the front door and rang the bell.

The house was very quiet, eerily so, since there was a blaze of lights streaming out from the uncurtained windows, but there was no answer to Alex's persistent ringing.

Perhaps Moira was entertaining, she thought, feeling half-resentful on Leanora's account, since she knew that not even a recent bereavement seemed to have the same effect on anyone in this family and their acquaintances as it did on normal people.

Perhaps there was a seance going on somewhere in a back room, while they all waited expectantly for Leanora to COME ON DOWN out of the ether, as if they were all contestants in some ectoplasmic TV game show... Perhaps Moira was conducting a *proper* ouija board experiment for Leanora's believers and giving them the benefit of tapping into her mother's psychic powers – for a fee, of course...

'What the hell am I doing here?' Alex muttered to herself. 'I don't like all this stuff and never did.'

And she deliberately pushed away the crazy feeling that Leanora was hovering somewhere near, and that if she looked over her shoulder she might well see her floating a foot above the ground, smiling benevolently at her new convert...

'Not in a million bloody years!' Alex said savagely out loud. 'Pull yourself together, woman, and find Moira.'

And if nobody was answering the front door, then she would find her way around the back. It was still a mellow evening, and maybe if there was a party, albeit a pretty quiet one, it would be taking place around the swimming-pool.

After the blaze of lights streaming out from the front windows, it took a moment or two for Alex's pupils to refocus to the darkness of the kidney-shaped pool in the tree-lined garden. There was no party going on then...

And then there was no need for her eyes to adjust to darkness as the electronic lights that sensed the warmth of someone's presence flooded the whole garden with light. She blinked as the brilliance hurt her eyes and she had to shield them for a few seconds.

The Wolstenholmes had clearly spared no expense in luxury here. But even as the thought entered her mind, she found what she had come for.

Moira was lying face down at the bottom of the pool, fully clothed, and seemingly ... apparently ... CERTAINLY, for God's sake ... very dead.

Anyone would naturally assume so. But Alex knew you should never assume anything. Even as the horror of it swept through her she was already rushing to the side of the pool and jumping straight in, gasping at the chill of the water as it closed over her head, and desperately grabbing Moira's inert body to haul it to the surface.

Alex rolled her over with difficulty, still floundering and treading water, as the dead, open eyes stared back at her. The mouth was open too, a great well of garish lipstick, and she shuddered as she dragged her gaze away from those eyes and that mouth. And then, acutely observant and with all her senses heightened now, she noted the bruise marks on her neck.

As if she was on auto-pilot Alex registered various bits of information in seconds. Remembering everything she had learned, both from experience and from the section on murder methods in the *Self-Help Manual of Detection* she guessed that Moira had been strangled and then thrown into the pool. But she couldn't have been in the water too long, because she wasn't bloated, and her skin wasn't wrinkled from immersion.

She pushed aside her distaste, gripping Moira beneath the arms and pulling her body in life-saving mode to the side of the pool before heaving it onto the grass surround. Moira was a heavy woman, and it took all Alex's strength to get her out.

And then she stood, dripping and shaking, catching her breath and feeling completely disorientated, before remembering what she had to do. Her mobile was in her car. She squelched her way back to it, and fumbled with the door lock, almost sobbing with tension, wondering if he was still here. The murderer. The strangler. The stalker. The one who knew she was involved with Moira and her mother.

She tried not to dwell on that thought, and punched out 999 on her mobile with fingers that felt as stiff as drumsticks. She babbled out a request for the police and ambulance, and gave her message as concisely as she could, considering her chattering lips. And when she had finished, she looked back at the house, so invitingly warm with the lights still full on, and shuddered from head to toe. It had been a warm summer's day in what seemed a lifetime ago, but when the daylight had faded and you had been immersed in cold water dealing with a dead body, you felt anything but warm.

Her intense longing was to get away from there at once. Nobody knew who had called the police, and a mobile number wasn't instantly traceable. But she knew she couldn't just leave. She owed it to Moira to stay and give a report, however much she disguised her real reason for coming here.

Nor could she leave Moira alone like this, looking so bloody grotesque. It was so awful. Whatever scam had been involved, the end of a person's life should be dignified, and neither of the Wolstenholme women had had that.

She tried to think sensibly. There was a car rug in the boot of her car. She could cover

Moira with it, but Moira didn't need it as much as she did. Instead, Alex cloaked herself inside the car rug to try to stop some of the shivering. And almost at once she heard the scream of the police and ambulance sirens and watched the lights coming towards her as the vehicles climbed the hill to the house.

'Were you the one who called us, Miss?' the scenes of crime officer said a short while later.

'Yes,' Alex mumbled. 'She's at the back of the house. I got her out of the pool – but I don't think she drowned. Strangled, I think – there are bruises on her neck–'

She didn't know why she was giving out this information, but she noted that it was being taken down by a subordinate.

You often got significant info while the suspect was in an anxious state, Nick had once told her. But she wasn't a suspect, for God's sake ... nor a witness...

She led the way to the pool. The place seemed to be swarming with people now. There were uniformed police, and men in suits, and ambulance men with a stretcher to take Moira away once the police doctor had done a brief examination.

Alex felt hysteria rising at the incongruousness of it all. Leanora couldn't have foretold any of this either...

'Are you ready to tell us what happened?' the officer asked her sharply as she stood there, shaking visibly. 'Where do you come into all this, Miss-?'

'Best,' she replied automatically. 'Alexandra Best-'

'Isn't that the name of the woman visitor who reported a stolen purse a short while ago?' the constable with the notebook asked. 'I seem to know the name-'

'Well done, Constable. Make a note of that. You don't live in Worthing then, Miss Best?' the officer queried, turning back to her.

'No, I-'

'And were you acquainted with the deceased?'

It gradually dawned on Alex that she was being treated less like someone who had just reported a murder, than as a suspect after all. It didn't scare her so much as astound her, and after the trauma of the evening, her temper snapped.

'Yes, I knew Miss Wolstenholme, and I was coming here to see her this evening on a private matter. When I got no reply at the front door I came around the back.'

She heard one of the suits murmur something to the officer.

'Is this Miss Wolstenholme a relation of the lady who was murdered in the town recently?'

'Her daughter,' Alex muttered.

'And how did you come to know them?'

'Look, Officer, I'll answer any questions you want to ask, but I'd like to go back to the guest house and get some dry clothes. I *am* soaking wet, in case you haven't noticed.'

'We've noticed,' he said grimly. 'So how do you explain that, Miss Best?'

Alex felt her mouth drop open. 'I'm soaking wet because I jumped in the pool and got Moira – Miss Wolstenholme – out of it. How else do you think it happened? I didn't push her under, if that's what you're thinking.'

'I'm not thinking anything at this moment,' he said. 'Until I get the pathologist's report, I prefer to keep an open mind. But you said you thought she wasn't drowned, and you noticed marks on her neck. Very astute of you, Miss, and perhaps not something most people might observe in a moment of panic. *If* they panicked, of course.'

'Of course I panicked. But I'm not blind, and those bruises were bloody obvious, even to an idiot–'

'You obviously need dry clothes,' he said, not giving her an opportunity to say anything more. 'A woman PC will escort you back to your lodgings and then bring you to the station for your statement.'

'I have my car—'

'You'll hand over your keys and someone will follow you in it. We shall also need the clothes you're wearing.'

Alex stared at him, engulfed in shock now. The nightmare was real. Somehow she had become the prime suspect for Moira's murder. The only suspect, caught in the act – allegedly. It was all so farcical she wanted to laugh, and to her horror, she did just that.

'You must be mad if you think I'm responsible for this,' she stammered. Why would I have been so stupid as to report it if I'd done it?'

'Murderers often do,' he said coldly. 'They enjoy watching the police arrive and they get a kick out of seeing the procedure in operation.'

'Well, I don't,' Alex snapped. 'I've seen enough of that, believe me.'

She bit her lip as his eyes narrowed.

'Really? You can also explain that remark when you give your statement. Now, we'll leave the forensic boys to do their job, and we'll get on with ours. Into the police car if you please, Miss. And I'll have your car keys.'

He held out his hand, and Alex handed them over silently. It was like a bad movie, she raged. The cops had got it all wrong, but would the sure but steady PI solve the crime and get the just rewards? So far they wouldn't listen to her. Not that she had tried to tell them much, and if she went to them now, would they believe the garbled story of a con man stalker whom she assumed had been paid by Mister Big to persuade Trevor Unwin to murder Moira's blackmailing mother?

The more the whole idea unravelled so untidily in her mind, the more she knew how unlikely it would sound to anyone who hadn't been there. Who didn't know the people involved.

Of course there was always Graham Johnson, she thought, finding in him a little ray of hope. However reluctantly, he would have to substantiate the fact that Trevor Unwin had paid two large amounts of money for his mother's well-being and upkeep at the Happy Days Home. But if she brought Graham Johnson in as a person involved in her own enquiries, she would have to reveal everything. And it was still her case...

Her heart suddenly lurched as the police car took her down to the town towards Mrs Dooley's guest house. How could it still be her case? She didn't have a case any more. The client was dead, and in any normal circumstances there could be no more case to solve. But this time was different.

The stalker was still out there, and he was still looking for something that Alex had.

The notebook had probably been the pot of gold at the end of the rainbow for a pair of unscrupulous blackmailers, Madame Leanora and her daughter – both of whom were now dead. The breath caught in her throat at the thought, and the woman PC beside her leaned forward.

'Are you all right? Not going to throw up, are you?'

'Well, apart from being virtually accused of a murder I didn't commit, I'm perfectly fine. How do you think I feel?'

The driver glanced back at her through the driving mirror. 'Have we met somewhere before?'

'I shouldn't think so,' Alex said resentfully.

And if this was a chat-up line it was the worst time in the world to try it on.

'Yes we have, and I'm trying to think where it was.' He snapped his fingers, making her flinch. 'Now I remember. You were with a Special Branch officer at that spooky woman's premises in the town.'

Alex groaned. She had a good memory for faces, but too much had been happening in the last couple of hours for her to register the guy. Besides, it was dark and she hadn't seen him properly, but the voice was vaguely familiar. Now she realized it was the constable who had nabbed her and the major at Madame Leanora's, and full of self-importance, he would surely report that fact now.

Including who she had been with on that day. Or supposedly with. Not that she thought the constable would have registered a name on the bogus ID card. But if they asked her ... and then they discovered that they couldn't trace a Special Branch guy with the name of Deveraux...

It was all getting away from her, Alex thought in a panic. It had seemed such an ordinary case at first. Trace a stalker, as far as possible. Produce reasonable statements of procedure, and get paid for your efforts whether they were successful or not. It beat walking the streets ... but it was never meant to involve murder...

'I suppose I'll be allowed a phone call?' she said huskily as they neared the guest house.

'When we get back to the nick,' the woman PC said.

Alex groaned. 'All right, but look, can we play this down while we're here? The landlady's a stickler–'

'You can say you've had an accident and need to change your clothes. I'll be with you at all times, of course,' she said crisply. 'If you wish to do so, you can say you're coming back to the station to give us all the details.'

'Thanks,' Alex muttered.

They hadn't *quite* read her her rights yet,

and she hadn't *actually* been accused of anything, but where the hell did they recruit these hard-nosed people? *Prisoner Cell Block H* soared into her mind... Come back *The Bill,* all was forgiven...

As expected, Mrs Dooley's face was a picture of disbelief, but the brief explanation apparently satisfied her, and the WPC's presence was enough to stem the flood of questions. They would come later though, thought Alex – providing she was let out of custody and able to explain anything.

Once in her room, she began to strip quickly, resentful of the WPC standing close enough to watch everything.

'I suppose a shower's out of the question?' she said sarcastically. 'I stink of pool chemicals, and I wouldn't want to contaminate your fragrant nick.'

'Five minutes then,' the woman said, bundling Alex's clothes into a plastic bag. 'We're not inhuman, you know.'

"No?' She dived behind the shower curtain without waiting for an answer.

'And you'll do yourself no favours by antagonising us. What are you doing here, anyway? Off the record.'

Alex grimaced, already running hot water over her hair and body and making it the quickest shower of her life. And knowing damn well that off the record was just as likely to be reported as anything official. But what the hell? It was all going to come out now, anyway.

'I'm a private investigator. I was following up an enquiry on Miss Wolstenholme's instructions.'

'Good God!' The WPC poked her head through the shower curtain. 'Are you having me on?'

'I'm not *having* you at all,' Alex snapped, grabbing a towel and wrapping herself in it angrily.

At the pointed words, she had the savage satisfaction of seeing the woman flush darkly and take a step back.

'If you give me a minute to get dry and dressed, I'll show you my card,' Alex went on more tolerantly. The WPC couldn't have been much older than herself, she thought, but she was as plain as a pikestaff.

She had always prided herself on being a quick-change artist at showering and dressing, and while she rough-dried her hair, she handed her card to the WPC without comment.

'You'll need to explain everything to my DI,' the woman said at last.

'I'd have done so earlier if I'd been given a chance.'

They both heard the car hooter from the road below, and the WPC went to the window and held up five fingers to the driver. Alex would have made it two.

'So who do you want to phone?' she said next, in an effort to be more amenable. 'My name's Tess, by the way.'

'Well, Tess, that's for me to know and you to find out, isn't it?' Alex said, in a pseudo-American drawl, and not giving a damn about how hammy it sounded.

'You should have told us who you were and what you were doing there right away,' the DI she hadn't seen before snapped. 'It would have saved an awful lot of trouble and paperwork. Not that your being a PI automatically makes you less of a murder suspect than anyone else. There are still questions to be answered, and you'll be required to make a statement. You can have someone with you if you wish. A solicitor or friend–'

'I don't need anyone watching over me to make a statement. I'd like to call someone first though.'

'Name and number,' he said, clearly not prepared to let her off the hook too easily, and annoyed by her frosty manner.

'Detective Inspector Frobisher–'

'*Nick* Frobisher?' His face was so comical that she dearly wanted to laugh out loud. But this was not the moment.

'The very same,' Alex said sweetly, her

self-confidence returning quickly now. 'He's a close friend of mine, and will definitely vouch for me.'

It was around midnight when they finally let her go, and by the time she had tried to explain to Mrs Dooley that she had only had a small accident, she learned that the sketchy outline of Moira Wolstenholme's death was already local gossip. And although Mrs Dooley didn't as yet connect the two events, Alex began to realize that her street cred was being sorely stretched.

She could see that her accident, hinted at wild orgies and drug raves and it wasn't the norm for Mrs Dooley's clientele to have such things to report. But once she invented the tale that her young man might be coming down to stay for a few days, Mrs Dooley visibly relaxed about the outlandish behaviour of this paying guest.

And then the sense of unreality about the nightmarish happenings of the past few hours really sank into Alex's brain. She sat on her bed, feeling as if her bones were dissolving with the release of tension.

She couldn't stop the tears streaking down her face, and she didn't try. Her father always said that as well as healing physical and emotional hurts, tears were there to help wash away all the hurts in your soul, and she had never missed his wise words more than she did at that moment.

They had so rarely been good communicators, but whenever he came out with one of his dour remarks, it had stuck in her mind more than she realized. It had been easy to ignore it at the time, but she was older and wiser now. Older, anyway.

It was almost impossible to get to sleep that night. She couldn't believe that she had virtually been suspected of murder, but in retrospect she could see how it had looked. But she would have a few words to say to Nick about the highhanded methods of certain police officers.

Thank God he had responded so readily to her call, and after she had blabbed out all that had been happening, and nearly lost it in the process, she had handed the phone over to the local DI and let Nick speak to him.

The reaction towards her had been very different then. Talk about an old boys' network ... but to hell with being pompous about that in the circumstances.

She shivered, curling up like a foetus in the bed, and finding comfort in the cocoon of the bedclothes. She wished Nick was here now. Here beside her, holding her and keeping her safe. She needed his strength and his love.

At the early morning knock on her door, she

groaned, assuming it was Mrs Dooley taking pity on her again. Her door was locked, and she staggered out of bed, dragging the duvet around her for quickness, and opened the door a couple of inches. Nick pushed it wide and strode inside.

'Well, do come in,' Alex stuttered. 'Have you been driving since dawn?'

But once the initial shock of seeing him was over, she forgot everything but sheer relief, ready to drop the duvet and hug him tight. He was her hero ... Sir Galahad in cop's clothing ... and she could forgive him anything for coming to her side so quickly.

He took hold of her shoulders and gave them a none-too-gentle shake.

'What the hell have you got yourself into this time, Alex?' he snapped.

She stared at him, all her good feelings vanishing in an instant. This wasn't what she had expected. If anything, she had expected him to take advantage of the situation, but she might have guessed that he'd probably been stewing all night over the report from that other supercilious DI.

'Well, I've hardly been knocking off a client, for a start,' she raged at him. 'And if that was the way all you coppers react to a 999 call, I'm not surprised that so many witnesses phone them and then scarper! I'm amazed that anyone bothers to phone at all!'

'I never thought you'd murdered any-body,' he said abruptly, seeing the sparkle of furious tears in her eyes.

'Well, *they* did.'

'Of course they didn't,' he retorted. 'But you know as well as I do that they had to find out what the hell you were doing there. And I gather they didn't get a very clear explanation.'

'They got enough to satisfy them. And if you're about to give me the third degree now, forget it. I told them all I intended to, and you're not getting another thing out of me.'

She was aware that she was sticking out her bottom lip, as belligerent as a child. She pushed away from him and took a step backwards, as if to ward off all comers, and the next moment he gave a smothered oath and pulled her back to him, folding her in his arms.

'My poor baby,' he murmured against her cheek. 'You've had a hellish night of it, haven't you?'

Her face was pressed tight against the cold morning roughness of his.

'You could say that,' she replied, finding it hard not to gulp in the childlike way she couldn't seem to stop now.

She registered that the duvet had some-how fallen to the floor. But it wasn't a bloody invitation, she stormed, seeing how

214

his eyes were noting her skimpy nightshirt. She grabbed up the duvet again and wrapped herself in it.

'It's a bit late for modesty, isn't it?' Nick said, his face a mixture of a frown and a grin. 'Considering the last time we were here–'

'That was a one-off,' Alex snapped. 'And I don't intend to repeat it.'

But she kept her eyes deliberately lowered, in case he thought she was remembering it all too well.

'So get dressed while I go and inform Mrs Dooley that I'd like breakfast. Then we'll talk,' he said, more aggressively.

'Don't you have work to do? And when are you going back to Plymouth?' she added. 'I'm surprised they can spare you. Haven't they found a replacement for Scott Nelson yet?'

'They have. And I'm not going back to Plymouth.'

He was gone before she could get any more answers. She should be glad that he was staying in London – presumably. She *was* glad, but she was too on edge to bother her head overmuch about anything but the fact that reaction from yesterday was setting in again fast.

She had been the one to discover Moira Wolstenholme's dead body, and she had no idea where that left her regarding the stalker. She still had Leanora's notebook, and presumably HE still wanted it. Therefore she was next in line...

She went into her bathroom and stood beneath the steaming shower water for the minimum amount of time, because for the life of her she couldn't stop thinking of *Psycho* now. The screaming in the guest ho water pipes didn't help, either...

But by the time she joined Nick in the dining-room for one of Mrs Dooley's hugely calorific breakfasts, she had got her wits about her.

'So why aren't you going back to Plymouth?' she forestalled him. 'I thought that was promotion. If they've offered you your old job, that's downgrading, surely.'

'I didn't say that. Actually, you're now speaking to Detective Chief Inspector Frobisher – acting at present. But old Kelsey retired, so the job was up for grabs.'

'Congratulations, Nick. That's great news,' Alex said, knowing it wasn't as easy as he made it sound. There were formalities and boards, and the usual mundane procedures before anything happened, but he had obviously got through them all, and hadn't even told her.

'Anyway, I discovered I didn't care for life down in the sticks after all. There were too many things I was missing. So what was your real interest in Moira Wolstenholme?'

He said it casually, throwing in the question before she was prepared for it. She continued with her scrambled eggs and bacon before she answered.

'I told you. I'd met her mother, and I came here for her funeral, and got to know Moira. She asked me to do a little checking for her, and I wanted a bit more information,' she finished lamely.

'About what? Whether she was all she professed to be?'

'Moira was a florist, and you couldn't have a more harmless occupation than that, I'd have thought.'

'And her mother was a fortune-teller.'

'I hardly think Leanora would have liked being described in that way! She called herself a psychic and a clairvoyant – but she did have some very odd friends. They turned up at her funeral, done up as if they were going to a party.'

She couldn't help a small shudder, remembering. It had seemed so very unnatural ... and she instantly wondered who would be organizing Moira's funeral, and if the same group of people would be attending. Including the major.

'What have you thought about now?' Nick said, too sharp not to notice her indrawn breath.

'I was just wondering if they would all be at Moira's funeral too,' she said, seeing no

217

reason not to share half her thoughts with him. 'And who would do the flowers.'

'Christ, Alex, you're really letting these cuckoos get to you, aren't you?' he said.

'You didn't know them,' she retorted. 'If you did, you'd understand. Anyway, what do you suppose will happen to the house now? Leanora's premises were on lease, and it's all in the hands of the estate agent. But the house belonged to Moira as far as I know, and I don't remember being introduced to any relatives at Leanora's funeral.'

Mrs Dooley was hovering close by, and Alex concentrated on her breakfast before she was asked if there was anything wrong with it. But she had clearly been overheard.

'Is that the poor lady who's just drowned in her own swimming-pool, Miss Best? Shocking affair, isn't it?' she said in a hushed voice.

'Yes, it is,' Alex murmured.

'I think there was a gentleman friend a long time ago,' Mrs Dooley confided. 'Their cleaning woman used to do for me a couple of days a week, and she mentioned it. He used to come down from London in a big car, so she said, but she only saw him once or twice. It was all a bit mysterious, but you couldn't always believe half-baked gossip, anyway.'

Her sniff said that she considered herself above such gossip, but the small piece of information was enough to send the blood pumping in Alex's veins. A gentleman friend in a big car was not what she had expected of Moira. But why not? She shouldn't have stereotyped her – and she shouldn't be surprised at anything.

Someone else caught Mrs Dooley's attention then, and Alex reminded herself swiftly that she didn't want Nick thinking she was interested in the fact that Moira Wolstenholme had once had a gentleman friend visiting her in a big car, and that her cleaning woman might know more…

'When do you have to go back to London then, Nick?' she asked him casually.

'You seem mighty keen to get rid of me. First you want to know when I'm going back to Plymouth, and now London–'

'I didn't say that.'

'Well, as a matter of fact I really should get back this morning. They can't spare me so often now I'm one of the bigwigs,' he said, self-mockingly. 'But I wanted to check that you really were all right. I do care about you, Alex.'

And you think I've only got half a brain and I should be leaving this kind of job to the experts.

'I know. And I appreciate it. But I'm quite capable of looking after myself.'

She mentally crossed her fingers as she spoke, but she couldn't wait for him to leave, and then quiz Mrs Dooley about Moira's cleaning woman, and where she lived. She also intended visiting Moira's shop, to see what she could glean there.

She began to feel more cheerful, thinking that there might be a glimmer of light in the puzzle at last. And then she sobered up, because a woman was still dead, and not from natural causes. But she also knew that Moira – and Leanora – would want her to go on with her investigations. She knew it as surely as if the pair of them were looking over her shoulder and urging her on.

'Mrs Dooley, you mentioned something to me about the Wolstenholmes' cleaning woman earlier,' she said, seeking her out the minute Nick left. The news about who had discovered the body would soon be in the local newspaper, so she had already told Mrs Dooley about her part in it all. She plunged on at the woman's vacant look.

'I think I might have a word with her, since she's sure to find the news upsetting. Do you know who she is and where she lived?'

'Cleaning woman?' Mrs Dooley said, more intrigued with the fact that one of her guests was a private investigator and had discovered a corpse in the town – and wondering how much of an anecdote she could make of it for future guests.

'I'm sure you said you knew the one who

had worked for the Wolstenholmes,' Alex said, trying not to sound too interested.

'Oh, you mean Enid Lodge. She's a bit short of a shilling, if you get my meaning, Miss Best. You'll get nothing sensible out of her.'

'All the same, I think it would be kind for someone to tell her before she reads it in the newspapers, don't you?'

'There's no likelihood of that. She can't read,' Mrs Dooley said positively.

God this really *was* like watching paint dry, Alex thought irreverently. But so much of her job was exactly like that.

'Her address?' she persisted.

Mrs Dooley shrugged. 'I think she lives in one of those cottages along the coast towards Lancing. You'd have to ask when you got there. I wouldn't bother if I were you.'

But you're not me, thought Alex, and half an hour later she was driving in the direction the landlady had told her. There were a number of decrepit little cottages way out of town and she assumed it would be one of those. She had to park her car some distance away and walk down a track towards them.

She knocked at the first door and got no reply. The second one was just as silent, and Alex began to feel as if she was in some kind of ghost hamlet. It was almost like a time warp here. A few miles out of fashionable

221

Worthing, and she was practically in Thomas Hardy country...

No, she amended. *Wrong county ... but same atmosphere*. Nothing moved, except the swaying of the grasses and the ripple of the sea beyond the ridges of wasteland. The only sounds were the screeching sea-birds, as if to taunt her...

'What d'you want?' she heard a voice say suspiciously, making her jump. She stepped back quickly, her foot going into something squelchy and unmentionable, and saw a woman peering out from a small upstairs window in one of the cottages.

'I'm looking for someone. Mrs Enid Lodge,' she said, wishing herself anywhere but here. Wasn't there an old Diana Dors movie where a buxom housekeeper in the middle of a wood drew people inside with sinister intent? But this wasn't the middle of a wood and she shouldn't be so damn stupid and susceptible to atmosphere.

''Tis *Miss* Lodge, and what d'you want with her?'

'I want to give her some information about her former employer. Miss Wolstenholme. Moira Wolstenholme,' Alex said, wondering why the hell she should feel so bloody defensive faced with this oddball, when she was city slick and perfectly in control. Supposedly.

'Wait there,' the woman said, and minutes

222

later she had opened the front door. Alex got a quick impression of a middle-aged woman with pepper-and-salt hair that stood on end as if she had misplaced her comb – not only that morning, but every other morning of her life.

She forced an encouraging smile. 'Are you Miss Enid Lodge by any chance?'

'Might be,' the woman said.

'I'm afraid I've got some bad news about Moira,' Alex went on, deciding not to be messed about by non-co-operation.

'Never called her that. 'Tweren't polite. She were Miss Woolly to me. Liked that, she did,' she said with a chuckle.

It *was* her then. Alex didn't know whether to be glad or sorry. But she had a job to do, she reminded herself.

'Could I come in for a few minutes?' she asked, resisting the urge to run. The smells coming out of the cottage were anything but sweet, and visions of the three witches in *Macbeth* kept entering her head now. She really must get out more...

'What for?' the woman said, staring.

Alex decided that shock tactics were clearly called for.

'Moira's dead, Enid. I wondered if you could tell me something about her, and about her friends.'

'She ain't dead!'

'I'm afraid she is,' Alex said, more gently.

'I can tell you all about it, if you like. Moira had a gentleman friend too, didn't she, Enid? I'm sure he would want to know. Do you know his name and where he lives?'

Enid continued to stare at her. She was clearly a slow thinker, to put it mildly, and was finding it hard to digest so much information all at once.

'What about a cup of tea while we talk?' Alex suggested, even though the last thing she wanted was to touch anything inside this hovel.

But you had to do plenty of unsavoury things in the name of research, and this would probably be one of them.

As the door opened wider, Alex stepped inside while Enid went off to the kitchen, muttering about Moira not being dead, and clattering the kettle and cups while Alex sat on the very edge of a chair and whisked a vicious-looking ginger cat away from her with the toe of her shoe.

Chapter 9

'I believe you used to work for Miss Woolly, Enid,' Alex said, ignoring the previous tea-stains around the rim of her mug.

'Sometimes. Not lately. Not since 'er mum

died, nor for a time before that,' Enid said vaguely.

'But when you did – sometimes – you saw Miss Woolly's gentleman friend, didn't you? The one with the big car.'

Enid frowned. 'Didn't like 'im. He never spoke much, and when he did, he was all lah-de-dah.'

'What was his name?' Alex said casually.

'Dunno. Sometimes he made Miss Woolly cry though.'

'Did he? Why was that, I wonder?'

Alex made a pretence of putting her mug to her lips, while Enid took a long slurp of tea before she answered.

'I heard 'em arguing once. He said her mum was getting too big for her boots, and it was time it stopped or he'd make things bad for 'em both. I dunno what it meant, but it made Miss Woolly cry.'

I'll bet it did, thought Alex. If the gentleman friend with the big car was getting tired of paying up whatever blackmail demands Leanora made, no wonder Moira would be upset. She knew it was all still conjecture on her part, but she had a gut feeling that she was on the right track at last. But she didn't think she was going to get anything more out of the woman.

'Do you know what kind of car it was, Enid?'

Enid shrugged and screwed up her mouth

as she tried to remember. It had the effect of making her look more prune-like than ever.

'It was black with one of them big cat things on the front,' she said at last. 'Not like my moggy, mind, but one of them silver things like a sort of little statue.'

'Cat things? Do you mean a Jaguar insignia?'

'Dunno,' Enid said, losing interest. 'Might be. D'you want some more tea, only I got things to do.'

'No, I won't have any more,' Alex said hastily, putting down her mug and standing up before Enid could realize she hadn't touched the tea. 'Thank you, anyway, Enid. You've been very helpful.'

'Have I? Oh well, you know best. I dare-say.'

Alex left the cottage with a sense of relief and headed back towards Worthing. It was a start, but not much of one. The gentleman friend had a big black car that sounded like a Jaguar. And if he could afford to fill up a Jaguar tank with petrol to swan around in, he wasn't hard up.

But she knew that. Otherwise why would Leanora be blackmailing him? And for what reason? It was a shame Enid hadn't been forthcoming with his name, but it was imperative now for Alex to get back to London to study Leanora's notebook and start eliminating.

226

In any case she couldn't stay here much longer, and after yesterday's happenings, she longed to be home again. But decency demanded that she stayed long enough to find out about Moira's funeral. She decided to visit the florist shop to pay her condolences, and suss it out at the same time.

She would also be required at the inquest in due course, which wasn't such a comfortable thought. But she knew the police wouldn't let her get away with less.

She got back to the guest house and was met by a low-voiced Mrs Dooley, a conspirator full of added importance now that she knew what her paying guest did for a living.

'There's somebody to see you, my dear. I tried to get rid of him, but these people stick like glue when they want something. He's in the guest lounge.'

'He? Did he give his name?'

Mrs Dooley sniffed. 'Yes, but I don't remember it. He's from the local newspaper.'

Alex groaned. Once the news of Moira's death was public knowledge it was inevitable that they would want to interview her, and she should have been prepared for it. The fact was, she wasn't. She had been too busy tracking down Enid Lodge to give much thought to anything else.

But she put on a professional smile as she

entered the guest lounge. It reeked of tobacco now, which wouldn't please Mrs Dooley, she thought fleetingly.

'You wanted to see me, I believe? I'm Alexandra Best.'

The reporter didn't answer immediately. He was around forty years old and scruffily casual, and his answering smile became a leer as he noted her tight black trousers and v-neck top. Then he leaned back in his armchair, his legs sprawled wide and his eyes showing an unwelcome interest.

It took no more than seconds for his reaction to register with Alex, but she was in no mood to waste time on pervs, and the leer was enough to make her smile freeze.

'If you have any questions to ask me, I'll answer them as well as I can, but if your sole purpose was to sit and stare at me, this interview is already concluded,' she said, in a voice sharp enough to cut crystal.

'Hey, I didn't mean to offend you,' he said, sitting bolt upright at once. 'But you're quite a looker, Miss Best, and you have to admit that nobody expects a private dick to look like you!'

Alex fumed at the sexist remark, realizing that either Mrs Dooley or the police would have given him the information.

'We don't come ready-stamped like something in Sainsbury's,' she retorted. 'Now, can we get on with it?'

'Right. The name's Ken, by the way. Ken Coombes – if you ever want to get in touch.'

She gave him a cool stare that said it was more likely she would kiss a hundred frogs, and had the satisfaction of hearing him give an irritated smoker's cough, and make a show of fiddling with his notebook with nicotine-stained fingers.

'You discovered the deceased's body, I believe?'

'Miss Wolstenholme, yes. Miss – Moira – Wolstenholme.'

She has a name, you bastard. She's not just a body ready to be dissected for discussion among pathologists and coppers and rat-faced reporters.

'Of course. Strange that she and her weird mother should have died so soon after one another, wasn't it? Did you know them well? I presume the latest stiff – victim – was more than an acquaintance if you were visiting her in the evening.'

The questions were innocent enough, if insultingly said, but Alex knew what was behind them. Trying to ferret out a connection between the women to see if there was any hint of intrigue or mystery involved. And so there bloody well was, but none that she was going to tell him about.

'I hadn't known her for long. We had some business dealings, and I needed to see her on a private matter.'

'And instead of that, you found her in the

229

swimming-pool. Must have been a bit of a shock. How did you feel about that, Miss Best?'

'Do you people have special training in asking the most inane questions?' she snapped. 'How did you think I felt? It was a *terrible* shock. It was also a pretty sure bet that Moira was dead, since she was at the bottom of her pool,' she added sarcastically, 'so I did what any decent person would have done. I jumped into the pool and got her out, and then I called the police.'

'And would you say she had been in the pool very long?'

'I couldn't answer that. If you need that kind of information you'll have to ask the police.'

And you're not trapping me like that, sonny.

'So was it suicide or did somebody push her in?' he said, apparently musing, but with his pencil poised over his notebook for her answer. 'The police aren't giving out any clear information yet, but I'm sure you have some theories of your own. You private dicks always like to beat the coppers at their own game, don't you?' he leered again.

'I have no theories on it at all.'

'But you did say that you and the deceased – Miss Wolstenholme, I mean – had business dealings. And you are a private di– investigator. You must be curious.'

'I have no theories whatsoever on the

cause of death,' she repeated coldly. 'And there's nothing more to say.'

She stood up and waited for him to do the same. He was a leech, and she loathed him. He snapped his notebook shut, and handed her his card. She took it automatically.

'Just in case you think of anything else – or fancy a night out on the town,' he added.

The minute he had gone she ripped the card into shreds. There was still a strong smell of tobacco lingering from his breath and his clothes, and she needed some air.

She was also sure that Mrs Dooley would be air-freshening the room as soon as it was empty. For once she was in full agreement with her fussiness, and since she didn't intend being quizzed on what the reporter wanted, she slipped out of the house again before anyone saw her leave.

She found Moira's florist shop easily enough. It was closed, with the shutters halfway down and a notice in the glass panel of the door to the effect that due to the owner's death, the premises would remain closed for a few days.

She should have expected it and come here first thing in the morning, before the news had infiltrated, and someone had had time to write out the notice. She wasn't sure it would be any use at all to come here, except as an insight into Moira's character from her employees' gossipy point of view, but it was frustrating all the same.

The next second she jumped at the sound of the loud female voice behind her. It was vaguely familiar, but she couldn't think for a minute where she had heard it before.

'They had to close the shop out of respect. You're that friend of Leanora's, aren't you? The one at the send-off?'

Alex turned around slowly, and saw two of the women who had been at Leanora's funeral; the one who had flitted around asking everyone what their zodiac sign was; and her bosom companion, a sombre-faced woman. They were both still dressed garishly, their hair a shrieking henna straight out of a bottle, their arms linked. Doreen and May. Alex resisted a shudder at the sight of them, and answered quickly.

'That's right. And now poor Moira has died. You've heard about it, then?'

Doreen nodded. 'Oh yes. As a matter of fact we were deciding how we should get in touch with you with Moira's letter, since she didn't write your address on it, but now you've saved us the trouble of finding you.'

'Dear Leanora would have expected that, of course,' the second voice said gushingly.

'Leanora?' Alex said without thinking.

Her voice was jerky, unlike its usual cool. She found herself wishing desperately that she had never set eyes on Leanora Wolstenholme, nor her daughter, and especially not

232

these two freaks. And easily disregarding any inkling of political correctness, she was damned if she could think of them as anything else.

'Oh yes. It was all ordained, you see.'

Alex groaned. She didn't want to hear this. She definitely DID NOT WANT TO HEAR THIS...

Doreen gave a half-smile. 'I know you're not a believer, Miss Best, but Moira was quite sure something of the sort would happen sometime, even though she didn't know how. She didn't have dear Leanora's gift, of course, but a short time ago she sent letters to all her close friends to be opened on her death. No ifs or buts, you see. She simply knew. There was a letter for you too, entrusted to May and me.'

Alex swallowed. There was a chilling matter-of-factness in the way Doreen spoke. Her friend was dead, but there were no tears or remorse. Just acceptance that this had been ordained, and that Moira was now in the Great Beyond with Leanora. Both gazing down on them indulgently like ghastly twins ... Castor and Pollux ... and Alex had a hell of a job not to glance upwards in the expectation of seeing two gruesomely distorted mythical faces in the guise of Leanora and Moira beaming down on her...

'Here you are, dear.'

Doreen had rummaged in her canvas bag and was handing Alex a large brown envelope now. She wished desperately that she didn't have to take it, but of course she did. The letter might provide clues. It might tell her who the gentleman friend was ... the friend who might be Mister Big ... was *undoubtedly* Mister Big...

'Would you like to have some lunch with us if you feel the need to talk?' May said next. 'It sometimes helps, and you do look rather pale, dear.'

'No – but thank you. I have to go–'

'Well, no doubt we'll be seeing you again when Moira's send-off is arranged.'

Alex hesitated. Her nerves were on edge and she was desperate to get away from these two, but she still had a commitment to Moira.

'What will happen to the house now, I wonder?' she said. 'Were there any other relatives?'

In her experience, they came out of the woodwork once there was a house and money involved. But both the other women shook their heads decisively.

'Not one,' Doreen said, disgustingly cheerful. 'It was all settled between dear Leanora and Moira and their solicitors years ago. When they had both been called, everything would be sold and the proceeds divided between the Psychic Society and a designated animal sanctuary.'

Alex puzzled for a moment over who had been calling them, and then realized what Doreen meant.

'Well, thank you for the letter,' she said quickly.

'Go with luck,' May said, and they both turned as if they were one unit and glided away into the crowds.

'*Shit,*' Alex muttered, using her least favourite expletive, but at that moment it seemed to express in a single word all the unease and abhorrence she was feeling.

'Come on, don't let them get to you,' she continued to mutter as she walked back to the guest house, and then she realised she was doing just that, as people began glancing her way.

Just as if she was the weird one ... either that or she had her name printed in sky-high letters above her head, announcing to the world that she was the one who had found Moira Wolstenholme dead in her own swimming-pool.

She let herself into her room with shaking fingers. It had been a hell of a 24 hours, and anybody could be forgiven for being slightly traumatized by it all.

She wasn't Superwoman. Definitely not. In fact, she felt more like Minnie Mouse right now.

Her stomach was gnawing, and she remembered it was almost midday, but she didn't really feel like eating. And *that* was a first, she told herself feebly. It was BB & EM at Mrs Dooley's, so she usually had a snack at a local beach caff, but not today.

But she supposed she should eat something, if only to dispel the emptiness in her stomach, which she knew damn well wasn't actually due to hunger. She had some crisps in her bag, and along with the small packet of biscuits on her room tray, she would make some coffee and that would do.

She knew she was simply putting off the moment when she had to open Moira's letter. Once she did, it would be as if Moira was standing over her shoulder, dictating the words. She would hear Moira's voice in her head ... instead of which, in her imagination, she suddenly heard someone else's.

Are you quite sure you're cut out for this job Alex?

'No, Gary, I'm not,' she snapped. 'I'm damn well not. Not this one anyway. And get out of my head, will you!'

At the mention of his name, she found herself wondering what he was doing now. It took her mind off Moira for a moment, and even thinking about him conjured up an image of his dark eyes and seductive mouth, together with the whiff of his leathers and the throbbing power of his motorbike. The powerful Harley Davidson that was an extension of himself. And as the images sped through her mind Alex felt her tension begin to unwind.

Which was the strangest thing, when she would never have thought of Gary Hollis as the catalyst to calm her down. He'd always had the means of arousing her, in more ways than one.

The sound of the kettle boiling pierced her thoughts. She made her cup of coffee and dunked the biscuits, and contemplated the brown envelope for a moment longer before telling herself not to be a fool, and ripping it open.

And after all, the envelope contained nothing more than an undated note in Moira's handwriting, and a second envelope. The note said that however long it was before she received the enclosed, it was for her services with grateful thanks. If it transpired that the job was still unfinished, then Moira hoped that this would help to see it through.

The message was vague enough to mean little to anyone but herself, Alex thought, but the packet of crisp fifty pound notes was an unexpected surprise. She counted them quickly, and the surprise turned to shock when she realized it amounted to five hundred pounds.

She had already been paid a good sum in

advance, and this was far too much ... but she instantly appreciated Moira's foresight in not making it a cheque which would have furthered the suspicion of her involvement in Moira's death.

But even as she thought it, she knew Moira could never have foreseen such a thing. She said herself that she didn't have Leanora's gift. Doreen and May had affirmed that, so whenever this note had been written, maybe it had been Leanora's hand guiding her daughter to enclose untraceable money instead of a cheque.

Alex shivered, forcing herself to stamp out such a thought. This was an unexpected bonus, and while she disliked the thought of profiting by Moira's death, she knew she mustn't see it like that, and she vowed to see through to the finish what she had begun. She would find Moira's stalker, and if in doing so she found the killer as well, she would feel she deserved the bonus.

As long as she kept that in mind, it would keep her sane.

As long as the stalker didn't get her first, the insidious little thought whispered in her head.

She made up her mind about one thing though. Whenever it was arranged, she wasn't going to attend Moira's funeral. She couldn't face the thought of seeing the same weird people again, nor the major – if he dared to turn up. And nor did she intend showing up for the benefit of any watchful police attendance, or the slimy oaf from the local rag. She knew Moira would understand...

'Christ, I've got to get out of here,' she found herself muttering. 'Or I'll be as nutty as the rest of them.'

'I'm checking out today, Mrs Dooley,' she told the landlady a while later, when she was packed and ready to go, and it was too late to change her mind. 'I've been called back to London on business.'

'Oh, what a shame. I'll be sorry to lose you, my dear,' Mrs Dooley said, clearly impressed at the importance of her paying guest. 'I hope I'll be seeing you again.'

'I hope so too,' Alex said, lying through her smile.

But if she never saw Worthing again...

It was a lovely summer's day as she drove away, and she kept her car windows open, breathing deeply. Almost without realizing that she did so, she slowed down near the road sign pointing to Beckingham, and she gave a little sigh of resignation.

'All right, Moira. I'll go and check that the rotund Mr Johnson knows what's happened to you.'

She didn't know why she said it or why she thought it, but it seemed like a humanitarian thing to do.

And a pretty stupid thing when she got the reaction of the Happy Days Rest Home boss.

'Dear heavens, what dreadful thing will happen next?' he said, practically wringing his hands in best movie-shock style. 'I hadn't heard, Miss Best, as our local newspaper doesn't arrive until this evening, and I shall try to keep the news from our people as long as possible. It's upsetting and very disturbing for those who are past the first flush.'

Oh God, any minute now he was going to turn into Jane Eyre, Alex thought faintly.

'Well, I'm sorry to bring you such news, but you're bound to hear it, and also that I actually found Miss Wolstenholme.'

'My dear young lady, how ghastly for you,' he said, his eyes near to popping. 'Would you like a cup of tea? Or perhaps a tot of brandy which we keep for medicinal purposes, you understand?'

'No, thank you. I have to get back to London, and I'm driving,' she said, her voice becoming strangled. 'I just thought I would call and let you know, Mr Johnson.'

And now all she wanted was to get out of there. Even here in Johnson's spacious office, certain smells were drifting through, making her feel slightly nauseous, and she wasn't feeling in the best of health as the trauma of the last few days began to take effect. A good night's sleep in her own bed was what she needed most of all.

London was full of the usual cacophony of street noise and traffic, and despite the frustration and the time involved in getting through, Alex didn't really mind, because it was familiar and it was home.

And then she paused, her hands drumming on the steering-wheel at the traffic lights as a thought with the force of a hurricane hit her. No, it wasn't home. Not really. She hadn't made all that many friends – not *close* friends – in all the time she had lived in London, no more than in the isolated community in the depths of Yorkshire where she had been born.

And suddenly, ridiculously, *infuriatingly,* she missed it. Not so much the dank, always misty fields in the dales where her father had farmed, but the wild moorland spaces with space to breathe, which you didn't get here...

An angry tooting from the car behind her made her realize the lights had changed, and she was sitting there like a loon on green. She resisted the temptation to hoist two fingers at the guy behind, knowing she was in the wrong, and shot away with a crunch of the gears.

She could still see his smirking face in the

car behind. *Bloody woman driver!* it said. Well, sod you, mate. Do you have an unexpected bonus of five hundred pounds in your pocket?

She sobered at once, knowing that the money wouldn't have come her way if it hadn't been for Moira's untimely death. Presumably she would have got it someday, unless Moira had withdrawn all the letters with their grim portents she had left for her friends.

She parked her car in her designated space at the block of flats and let herself into her flat with shaking hands. She scooped up the mail without much interest, aware that she did indeed feel unwell. And it had to be that that had brought on the small surge of nostalgia, for a simple life in the country, for being Audrey Barnes again without any of the complications in the life of Alex Best, private eye...

'God, what's the matter with me?' she said out loud, and switched on the radio to the blare of Radio One, before switching it off again just as quickly, as her head throbbed to the remorseless beat of the music.

She felt her forehead, and it was burning. Somewhere in her bathroom she had a thermometer, but as usual you could never find such a thing when you needed it. There was a half-empty packet of hot lemon powders, which would do for a start.

First resolve – get a properly equipped medicine box.

But she didn't need a thermometer to know that the only place for her now was bed. And if this was the flu, she would be quite happy to hibernate for however long it took, and to hell with the rest of the world.

Except that her answer machine was flashing, and she could never ignore it … she tottered across to it and pressed the rewind button, already starting to shed her clothes and put the kettle on for coffee and a flu powder.

'Call me when you get back, Alex,' said Nick Frobisher's voice. 'I've got some news.'

She groaned. Not now. Not yet. Whatever it was, it could wait. She only half-listened to the next message on the machine, not recognizing the voice at first, and then she felt her heart give a jolt.

'How's this for a blast from the past, doll?' Gary Hollis's arrogant voice said. 'I might be seeing you soon, so keep the bed warm for me. Bye for now.'

He had a bloody nerve, thought Alex, but she couldn't help a small smile all the same. Gary was the type who would expect to waltz right back into her life as if the last six months or so never existed. They had never been more than fair-weather friends, any-way – well, that, and a couple of spec-tacularly torrid lovers for a brief time, the

243

honest part of her admitted – but that was it. It had never been a forever kind of partnership – so why the hell did it matter if he looked her up from time to time?

There were no more messages, and the mail could wait. She had checked the envelopes and there seemed to be nothing dodgy-looking about them, so she tossed them onto her sofa, made her coffee and hot drink, and fell into bed. If this was flu, she prayed it was the short, swift variety, and found herself wishing feebly and miserably that she had someone to tuck her in and look after her.

She didn't remember anything about the next 48 hours except for floating to the bathroom from time to time and then crawling back into bed. Providing she didn't die from hunger an enforced fast must be good for the diet, she thought – when she could think lucidly at all.

Halfway through the third morning she heard an urgent knocking on her door. She turned over, ignoring it. Her head still throbbed, but with not quite as much of a battering as before. But the knocking went on, and in the end, she pulled on her kimono, staggered to the door and croaked:

'Who is it?'

'Alex, it's me, Charmaine from downstairs,' came the bright young voice making Alex feel even more like Methuselah than usual, considering her flu. 'I saw your car so I knew you were back, and I was dying to tell you about the job.'

'Job?' Alex said vaguely, and suddenly feeling ridiculous in acknowledging that she was talking to a door. A bit like Shirley Valentine talking to the wall ... she opened the door a fraction, and saw Charmaine's eagerly smiling face change at the sight of her.

'My God, Alex, you look awful. Are you ill? I could come back – or can I do anything for you?' she added as an afterthought.

Care in the community obviously didn't come high on an out-of-work model-cum-actress's agenda, Alex thought sourly, and then felt ashamed of herself for her lack of charity.

'It's only a touch of flu,' she croaked again. 'And you wouldn't want to catch it if you've got a new job–'

'Don't be silly,' Charmaine said, pushing open the door and belying Alex's earlier uncharitable thoughts. 'You should be in bed, and I'm going to make us both a cup of coffee and tell you about the job, and then I'll come back later and bring you some food. I'm making chicken curry tonight, so we could share it, though I probably shouldn't get too close to you. Germs, you know,' she added.

My God, I don't know you at all, Alex

thought in amazement. *I didn't know you cared – or that you could cook!*

'That's very sweet of you, Charmaine, but I think I'm better off without eating,' she said huskily, mentally resolving to be nicer to the girl in future, and practically revelling in the groans from her stomach as she pulled it in. 'But coffee sounds wonderful, and you can tell me your news before you go.'

'News?' Charmaine said vaguely, always easily distracted. 'Oh yes, the job! Well, I got it. It's just a small part in an ad for dog food, and somebody else will be doing the voice-over. But it's a start, isn't it?'

'It certainly is,' Alex said. 'Good for you.'

She was so elated it would be awful to put her down, even though it didn't sound like much. But once Charmaine had made the coffee, and brought the biscuit tin with it, she edged her way out of the flat as Alex began coughing. She didn't blame her. A budding TV star couldn't afford to catch germs...

'I'll let you know about the party when it's all fixed,' she said as she left.

'What party?' But the door had already closed behind her.

Whenever it was, she wouldn't go, anyway. She'd hardly have anything in common with Charmaine's friends. They'd all be under twenty, fresh-faced and brimming over with libido and on the hunt. And what the hell was she thinking of, Alex thought, appalled at such a mid-life-crisis reaction. Wasn't she twenty-six years old and in her prime, as Miss Jean Brodie would say?

And wasn't she trying to fight off a flu bug with the energy of a flea, and feeling bloody sorry for herself? And it was no good, the biscuit tin was just too tempting to resist, and a lot of good she'd be to anybody if she simply faded away without anybody knowing. She had to have *something* to keep up her strength, and that proved that she must be getting better even if she didn't feel it.

Half a dozen digestive biscuits heavily laced with butter and Branston pickle later, she felt strong enough to get dressed and to open the small pile of mail that seemed to be facing her reproachfully. Just as long as there was nothing from HIM, whoever he was – and until that moment she hadn't even thought about it.

But the flat had been intact when she got home. Leanora's notebook was still safely where she had left it – and she vowed to study it properly today, providing her head allowed her to concentrate, since she had no intention of going into her office. But first there was the mail.

Sniffing her way through a box of paper handkerchiefs, she slit open the envelopes. There were the usual business statements among several offers to make her a millionaire if she replied within ten days, providing she purchased a few useless items that nobody in their right minds would ever want. There was one small but welcome cheque from a client.

The final envelope contained a brochure advertising cosy cottages in the West Country for sale or rent, and her name had obviously come up in the junk mail lottery. Because she intended spending one more day giving in to her flu – and cossetting herself because nobody else was likely to do so (Charmaine apart), she browsed through it with more attention than she normally would have done.

It looked idyllic. Some of the cottages in their lovely rural settings reminded her of her last big case – the one that had paid for the cruise, where she had met Leanora and begun the chain reaction that had culminated in discovering Moira's body in her swimming-pool.

Alex gave a shudder, and closed the brochure at once, deciding to look at it later when she felt more like herself. Next time she took a brief holiday, maybe she'd go down to the West Country, to one of those sleepy little places where nothing ever happened.

Exmoor looked wonderful, and there were big towns near enough to go shopping if she felt the need…

'What the hell am I thinking about?' she muttered. 'I'm a fixture here now. I'm a Londoner, a city girl, remember?'

The hell of it was that she wasn't, not deep down, and she had no idea why that thought should keep drumming itself into her. Maybe she should see a psychiatrist to find out why she was so unsettled. Or maybe she already knew.

Dealing with the likes of the ill-fated Madame L. and her daughter, and their spooky hangers-on who thought so little of death claiming their friends, was enough to send anyone round the bend. And Alex wasn't ready for that yet.

As the day wore on, she realized she wasn't feeling so bad, and decided that she was beating the bug after all. She nobly ate a miniscule lunch of soup, and then ruined it all by eating a great hunk of stale bread, which she had to soften in the microwave and then liberally spread with butter because it was solidly past its sell-by date, but which made her feel decidedly better for all that.

'Now then, Leanora, let's see what we can make of your notebook,' she said to herself. 'If you're really up there, and you want me to solve your case, you'd better give me a sign or two. But nothing too obvious, thanks all the same,' she added hastily. 'Just direct me to the right name, OK?'

Oh yes, she *must* be feeling better to be able to direct her thoughts 'upstairs' without a qualm. She fetched the notebook and curled up on the sofa, feeling reasonably at peace with the world, considering. And as long as Leanora didn't take her at her word, and start giving her ouija board signs and making her fingers judder over the pages...

It was all meticulously written in Leanora's spidery handwriting, and although many of the names were in ciphers or initials, others were not. The dates went a long way back, so it looked as if the Wolstenholmes had been doing their scam for some time, and Alex wondered how many of the prominent businessmen regretted ever visiting a psychic – or subscribing to the advertisement to consult her privately.

Alex hadn't noticed it before, but there it was, slipped into a pocket at the back of the notebook, detailing Madame L's credentials, and offering advice on everything from financial matters to affairs of the heart. There was a smudgy photograph of Leanora on the ad, suitably tarted up from the dun-coloured woman Alex remembered on the cruise ship. The small print added that more personal consultations at an undisclosed private address could be arranged with all discretion.

So there were obviously two sides to Leanora's business. There were the casual holidaymakers just calling in at a seaside clairvoyant's on impulse for a bit of fun. Then there were the more serious ones who probably never visited the Worthing business premises at all, but would be invited to the house on the hill for a more personal and discreet consultation. They would know the house. They would know the place where Moira had been murdered.

And one of them had to have been Mister Big, arriving in his big black car that was probably a Jaguar, consulting Leanora about his special problems, and turning Moira's head into the bargain. The mysterious 'boyfriend' that Enid Lodge had mentioned.

Alex's heartbeats raced now, because one thing was certain. They surely had to be pretty big problems for someone to want such discreet consultations, and if Moira had continued with the scam after her mother's death, Mister Big had to be getting desperate to have killed her too. She must have been fleecing him rotten.

You had to go through the possibilities of such a Mister Big. Royalty ... politics ... the church ... financial wizards ... some of the names in the notebook were fairly recognizable, but there were none that would cause the country's downfall, and unfortunately, political and royal scandals were two a penny nowadays.

Alex's fingers suddenly paused over the pages. Something was wrong. Here and there the dates skipped several weeks. There was nothing odd in that. Clearly, Leanora didn't bother recording her dealings with small-fry, and there were frequently missing weeks.

But if she looked closely at the notebook Alex could see that some of the pages had been taken out. Very *carefully* taken out, so that an ordinary reader would hardly notice.

As if someone had gone to great pains to slice down the inner folds of the pages and lever them out. If she hadn't looked at them minutely she wouldn't have noticed it at all.

Alex felt a cold shiver run through her. She was perfectly certain she *would* have noticed it before now, because it was the kind of thing she had trained herself to do. So it must have happened recently. She couldn't even be certain whether or not someone had intended her to pick up in it. What she *was* certain about, was that the notebook hadn't been in this state before she went down to Worthing. She knew it.

She tried not to fall apart with nerves, reminding herself that she was in a vulnerable state after her sharp flu bout. But she knew that whoever had done this was skilled in taking just what he wanted and no more, and was capable of arousing no suspicion that anyone had even been here.

Her thoughts raced on, tumbling over themselves. Either someone had been in her flat and found the notebook while she was away. Or he had been here while she had been half deliriously fighting off the flu in the next room.

That was the worst thought. But whenever it was, he had *been* here. Touched her things. Maybe opened the bedroom door and watched her while she slept. Touched *her*. Leered at her silently while he went about his business. Maybe he had looked in her bathroom.

Knowing what shower gel she used, what deodorant, what perfume. Invading her privacy, her intimate self. Touching her knickers in the laundry basket. Running his fingers around them. Smelling them. Burying his face in them and getting off in the process...

Revolted and sickened at the bizarre images that she couldn't stop, Alex tottered into the bathroom, ripped open the top of the laundry basket and grabbed the few items inside.

There was only what she had brought back from Worthing. A couple of pairs of knickers, a bra and T-shirt. She could hardly bear to touch them, but when she did so, she threw the lot into the bin.

The logical part of her brain that was still working told her there was no point in keeping them for fingerprints. Whoever had been here – if he had been in the bathroom – was far too expert to have left fingerprints.

And then she went back to the living-room to try to think sensibly – and to stop shaking.

Chapter 10

'*Nick*,' she croaked at his pager's polite request to leave a message. 'Can you come round to the flat sometime? The sooner the better. I have to talk to you.'

She slammed down her phone. Why couldn't he have been there? she raged. Why, when she needed him? And why expect him to be there at her beck and call, when she had so often snubbed him in the past? She felt abject and humbled and very, very sick.

Without warning, she slapped her hand over her mouth as she began to retch, and tasted bitterness. She rushed back to the bathroom and just made it before she violently heaved up everything she had eaten into the lavatory bowl. So much for stale bread, and the stupid hope that the bluish crust may have provided some unrefined penicillin, she thought, with a pathetic attempt at humour.

But once she had swilled her mouth and cleaned her teeth several times, she crept back to the sofa and closed her eyes for a few minutes. And far from making her feel even more vulnerable, she gradually realized that the vomiting had had the converse effect of calming her down.

You're as contrary as an unbroken filly, Audrey, her father used to blather.

Well, this time he was right, because she was finally starting to see things more clearly now. And what she saw was that this whole thing had got beyond her.

It was too big, and she needed Nick's help. It wasn't failure. It was common sense. No man was a bloody island ... nor woman, either.

Nick didn't get to the flat until late that afternoon. By then she had tentatively walked to the corner shop that grandly described itself as a twenty-four-seven, and bought some fresh provisions and a couple of ready-meals for the microwave. She had made herself a comfort dish of bread soaked in hot milk, which was her mother's cure-all for lining delicate stomachs. In Alex's opinion it was a revolting mush until it was well sprinkled with sugar to make it less pappy, but she had to admit that it always did the trick.

Nick came in to the flat with a broad smile that changed to alarm when he saw her pale face and the unkempt stringiness of her usually sleek red hair.

'Good God, what's happened to you, Alex?'

'Flu. I'm over it now, but you'd better not get too close,' she said, with an uncharacteristic urge to weep at his obvious concern.

'Have you seen a doctor?'

'No need. I told you, I'm better now—'

'You don't look it. How long have you been like this?'

'A couple of days, maybe more,' she said vaguely. 'I don't remember, and it doesn't matter anyway. That's not why I asked you here.'

'Well, it should be. What are friends for?' he said, starting to get the angry look in his eyes that she knew so well. 'Honestly, Alex, sometimes I despair of you.'

'Well, don't. I can take care of myself.'

But she couldn't, not right now, and she knew it. She tried desperately to fight back the tears, but this time it was impossible, and the next minute she found herself wrapped tightly in his arms.

'God, Alex, don't you know I'd be happy to take care of you all the time if only you'd let me?' he said roughly against her cheek.

'Except that there's a rather disgusting smell in your hair, darling, and it's enough to put anybody off. It's hardly your usual perfume. What the hell is it?'

'Sick, I expect,' she muttered, feeling even more wretched to think that she hadn't noticed it herself. 'I'm a real mess, aren't I?'

'It's nothing that we can't put right, my love,' he said gently. 'And I'm a dab hand at hair-washing. Lead me to the bathroom and we'll soon have you smelling sweet again.'

'You needn't – you can't – I'm not up to it–'

But he led her to the bathroom, and she had no more fight left in her. He sat her on a stool and ordered her to lean back over the wash-basin while he ran the hot water over her tangled hair. And then he began slowly massaging the shampoo into it with strong, deft fingers, and Alex closed her eyes, becoming aware that it was not only soothing, it was immensely sensual ... almost orgasmic, in fact ... and she had to hold herself together before he became aware of it too.

'Conditioner?' he enquired, his face very close to hers.

'On the shelf,' she said huskily, praying that this wouldn't go on much longer ... and at the same time hoping that it would.

'Next time we do this, we'll do it in the shower, when you're feeling as up to it as I am,' Nick said finally, his mouth touching hers, and with a definite smile in his voice.

Oh God, he knew!

She smiled back weakly as he moved away to reach for a towel to wrap around her head.

'Who said there's going to be a next time?'

'I think we both know that there will, however long it takes you to make up your God-damned female mind,' he said, arrogant as usual. 'Now, where's the hairdryer?'

'Not now, thanks. I'll do it later,' she said hastily, knowing this had gone on long enough. 'I want to talk to you, and it's important, Nick.'

'And this isn't?'

Then he held up his hands, palms towards her as she made to protest. 'OK, OK, so what do you want to talk about?'

She suddenly thought of something. 'My head went totally woolly with this flu, but I seem to recall that you left a message for me to get in touch with you too. Was it something to do with major-whoever?'

Nick frowned. 'Oh yes, the Harold Dawes character. I got his address, if you're interested. Some seedy little place south of the river, by the sound of it.'

'Good. Because I think he may have been in the flat, and I want it stopped,' she said, choking up again at the thought of someone touching her things.

'What do you mean? Has he been threatening you?'

His aggression on her behalf was absolute, and she loved him for it. But she needed a moment more to gather her senses.

'Nick, I think I'll have to make some coffee before I can say any more. My mouth's horribly dry and I'm starting to feel dehydrated–'

'Sit right where you are and I'll do it. Do you want it laced with anything?'

'At four o'clock in the afternoon?' she said weakly.

'To hell with the time. A drop of brandy would do you good. Do you have any?'

'In the sideboard. All right, but you'd better have some too. You may need it.'

Though she knew he would have seen and heard far worse things than she had to tell him. What was one tin-pot little blackmailing scam and a couple of murders to an experienced copper who had experienced far more grisly things in the course of his career? But this was a copper with a far more tender streak in him than she ever gave him credit for...

You thought you knew somebody, but there were always things you didn't know. Everyone had secrets. Private thoughts. And not all of them were bad.

He came back with two large mugs of

coffee with a good swig of brandy in each. It tasted hot, strong, and deliciously decadent. And at this rate, any remaining bugs in her system would be well and truly snuffed out, she thought. Or doped to the eyeballs, if bugs had eyeballs....

'So now tell me,' said Nick the professional. 'What do you mean by saying you *think* this major who isn't a major, has been in the flat? Didn't you see him? And if you did, what did he say to get you so jittery?'

'He didn't *say* anything. And no, I never saw him. I don't know for sure that it *was* him. Maybe I'm getting it all out of proportion,' she said, knowing how impossibly vague it all sounded to somebody who dealt strictly in facts.

'And maybe you're not. Come on, Alex. Don't back down now. I know something's been getting at you for weeks, and that it's something to do with these Wolstenholme women. So just where does this Harold Dawes character come in?'

She drew a deep breath, ignoring the question for a moment. 'Nick, I don't like admitting defeat in any of my cases, but I think this one has got a bit ugly.'

'In what way?'

'Moira was being stalked. It was why she got in touch with me in the first place. It didn't sound terribly sinister, just the usual stuff, phone calls, letters and so on, and I didn't think it would have worried such a strong-minded woman unduly. But I always sensed there was something more behind her contacting me in the first place, and that it was to do with her mother's murder.'

'There was no doubt about the loner who did that. It was an open and shut case. And you know bloody well that stalking is a legal offence. If the woman had had any sense, she should have reported it officially.'

'I know all that. But she chose me instead. Anyway, that's not what I'm concerned with at the moment. The police knew who killed Moira's mother all right, but they never got to the bottom of *why* he did it. They didn't even try, as far as I could see. They were just happy to get a result.'

She caught the snappy look in Nick's eyes at the implied censure of the police force *en masse*, and rushed on. 'Well, he was hardly the type to have been one of Madame Leanora's clients, was he? But apart from the murderer, there was the major's appearance at the funeral. I never really knew why he was there, and Moira said she didn't even know him, nor why he pretended to be a Special Branch bloke when we went to Leanora's premises in Worthing–'

'Hey, hey, slow down! You're losing me now. There's obviously been a hell of a lot going on that I don't know–'

'That's why my clients trust me. I'm

discreet,' she said defensively, 'and when they don't want the police involved, I have to respect their wishes.'

'But now you don't have a client any more, and yet you say it's getting ugly,' Nick repeated. 'The woman's dead, Alex, and it's out of your hands. It's a police job to investigate a murder, but if you have any information to give them, you'd better open up. You know that.'

'That's *not* why I called you,' she repeated, hardly knowing why she was prevaricating again. 'But now I'm the one getting the occasional weird phone call, and a bunch of dead flowers was sent through the post, and then some slimeball had broken into my office and left his mark – and I know damn well someone's been in the flat too, without leaving any evidence except the nasty feeling of having my privacy invaded–'

She gasped for breath as she rushed on without pause. She had to say it like that, or she knew she would never say it at all. But she had to admit that the way the words came out made her sound more paranoid than anything else. And she was well aware that something had stopped her mentioning the notebook.

'So you think you're being stalked,' Nick said flatly.

'I don't *think* so. I *know* so! Haven't you been listening at all?'

All the same, she knew it was small fry compared with the way the real celebs of this world were stalked. She honestly couldn't say she felt as if someone was constantly watching her, noting every move she made, and bombarding her with obscene phone calls or notes. It was hardly death-threat stuff, and she hadn't been physically abused – yet.

'You did right to come to me if you think this self-styled major aka Harold Dawes is behind it all. I can put a surveillance on him if you do, Alex,' Nick went on.

But already she sensed from his tone that he thought she could be making too much of all this – and in his job he had far more important cases to follow up than to plant an officer on house-watch because of a girlfriend's whim. Nor did she want to seem too interested by asking him outright for the address. Not yet. Her instinct to conclude the case herself hadn't been entirely dampened or scared off.

'No. I'm not making an official complaint, and now that I've said it out loud, I think I probably *am* over-reacting.'

'As you so often do,' Nick said coolly.

But his eyes were still alert, and she knew he didn't altogether believe her sudden back-tracking.

'Anyway, if somebody was getting at me because he wanted me to stop prying on

Moira's behalf, there's no more need, is there? She's dead, and the case is closed.'

'You're sure about that?'

'Yes, I'm sure she's dead,' she said, tongue-in-cheek, and trying not to shudder at the memory of Moira's open-mouthed face staring up at her with those glassy dead eyes.

And she wasn't telling him about the surprise of getting Moira's post-demise retainer, either. Any more than she was letting on that his words had given her a new purpose.

Surveillance on Harold Dawes was exactly what she intended to do for herself, once she had got hold of his address. And she was angry to think that she hadn't tried looking him up in the telephone book before now. So much had been going on ... but that was just a sloppy excuse for incompetence, and she was definitely slipping.

Because she was quite sure now that he was working for somebody, and the sooner she found out who it was, the sooner she would know who she was up against. She owed it to Moira. And to Leanora. And the silent cheer at the back of her senses had nothing to do with either of them. It was more to do with her professional need to conclude a case satisfactorily.

'Nick, I think I just panicked, and I needed to see you to feel reassured. But this definitely *isn't* an official complaint. I've no intention of making a statement, so you can forget that. If I hadn't been feeling so bloody weak after the flu, you know very well it wouldn't have been my style to call you in on such a feeble pretext.'

'Pity,' he grinned, pulling her closer and not wasting the moment. 'I rather like feeling needed.'

'Well, you'd better make the most of it, because it sure as hell won't last!'

But she submitted to a few very enjoyable kisses, and then felt guiltily relieved when he got a call on his mobile, recalling him back to base. If he hadn't, God knew how this day might have ended. As it was, as soon as he left, she checked her phone book, only to find that there was no H. Dawes or Harold Dawes listed at all.

The whole episode was beginning to make her feel claustrophobic with frustration, and she needed some fresh air. The staleness of the flat after her incarceration inside it was getting to her now. She dried her hair and made herself look reasonably presentable for the first time since returning from Worthing, and then she went out.

This time, Leanora's notebook was safely in her bag, and she didn't intend to make a move without it, ignoring the fact that it didn't matter anyway, since the intruder had already got what he wanted out of it.

She let herself into her office cautiously, breathing a sigh of relief to see that the slight film of dust everywhere after a week of disuse was completely undisturbed.

As a last piece of self-acknowledged paranoia now, she knew she had to check that there was nothing untoward in the post here before she did anything else. But the letters were all harmless, and mostly advertising junk that went straight into the bin.

Only then, did she pick up the office phone and get through to directory enquiries. She couldn't give a definite street address, but she said she thought the place she wanted might be in the Lambeth area. Nick had said south of the river, and it was the first name she thought of.

Firstly she requested the number of a Major Harry Deveraux since it sounded more upmarket than asking for plain Harold Dawes. As expected, there was no joy in that, so then she gave his real name.

'What street, please, caller?' the voice requested.

'Again, I don't know exactly, only that it's also in the Lambeth area,' Alex said crisply, her accent becoming more cut-glass as she sensed the operator's growing impatience. 'There's one more thing, though. The number may be ex-directory, but it's vital that my department traces the gentleman, so if you could just confirm the address for us that will be enough,' she improvised.

And the woman could do her own bit of guessing about the fictitious department.

'I'm sorry. I can't help you if the number is ex-directory,' the operator's terse voice came back at her before the line went dead.

Shit. She should have known that, Alex fumed. She *did* know it. She wasn't born yesterday. It had just been a long-shot, and it was a blip in her memory not to have remembered that she wouldn't have got the information. Anyway, if Dawes had a phone at all, it could just as easily be a mobile. Now she had no option but to ask Nick for his address.

She sat limply on her office chair, only just noticing that she was sweating profusely. She felt a hundred years old instead of twenty-six, and even driving her car to the office in the London traffic had been a traumatic experience in the aftermath of flu and a few days in bed. She longed to be there now, and bed was exactly where she was going to spend the next few hours.

But once she got there, the hours stretched into another day and another few bouts of sickness, by which time Alex decided that blue mould on stale bread was definitely not to be recommended. The only thing in favour of all this throwing up was that she was sure she must have lost a stone in weight, and she snarled at the bathroom scales when they confirmed that she had only lost two miserable pounds.

And to hell with Harold Dawes for now. She needed to get properly fit if she was planning on spending hours watching his comings and goings. As her stomach gnawed in rebellion, she grudgingly heated a ready-meal of lemon chicken and rice in the microwave, and was mightily relieved to keep it down.

The digestives were all gone, but she discovered the remains of a packet of chocolate biscuits in the bottom of a cupboard, and just one, or even two, wouldn't hurt. She needed pampering, for God's sake.

She was feeling fractionally better by the following day, and resolved to be back at work on the next. When her phone rang around eight o'clock that evening, she switched off the inane quiz show on the television, and picked up the receiver without a second thought as to who it might be.

She had made up her mind that she wasn't going to be scared or intimidated by Dawes any more. Remembering how he had flaunted his way around the cruise ship in the guise of the appallingly arrogant major, she could soon cut him down to size now.

Screw you, major...

'Alexandra Best,' she said coolly into her phone.

'Do you want to come to a party, doll?'

She didn't know *what* or who she had expected to hear, but it certainly wasn't that particular voice again.

'Gary! Is that you?'

'The one and only. So whaddya say? Are you up for it?'

Alex began to laugh. Only Gary Hollis could phone her out of nowhere and expect her to be ready and waiting for whatever mad idea he had in mind.

'Up for what? No, don't answer that, Gary,' she said, as she heard his sexy chuckle. 'I'm quite glad to hear from you, actually. It's been a while. So how have you been?'

She groaned, listening to herself. She sounded like one of those bright and jolly middle-aged counsellors you heard on TV documentaries. 'And where are you?' she added.

'Not a million miles away. So are you coming to this party or not? You'll need to be ready in three minutes.'

'For God's sake, Gary, don't be stupid! How can I possibly be ready for anything in that time?'

She bit her lip, knowing his expertise at seeing innuendoes, even when there were none intended, and she had just let him right in.

'Hey, I seem to remember–' he began

sexily, and then she heard other voices in the background, and she frowned, because one of them sounded familiar.

Then Gary spoke again. 'Somebody else wants to talk to you, Alex. I'll put her on.'

Her? What the hell was this? Before Alex could think properly, she heard Charmaine from the flat below.

'Alex, I've only just discovered that Gary knows you, and I know you haven't been well, but remember I told you about my party. You must come. It'll do you good.'

At the bright, giggly young voice, Alex felt even more like the middle-aged neighbour who needed taking out of herself now, and she bristled at once.

'Oh, I don't think so. I'm still a bit under the weather, and I'd only be a drag–' she said resentfully.

'Hey baby,' she heard Gary's voice break in. 'I'm coming up to get you in three minutes, and if you're not dressed and ready – well, that's OK by me too–'

Charmaine evidently grabbed the phone from him again, and Alex had to hold the receiver away from her ear to ward off the screaming laughter coming through.

'Isn't he just wild, Alex? And I'm green with envy that you got to him first. Now, are you coming or not?'

Please, Gary, don't make anything of that remark, Alex begged silently, knowing it would be in his head, and probably elsewhere too.

'I can't be ready in three minutes. Tell Gary to make it ten,' she said quickly.

She hung up, knowing she must be mad to even think about going to one of Charmaine's parties. But she knew Gary too.

He'd be here sharp on time, and if she didn't appear with him, she'd never hear the end of it from Charmaine, and her reputation would be in shreds. And who was acting prudish and middle-aged *now!* And as if anybody cared.

She was out of her jeans and t-shirt before she thought twice. A shower took all of two minutes – just the vital bits – and her hair was OK, thanks to Nick. She pushed the memory of his sensual hands out of her mind as she wriggled into a slithery black dress, cheering silently as it slid over her hips with the minimum of effort. Flu wasn't all bad news.

She was just fixing her lipstick and applying blusher to get some more colour into her cheeks when the doorbell rang. And her heart was beating wildly as she went to answer it.

Gary whistled loudly. She had forgotten that whistle. He did it incessantly when he was thinking, and it had often driven her mad ... but right now all she could think about was that it was good to see him again, and that he looked great.

He came into the room, kicking the door shut. He hugged her tightly, and she could smell the freshness of his aftershave as his hands reached down to caress her buttocks.

'I always said you had a great arse, didn't I?' he whispered wickedly in her ear.

Oh yes. Same old Gary. Same old finesse ... or lack of it.

She pushed him away from her, laughing.

'You don't waste much time, do you?'

'You know me, babe,' he said with a grin. 'So are we going to this party – or what?'

'We're going to a party,' Alex said determinedly.

She hadn't wanted to go, but now she did. And she didn't want to spend the evening fending off Gary Hollis's tentacle arms. In fact, she didn't want him at all. The surprise of it hit her forcibly. He was fun. He was sexy. He was great in bed. But she didn't want him. And if he expected to be sharing her bed later on, he was in for a bigger shock.

'What's up?' he said, holding her away from him.

'Nothing. Why?'

'You're different.'

'I've just had the flu, for God's sake. You can't expect me to be jumping through hoops.'

'And that's all?'

She had also forgotten how petulant he could be at times. Like a small boy seeing his treasured toy about to be taken away from him.

She touched his cheek. 'Gary, don't rush me, OK? Let's just go to a party – and how did you get to be invited, anyway? I didn't know you knew Charmaine.'

At his cocky grin, she recognized the Gary of old, on the night she had first met him, all biking leathers and brimming with testosterone.

She got the weird impression now of the hunter having caught his prey (Charmaine), but still wanting to keep another possibility dangling. Alex.

'Met her a couple of weeks ago, and when she said she had this private di– eye – living in the flat above, and then told me where she lived. I latched on at once. Good bit of detective work, huh?'

'Amazing,' Alex said, straight-faced. 'So are we going to this party?'

'Or what?'

'Or nothing.'

Four hours later, Alex was thankful that he had latched on to that too. Either that, or the luscious and nubile talent in the flat below was far more to his taste. It was a relief, anyway, and when she managed to yell through the disco noise to Charmaine that she'd really had enough, she was able to get away while the music was still throbbing, and the answering throb in her head was just about bearable.

'It was nice to see you, Alex,' Charmaine screeched. 'Take care of that flu now.'

'I will, and say goodbye to Gary for me,' Alex yelled back, seeing him wrapped around a long-legged girl in a scarlet sheath that was little more than a belt, and hardly able to distinguish which of them was which.

And she didn't give a damn. Good luck, Gary, she mouthed at him, before she took the lift up to her flat, and entered its blissful silence. Her answer machine was flashing, and she switched it on automatically.

'Hi, Alex. I guess if you're out you must be feeling better. Anyway, I forgot to give you that address,' came Nick's familiar voice. 'It's 84 Battery Mews, Lambeth. See you around.'

She could have kissed him. She was warm and mellow with wine, and thankful to have shaken off Gary, and here was Nick, in spirit if not in body, giving her the information she wanted without the need for any more subterfuge on her part.

She could definitely have kissed him. All over. She had even guessed right about Lambeth too, which did her ego good, and if she'd seriously believed in omens, she'd have said Leanora had guided her towards the right location. But she was right off omens for the moment, and preferred to believe in her own instinct and logic.

But she was still in the lingering haze of too much wine, and she found herself waltzing around the room, wishing Nick was here, so she could show her appreciation.

Not that she had she ever paid for favours with her body. Well, not seriously. So maybe the feeling had to mean more than that. Wanting to share special moments with one special person had to mean something, didn't it? She didn't want to examine that crazy thought too closely, but right at that moment she wanted him with a fever that shook her rigid.

Because they were mates, for Christ's sake. Good mates, best mates, even though he'd never made any secret of the fact that he wanted more, and she had always held him off except for one magical night in Worthing.

But it was never a good idea for people like them to get close. Their jobs were too similar – and too opposite. It never worked. Service occupations were high risks for marriage breakups. The army chucked out higher ranks for consorting with lower ones and mixing business with pleasure. The medical profession frowned on it. And what the devil was she doing, even *thinking* about marriage? It wasn't on her agenda.

The combination of getting over the flu, and tonight's party – which, for a short while had been more fun than she had expected – and now the bonus of getting Harold Dawes' address so painlessly – must be filling her head with romantic tosh. A good night's sleep was what she needed, and tomorrow she vowed to be at her sharpest again.

So *Goodnight Vienna* ... without warning, one of her father's favourite old songs floated into her head, as sung by Richard Tauber on a well-scratched gramophone record of 78 rpm vintage, if she remembered correctly, and played on an ancient gramophone that needed winding up. And she had no idea what had made her think of *that*, when the blare of Blur's best should still be ringing in her ears.

Bed, she thought again, *before I go completely to pieces.*

Alex slept in late the next day, but by the time she awoke, her head was clear. The cocktail of wine and music had evidently done its job well, and knocked any remaining bugs out of her system. She was ready to go – and today she was going to Lambeth to check out where Harold Dawes lived.

She remembered the boisterous arrogance of the major on the cruise ship, and then the damn cheek of him, pretending to be a Special Branch bod when confronted with the constable at Madame L.'s premises. He wasn't exactly the Brain of Britain when it came to disguises, but she was.

Instead of wearing her trademark black, she dressed in jeans and a check shirt, twisted her hair on top of her head and bundled it all up under a peaked baseball cap.

She had no idea if Harold Dawes had been the one to kill Moira, whether or not it was on Mister Big's instructions. But he was definitely involved somehow, and she couldn't afford to let him see her, or that she had tracked him down. He would also know her car, she remembered, so she splashed out some of Moira's money and hired one at a hefty discount from a private hire company where she had done some business in the past. It always paid to know somebody...

She ate a ploughman's lunch at a pub near the river, and suffered the catcalls of some building site yobs before heading for Lambeth. The yobs were probably harmless enough, despite their threatening tattoos, and she bet that if she whistled at their bum cleavages they'd run a mile. Maybe. She decided not to risk it.

She reached Lambeth in the early afternoon. Having studied her *A to Z,* she had easily sussed out the route to Battery Mews. Nowadays, Mews premises could be hellishly expensive and trendy places, or just dumps. The major would have lived in the former, but Harold Dawes...

This particular Mews turned out to be a seedy little cobbled backwater in a maze of nondescript streets, but it was thankfully wide enough for parking. The houses were cramped, with tiny front yards, in which there was a motley collection of old bicycle tyres, rusting prams and other debris. From the range of different curtains and tatty window blinds, Alex guessed that some of them were let into flats or bed-sits.

She drove slowly up the street, glad of several old bangers parked haphazardly so that she had to negotiate them carefully enough not to draw attention to herself, until she located number 84. It was nothing special, and from the look of it, Alex guessed that it was a bed-sit. The net curtains were more grey than white. They still hid any occupant inside, though. He could see out, while no one else could see in.

She felt a shiver of excitement. Whatever Harold Dawes was up to, she intended watching him. The fact that he had no telephone was annoying, because if he had been the one calling her and sending her the dead flowers, she would dearly have liked to play him at his own game.

But that was not an option. The only thing to do was to play a waiting game – not that she could imagine Mister Big deigning to contact him here, so it figured that if any contact was to be made, he would go to Mister Big.

Unless, of course, their whole association was now at an end, with the demise of both the Wolstenholme women.

There was no need now, for Mister Big to fear anything from either of them. And now that the pages of Leanora's notebook had been removed as well, Alex had no idea whose name was involved.

It was more than possible that Harold Dawes was now expendable. If so, the trail could easily go cold right here. And Alex could waste a hell of a lot of time sitting around in frustration, when she could be taking on another case.

But there were several more nagging thoughts in her mind that wouldn't go away.

The first was that Harold Dawes might be so vindictive that he would continue targeting her with his feeble stalking methods for the sadistic fun of it.

The second was that Mister Big might decide not to risk any repercussions from his partner, and get rid of him. Someone who had already masterminded the murder of two women wouldn't hesitate to deal with a third.

And there was something else. Despite the warmth of the summer day, the shiver inside her was colder now. She had never really imagined that she was in serious danger, especially since all the evidence in the notebook had been neatly removed. But how did the thief know that she hadn't already seen it, and noted it, and decided to report all that she knew to the police? And while she was watching Battery Mews now, was somebody else already watching her?

The Mews was as quiet as the proverbial grave, and at the thought, she switched on the car engine with shaking hands and shot away down the cobbled street and out into the mainstream traffic, her heart thudding. She drove around for ten minutes, keeping a regular watch in the rear view mirror, but no one was following her, and gradually her heartbeats slowed down.

She parked in a nearby street and called herself a fool for panicking. She had two choices, anyway. Either she could give the whole thing up and forget it ever happened, or she could go to Nick and tell him every-thing – or she could get on with the bloody job she had been paid to do, and stop acting like a wimp.

'That's three choices,' she muttered. 'And if you want to hold up your head at the end of it you know what you've got to do, girl.'

That was her father speaking again. But at least it wasn't Leanora. Nor Moira. It was the Barnes stubbornness that said you were only half a person if you gave up on a job. He never had, and nor would she.

Without realizing it, she saw that she had parked with a reasonable view of Battery Mews. She could make out exactly where number 84 was from here, because of its proximity to the old bangers in the road. It must have been instinct to park where she had, and if nothing else told her she had to go on, that did it.

She stayed for half an hour with no sign of Harold Dawes, or anyone else. In the meantime she had made a few sketches of the whole location. She took some camera shots too, but the sketches were more immediate, and were enough for her needs. Only if Dawes appeared, or had any visitors, would she need to take more photos.

God, this was boring, she thought, some while later when the sun grew higher in the sky, and it became uncomfortably hot in the car. The Mews was far enough out of the city not to warrant a one-way system, and she had already noted that it was open-ended, so cars could approach from either end, but today it all seemed as quiet as the proverbial.

He could be a night owl, of course. After a fruitless wait, Alex decided it was time to go away and come back after dark. In any case, if she intended taking a closer look around the premises and the area, it would be safer to do it at night. He knew her, so there was no way she could go right up to his door in daylight and pretend to be somebody doing a mail order survey or canvassing for double glazing.

Gary could, though. He'd helped her out before, and she knew he'd do it again, even though he'd expect payment in kind for his trouble. But she didn't really want to get him involved, and she put the idea on hold unless it became absolutely necessary.

Just as she was about to switch on the car engine again, there was some movement from number 84. Alex sank down in her car seat and pretended to be fiddling with something in the glove pocket. But it was definitely him, and he was coming this way.

She was shocked at the sight of him. He was unshaven, and shabbier than she ever remembered him, and a world away from the brash and boisterous major on board the cruise ship. Whatever money Mister Big was paying him, it certainly wasn't doing him a lot of good.

He came around the corner of the Mews to where there was an off-licence, and disappeared inside. A few minutes later he came out with a carrier bag that obviously contained a quantity of bottles. So that was where his money went, and from the look of him now, he was probably an alky.

Alex thought rapidly. From any Mister Big's point of view, alkies were dangerous. Alkies would do anything for money. But if their regular suppliers dried up, they would be just as ready to turn snout to the police for payment. Alex wondered just how far down the slopes Harold Dawes had already gone.

And if his Mister Big was aware of it, she didn't give much for his chances.

Especially if he had been the one to kill Moira. Maybe the memory of actually doing the ultimate crime had tipped him over the edge, the way it had finished Trevor Unwin.

And maybe it was time for her to confront Harold herself, and offer him some of Moira's money, in return for giving her a name. Even if it meant that he – and whoever was working his strings – knew for sure that she was on to them.

She would be putting herself in a highly dangerous position, considering that two women had already been killed, and one man had committed suicide because of his part in it.

It was such a huge decision to make that she could no longer think straight. Her heart was beating erratically as she drove off at speed, needing her own four walls around her like a security blanket as she tried to work out the best course of action.

Chapter 11

The temptation to call Nick Frobisher and have the power of the police behind her had never been so strong as it was right then. But she still felt it would be letting Moira down if she did so, and there was still a part of herself that said she wanted the power and glory of solving this crime. It would definitely be one up for woman power.

It might also send her to an early grave, Alex thought grimly, but she wouldn't let herself worry about that. Instead, while she waited for darkness, she carefully dusted the pages of Leanora's notebook adjacent to the missing ones. With the aid of a very large magnifying glass and a very strong light behind her, she could make out the faint indentations of Leanora's handwriting.

It was surprisingly strong. Some of the indentations were quite deep. There was a capital L, then a small gap, then a capital I and a longer gap. Or it could be a J. Or even another L. There could also be two words after the first L.

'Damn it, Leanora, why couldn't you have been more explicit!' Alex said out loud. 'Is it Les, or Liam, or Luke? Or is it Lord? *Lord* somebody starting with I or J or L?'

She felt the adrenalin begin to tingle. Someone who had arranged two killings and hidden his tracks so cleverly, wasn't going to be somebody run-of-the-mill.

Remembering the large amounts with which he'd paid off Trevor Unwin, he had to be a Somebody, with plenty of money and influence.

Would Harold Dawes have been paid a similar amount for getting rid of Moira, or did his puppet-master have such a hold over him now that he could afford to pay him far less? Which would account for the fact that Harold looked such a miserable figure compared to his jauntiness as Major Deveraux. MB would presumably have paid for his cruise passage, in order for him to keep an eye on Leanora.

There were two strands to MB's operation, Alex decided. One involved Harold Dawes, and the other involved Trevor Unwin. She doubted that either knew of the other's existence. And Alex doubted that Mister Big was an ordinary mister at all. So she was looking somewhere much higher up the social scale than your average next-door neighbour.

'Maybe it wouldn't be such a crazy idea to have a few words with you, major dear,' she muttered. 'Especially with a few bottles of whisky as an enticement, and waving a few quid of Moira's money at you while we got quietly sloshed and mused over old times. Or at least, while *you* did.'

She still felt guilty over Moira's retainer. She had already been paid a far larger sum in advance than she had expected, and then there was the bonus of the five hundred pounds. But her conscience wouldn't let her do other than follow Moira's wishes through.

'It's the Audrey Barnes syndrome,' she told herself. 'It will always catch me out when I least expect it. But at least Dad would be proud of me.'

And she was probably never going to be as ruthless as a hardnosed copper...

She had never needed to look up *Debrett's Peerage* before, and she had nothing more substantial than a general *Who's Who* on her shelves. But she knew she could find the information at the reference library that stayed open late.

It had to be her first stop, before she surprised Harold, armed with whisky and cash. She remembered he had drunk heavily on the cruise. But she still didn't know whether or not it was a sensible thing to do. Harold was presumably a murderer – and she could be putting her life on the line.

It would certainly surprise him to discover she had tracked him down, she thought uneasily, and maybe it was the craziest idea she had had yet. But she was counting on the fact that once he knew she was aware that he had made the phone call to her, and sent her the dead flowers, it would shock him into telling her more.

Especially if he thought she had contacted the police ... as the ideas spun haphazardly in her head and got her nowhere, she pushed them away and concentrated on the immediacy of the job in hand.

The reference library was nearly empty, and a tired female assistant located the directory she needed.

Everything was on microfiche film these days, and Alex knew she could consult it that way if she chose, but she still preferred the good old page-turning methods. There was nothing quite like the smell and feel of a book, whether brand new or musty with age. And the photocopier was close at hand.

She discovered that there were seemingly dozens of peers of the realm with names beginning with I, J or L. Well, she was pretty damn sure her target wouldn't be Lord Lucan, she thought with a feeble attempt at a joke, so she could dismiss him for a start.

She ended up with a formidable list of possibles, but since the man was Moira's sometime boyfriend, the elderly ones among them would seem to be unlikely. Alex would never have considered Moira to be a raving nympho, but there had to have been some kind of attraction between them.

Unless Moira had done all the running, and threatened to compromise her lover unless he continued to pay up whatever blackmail amounts she and her mother were demanding from him.

She shivered. There would obviously have been a lot at stake for a man in the public eye. However high up the social scale he was, the more he would have to lose. And whoever he was, he had known both women, and now both of them were dead. And Alex had no wish to be his third victim.

'Will you be finished here soon?' she heard the librarian say. 'We're about to close.'

'Sorry,' Alex said hastily. 'Anyway, I think I've found everything I need.'

That was an understatement, if you like. But she knew she had been at the photocopier far too long. She paid for the privilege, put the papers in a folder, and gave the librarian a smile before leaving the building, knowing that she didn't really have much to go on except a long list of people whose backgrounds all appeared to be impeccable.

Common sense told her there would be any number of hereditary peers with shady pasts, as well as the *nouveau riche* and the New Year annuals – and whether they were

288

true blue or a dubious grey, they would all have the means or the contacts to hide those pasts. That was the problem. If she was going to investigate every damn one of them, she'd be whitehaired before she found the one she wanted.

So she would have to weed some of them out. But it looked like being a lengthy job, and before she even began to tackle it, she was going to do a little more night-time surveillance on Harold Dawes as she had planned. First things first, and it was always useful to establish if a suspect had a regular *modus operandi*.

Alex debated on whether or not to don her disguise again, and then decided it would be sensible. There were too many street lights around the area of Battery Mews. It was pretty crummy, and may be well-lit for a very good reason, and she reminded herself to lock her car doors before she reached the end of the street where she had a good view.

There was no sign of life, and after nearly an hour she got out of the hire car to stretch her limbs, and walked purposefully towards the off-licence. She bought a couple of cans of coke, while she casually chatted up the elderly guy behind the counter, trying not to notice the huge beer gut beneath his stained woollen pullover.

'Quiet tonight, isn't it? I thought you'd be

full of customers,' she said, adopting a south of the river accent.

He looked her up and down with a small leer of appreciation, apparently glad of a diversion from his racing paper, and she was glad she wasn't wearing her usual black gear with her distinctive red hair hanging loose. He might be old, but he still had a lecherous look in his eyes.

'It gets busy later, darlin'. I get my reg'lars from the streets and the Mews, and there's always folk that are glad of an all-nighter once the boozers shut.'

'You stay open all night?' Alex said, immediately wondering just how late a night-owl Harold Dawes would turn out to be. 'Bit risky, isn't it? You hear all sorts of things about all-night shops being turned over these days.'

The man shrugged. 'I got my alarm system, duck, and I ain't had any trouble I couldn't handle yet. You don't go into this business without some know-how if you've got any sense. I ain't seen you around here before. Visiting, are you? Or just passing through? If you're looking for a bed for the night, I could put you up, and you'll be quite safe wiv me–'

Alex laughed. 'I'll bet!' she grinned, giving him the benefit of the doubt. 'No, I was meant to meet a friend, but I don't think she's going to show now. She lives somewhere around here, but I'm not sure exactly where.'

'Bleedin' waste, a lovely gel like you waitin' for a *female* friend, if you ask me.' The guy leered more boldly. 'Unless, of course – well, pardon me for mentioning it, but you meet plenty of both-ways these days, doncher?'

Alex looked at him blankly for a minute, and then got his meaning. 'Oh God, no. She's just a workmate, that's all.'

He chuckled. 'That's all right then. Live and let live, I say, but there's some you wouldn't want to give house-room to, ain't there? But like I said, if you're wanting a bed for the night–'

'I'm not, but I'll keep it in mind if I ever get desperate,' she said teasingly, as if she could actually be interested in the creep. 'So where are all these regulars then? Not very keen tonight, are they?'

'Oh, they'll turn up when they're ready. Couple of old ducks from the Mews will be in for their bottle of gin, and the sergeant will be back for a fresh supply later. He's a midnight man, as reg'lar as clockwork. Goes through drink like a dose of salts too. I can't make head nor tail of him, but I reckon he's trying to drown his sorrows.'

'Sergeant? As in police sergeant?' Alex said coolly.

'Christ, no. Army. Or so he says. Sometimes you can't understand the nonsense he talks, he's so puddled. Don't get him talking if you're still here when he comes in,' he warned her. 'He's always aggressive, and he don't like women much.'

Except when he was sucking up to them in his major guise on a cruise ship.

'Thanks for the tip, but it's time I was going, anyway.'

'Oh yeah. Your friend will be looking for you.'

She looked at the shopkeeper blankly, and then remembered the non-existent friend she was supposed to be meeting. She looked at her watch quickly.

'God, you're right. I'd forgotten the time. Well, it was nice talking to you.'

'Yeah. Well, any time you're passing, darlin' – or feel like stopping–'

She laughed as she went out, feeling his gaze on her backside as she clanged the door shut.

Some of these lusty old guys never lost their urges, or knew when it was time they hung up their tackle. They all thought they could get any woman they fancied, whether it was their hair or their teeth that were dropping out, or their beer bellies had prevented them seeing their feet – or anything of more importance – for years.

Most of them could probably do nothing more than dream about it, anyway ... but even if it was only the thought that kept them alive, she supposed it was preferable to mouldering away in front of the TV ... and you were a long time dead.

And why the hell she should care, anyway!

She stopped her meandering thoughts as she slid back into the hire car, opened a can and took a long drink of coke. She needed to concentrate on her own cause, instead of wondering about a geriatric's loss of libido. She gave a little shudder. Whether he could or couldn't do the business, it was hardly a thought to make her heart beat faster.

But by now, she was quickly revising her idea of meeting Dawes tonight. If he was going to be as aggressive as the shopkeeper said, she would do better to leave it until another time – and earlier in the evening before he got legless. She had no wish to encounter the rage of a madman. Nor could she guess how he would react to seeing her, either, knowing that she had tracked him down.

So for tonight, she decided to keep up her watch until she saw him come out of 84 Battery Mews and make his way to the off-licence, just to establish that he did indeed have a regular pattern. There was only another hour to go until midnight, she thought with a groan. But boredom went with the job. It wasn't all excitement and thrills. Hardly ever.

As the time dragged on, she heard a clock strike somewhere in the distance. Fifteen more minutes to go, and then she could observe as long as necessary, and go home. Her normal amount of energy was flagging fast, and the aftermath of her recent flu was still lingering. She needed sleep – and some extra vitamins to pep her up.

A short while later she sat up more stiffly as a couple of young guys in jeans and sweatshirts came swaggering down the street towards her, mouthing drunken obscenities and thrusting their hips towards her suggestively.

'*Bastards,*' she muttered, forcing herself not to retaliate or make obvious eye contact, and feeling thankful she had locked the car doors again.

It was almost exactly midnight by her watch when she noticed movement from Battery Mews. Halfway down the street a door opened, spilling light out on to the pavement for a moment before it was closed again. From her observations she knew it came from number 84.

'Hello, sergeant cum major, whoever the hell you really are,' she said silently. 'Stay still long enough for me to take some pics for posterity–'

But it hardly mattered, because he shuffled slowly, like a very old man, as if it was an effort to move anywhere too quickly. Or else his brain was too addled to bother, and Alex guessed he was pretty drunk already. She watched him begin to cross the cobbled street to get to the side leading to the off-licence, wondering if he really enjoyed drinking himself into a stupor. Or was he just drinking himself to death because he had so little else in his life?

Alex kept her camera clicking to get a series of reference shots. He was in the middle of the Mews street now, seemingly oblivious to the car that was approaching from the opposite direction. It was behind him, and it didn't have its headlights switched on. Curious ... but presumably it was a resident's car, and it was going to slow down and stop...

In a split second of complete shock, Alex knew it wasn't going to happen. For one thing, the car was too large and impressive to belong to anyone in this seedy street. And for another, she was suddenly aware that it was gathering speed, and that the headlights had been just as suddenly turned on, blazing into life, and dazzling anyone near enough to be in their way.

Like a crazed animal scenting its kill, the car was heading straight for Harold Dawes. And in the same split second, he realized it too.

He turned as if bewildered, and was

caught full in the headlights, frozen for a moment in time before he screamed in terror as the car ploughed into him, tossing him into the air like a rag doll.

Then the car hurtled on into the night, passing Alex's car, while she threw herself sideways on to the passenger seat, flinging her camera to the floor.

'Christ,' she whispered, her heart pounding, and forcing down the vomit in her gut. 'Oh, *Jesus Christ!*'

Half of her brain was completely disorientated. The other half was furiously registering that she had neglected to keep filming at the vital moment. She had just lost it. She had witnessed a cold-blooded murder for the first time ever, and she hadn't got it on film.

But her fury was just as instantly submerged by what she had just seen. The sight had been just as sickening and shocking as she always imagined. No. It was worse than imagination, because she had not only seen the impact, she had heard the dull thud of the body as the car struck it, and the screams of terror from Dawes as he saw what was coming...

It had all happened so fast, and there was nothing she could have done to warn him that somebody was coming for him, deliberately targeting him. Somebody who must have known his movements so well ...

the truth of it was so bloody merciless.

Alex's mouth was so dry now that she almost gagged. She knew who the hit and run driver had to be. She had registered the size and shape of the car, even if she hadn't fully recognized it as a Jaguar. But it was black, and it was large.

So it had to be him. MB. Mister Big. Taking charge of things himself, now that his henchman was habitually too drunk to be trusted any longer, and might well start blabbing or boasting about what they had done.

The stupid nickname Alex had given him was too infantile to credit any longer. She sat crouched over the steering-wheel while the terror of it stunned her mind, knowing that she should go to see if anything could be done. Dawes might be horribly injured, and although she balked from going anywhere near him, it was only common decency to do so.

And if he thought he was about to breathe his last, he might be willing to give her some information. She was further sickened by her own thought, but she knew it was the way Nick's mind would have worked. Always the professional, no matter how ghastly the circumstances, putting personal feelings aside to get at the truth.

But Dawes might already be dead. Was almost *certainly* dead, she thought, seeing that there was no movement at all from the heap of humanity lying at the side of the road now. MB would have made certain of that. He would have done his job well and made no mistakes.

While she dithered in those moments, a mass of shivering indecision, she saw that curtains were being pulled aside from windows in the Mews. Other people had clearly heard the roar of the car and the terrified screams.

And then she saw that doors were opening, and people were rushing out of the houses to bend over Harold Dawes' mangled body, and there were more shrill screams mingled with voices shouting for someone to send for an ambulance and the police.

Alex could have done all that, but so could someone else. There were plenty of people with access to phones, and she had to get out of there fast, before somebody came running to the end of the Mews to see if she had seen or heard anything. The last thing she wanted was to be called as a witness, and to have her name blazoned in the newspapers for MB to see and recognize, and to wonder if she might be on to him.

The fact that he almost certainly knew it already made her blood freeze. It also made her his next potential target.

She fumbled with the car's ignition switch,

crashing the gears as she shot away from the scene, desperate to get away from anywhere remotely near Battery Mews.

He hadn't seen her, she kept telling herself. He couldn't have seen her. She had had her head well down by the time his headlights had lit up her car and moved on, and she was still wearing her baseball cap and check shirt.

If he had ever seen her, or had a description of her from Dawes, he couldn't possibly have recognized her tonight...

She tore off the baseball cap and flung it on the floor, then drove around for an hour before she had calmed down enough to think logically. If he *had* seen a car parked near Battery Mews, he would have seen a green Mini, and not her own car. So she had to get rid of this one as soon as possible. The hire place was closed now, but from past experience she knew she could leave it in the yard and post the keys through the office letter-box.

Long hours of surveillance could get very cold, and she thanked God she'd had the nous to bring a dark jacket with her, and she put it on over the check shirt as she walked back to her flat from the hire car place, her hair hanging loose.

The time it took to get home was sheer torture. Every large car she saw made her want to shrink into the shadows, as if he had truly stalked her now.

She felt as if she knew how it felt to be hunted, and no matter how many times she told herself she was being completely irrational, she couldn't shake off the terror.

'Christ, Gary, you were so right,' she whimpered, when at last she reached her own building. 'I *am* in the wrong bloody job, and the sooner I get out of it, the better.'

And she refused to give credence to her father's usual remonstration that *everything will look better in the morning, Audrey...* Because everything wouldn't. Not this time.

In any case, she wasn't waiting until morning to see how things looked. She had to get away. Her own flat didn't feel safe any longer. He knew where she lived. And now that Leanora, and Moira – and now Harold Dawes – had been disposed of, she was the only one with any real information about the blackmailing scam the two women had been operating.

She no longer felt as if she was doing a noble service to help people. It was just bloody stupid, meddling into other peoples' lives, and pretending you were some godlike creature who could do miracles. Well, she couldn't, and she hadn't, and the sooner she got out from it the better.

She flung some things into a bag and had vacated the flat again within fifteen minutes. She got into her car, and once through the city, she headed for the south coast with no clear idea of where she was going. Worthing? Mrs Dooley's guest house? And how stupid would *that* be!

The temptation to prowl around the Wolstenholme house looking for clues had lost all its allure. Besides, the boyfriend may have keys to it. He wasn't brainless, and he might figure out that she would go there, and lie in wait. And she might well be the next one to end up in the swimming-pool and not just for a moonlight dip.

There was one place she could try for refuge. The Happy Days Retirement Home might not be her first choice, but it would be a good place for cover, until she could get her scrambled thoughts together. She was sure Graham Johnson would give her a room for the night, if she invented some trouble with her car and couldn't find a garage open at this hour.

'Calm down – and *slow* down,' she muttered out loud, as another car flashed its headlights at her and honked its horn as she shot across its path. 'A fat lot of good you'll do if you get stopped by the police.'

But maybe that wasn't such a bad idea, either. If she was stopped for reckless driving and forced to spend a night in the cells, at least MB couldn't get at her there. But her pride quickly reasserted itself. She'd be damned if he was going to make her hide away like some snivelling criminal. He was the villain, not her. All the same...

She reached The Happy Days Retirement Home at Beckingham and roused Graham Johnson after a short while of futile hammering on the front door and getting no response. Weren't these places supposed to have all-night vigilance for their residents?

'Yes? What the devil do you want? This is a respectable establishment, and we don't take in casuals,' Johnson snapped, blinking owlishly at this unwelcome visitor at three in the morning, his purple and green striped dressing-gown pulled ludicrously tightly over his portly frame.

As if anyone would want to see anything that was underneath that towelling monstrosity, Alex thought. She was starting to feel light-headed, and the image of pink chipolata sausages flitted unwillingly through her mind.

'Mr Johnson, I'm sorry to disturb you. My car's broken down, and if you could let me have a room for tonight, or what's left of it, I'd be awfully grateful,' she almost gasped.

And then to her fury, she staggered, and was forced to lean against him as her legs threatened to give way. His arms went around her at once, and she could smell the sleep on him.

She forced down the sudden urge to throw

up, and struggled out of his embrace, but he still gripped her arms as if afraid she was going to fall down at any moment. Which wasn't so far from the way she felt.

'My dear Miss Best, please come inside, and I apologize for my lack of manners,' he oozed when he recognized her.

'Oh, I don't blame you. Mr Johnson – I just need a bed for a few hours if it's not an imposition–'

'Of course it's not,' he said, fussily efficient at once. 'We have a few vacancies at the moment–'

Alex didn't need three guesses as to why. She just hoped the room had been cleaned and fumigated from the elderly patient who would have breathed her last in it ... and that wasn't being churlish, it was just being bloody hygienic.

But a short while later she was lying on a narrow bed in one of the plush rooms the well-off residents paid so dearly for. She had curled up beneath the duvet in a protective foetus position without bothering to take off anything except her shoes. And she was shivering with relief that she was here, and she was safe. For now.

She was woken by the sound of someone tapping on her door, and as she opened her eyes a fraction, she didn't have the faintest idea where she was for a moment or two.

And then she remembered – and wished she didn't have to.

A young girl came in with a breakfast tray, and Alex suddenly felt very old at the sight of the bright young face and pony-tailed hair and big blue eyes. Baby blues, Gary would call them.

'Mr Johnson says you're to come to his office as soon as you feel like it,' the girl recited.

'Thank you–' but the girl was already gone, before she could say that she didn't want bacon and fried egg, thank you very much.

Except that the smell of it was wafting into her nostrils now, enticingly mouthwatering, and without another thought, Alex devoured the lot, only just realizing how long it was since she had eaten anything at all.

She felt decidedly better once she had finished, and was thankful that she hadn't had to join the old dears in the dining-room, where questions would certainly have been asked. All the rooms were en suite, so she didn't have to use a communal bath-room, thank God.

Half an hour later, she went to Johnson's office, more refreshed than she had expected to be, and with last night's memories a fraction less nightmarish now. Just. This place was definitely a haven, though, and thank God she had thought of it before heading off to nowhere in particular.

She realized she was thanking God a lot lately, despite not being overly religious, and she hoped fervently that He was feeling benevolent towards her.

'Come in, Miss Best.' Graham Johnson beamed at her now. 'I'm sorry if I was a little brusque when you arrived–'

'Good Lord, you don't need to apologize to me, Mr Johnson. You must have thought me a madwoman, barging in on you like that in the middle of the night–'

'Not at all, dear lady. I understand the needs of a person such as yourself, and I've no doubt you were on a case, and needed sanctuary for a while.'

And how many Agatha Christie novels have you been reading lately? Alex thought, resisting the urge to laugh as he looked at her eagerly, obviously fancying himself as a Captain Hastings to her Poirot...

'It was something like that,' she murmured, seeing no need to disillusion him. Though Miss Marple would be more like her *alter ego*, she thought, bumbling about as she did...

'So how can I help you? If you want to stay here for a few more days, I could accommodate you, although–'

'Although you would naturally expect me to pay for the room,' she finished for him.

He fluttered like an oversized cabbage-white in his anxiety not to embarrass her by speaking about money. But Alex knew very well he was as grasping as the next man when it came to getting his fat fees from the old dears in his care. They certainly got every care, though, and compared with some of the oldies she had seen living a wretched existence on the streets and in the subways, she could forgive him anything.

'I would like to stay, if it's no inconvenience,' Alex said. 'I'm travelling incognito for the moment,' she added, knowing he would savour the detective lingo, as well as the fact that she was apparently taking him into her confidence.

'I understand,' Johnson said, tapping the side of his nose with the tip of a pudgy finger.

God, it was like watching a bad movie, Alex thought. And she was playing the star role, even though it didn't feel much like it. Did Poirot ever have such jitters?

'An important case, is it?' he went on.

'Now, now, Mr Johnson, you know we private eyes never divulge any information while an investigation's going on,' she chided him, and cringing at her own twittering. But it was an approach that made him smile with satisfaction.

'I can arrange for a mechanic to come up here from a local garage if you like–'

'What?'

'Your car. You said it had broken down.'

So she had. Shit. 'Thanks, but I'll try it first. It's temperamental, and it may be all right again now that it's cooled down. I've been racing the engine a bit recently.'

And if he thought she had been involved in some high-speed car chase, so much the better. He was clearly a man who had only ever lived a vicarious life, and she was adding a little spice to it.

She was glad to leave his office and go and sit in her car. She needed to think what to do next, while revving up the engine now and then as if to check that it was still serviceable.

The village of Beckingham was little more than a dot on the map, but it would almost certainly have a newsagent and/or general store. With luck, it would have the national newspapers as well as local rags, although there was unlikely to be any mention of a hit and run accident in Lambeth until the evening editions. If there was any mention of it at all.

Such statistics were depressingly frequent these days, and Harold Dawes' death would be seen as just one more tragic incident. Unless there was information to the contrary, no one was going to connect it with a murder.

And remembering how deserted the

Mews had been before he had come out of his home, there was almost certainly no other witness but herself. She could tell...

If she chose, she could give Harold Dawes a little posthumous dignity, and even deny that he had been lurching drunkenly across the street and had just been in the wrong place at the wrong time ... but why should she?

He hadn't shown any mercy when he had strangled Moira and drowned her in her own swimming-pool. Either him, or MB.

Whichever one of them it was, they deserved what they got, Alex thought viciously, and eventually MB had it coming to him too. If she could nail him, she would show as little mercy as he had shown his victims, whether or not he had stabbed them in the back, or drowned them, or run them down.

She jumped as she heard someone tapping on her car window, and she wound it down as she saw a man she didn't know leaning towards her.

'Having trouble, love? You won't get much joy out of the old geyser here,' he said.

'It's all right, I know Mr Johnson, and I'm staying here,' she said quickly.

The man whistled, reminding her of Gary for a moment. But that was the only similarity, because this guy was around forty-five years old and running to seed.

'Well, whatever pep-up pills they're giving you, I want some!' he said with a laugh.

Alex didn't follow for a moment, until she saw the way he was peering down at her legs in their tight black trousers.

'I'm not an *inmate*,' she said, laughing back.

'Pity,' the guy said cheekily. 'Me and old Johnson might have made our fortunes if I'd got you in the frame.'

'What?' she said, startled by the hint of police jargon. But it clearly had a different meaning for this guy.

'I come here quite often to photograph the old dears. Makes 'em feel good when I touch up their pics to make 'em look like film stars. They know I do it, of course, but it makes 'em happy. But you wouldn't need any of that!'

'You're a photographer?' she said, ignoring his last words, and echoing him as if she was a bloody parrot.

Well, part-time. I do it as a favour, because the old loves know me and don't get flummoxed because there's a stranger in the camp.'

Alex got out of the car, and leaned against it, giving him the benefit of seeing her long-limbed body in her well-filled skimpy black t-shirt and trousers.

'Do you do it commercially, or privately? What I mean is, do you do all the developing and printing yourself, or do you have to send the films away?'

'Gawd no, begging your pardon, love. It's just a hobby, but I've got my own dark-room at my cottage in the village. You could come to see it if you're interested. When I've finished here, of course.' He grinned. 'Makes a change from asking somebody to come and see my etchings, eh?'

Alex agreed with him, trying to hide her excitement. And oh yes, there *is* a God, she breathed inside her head.

'I might just do that. And maybe you could do me a little favour too.'

Chapter 12

The photographer told her his name was David Bailey. Alex started to laugh until she realized he was serious. Well, why not? Somebody had to be.

Not *the* one, she asked solemnly, and he assured her just as solemnly that unfortun-ately he didn't have that honour.

The old ladies at Happy Days clearly adored him. He was definitely a ladies' man as he encouraged them to look at the camera, think of sex, and smile. He could coax the old boys into a grudging grin by the same method, though with some of them it was more of a lecherous leer.

And by now Alex was acting as unpaid assistant, suggesting how the ladies with good hands should hold them loosely in their laps, or sit three-quarters on to the camera to hide thickening chins for the best profiles.

'Have you ever done any modelling?' David asked.

'God, no. I'm just a woman, but I know how to pose.'

'I'll vouch for that,' he said cheekily. 'When it comes to arranging different angles, I'm still an amateur, but you seem to know how to get the best out of them.'

'It's just luck, but why shouldn't they end up with the nicest and prettiest photos they can have? They weren't born old, and a bit of pampering never did anyone any harm.'

She wouldn't admit, even to herself, that she might be giving more than half a thought to her own parents at that moment, who'd never had any pampering in their lives, and had endured the rigours of the harsh Yorkshire winters.

And if she was getting soft, it was a welcome diversion from last night's trauma, enabling her to push aside the memory of the hit and run killing, if only for a little while.

'We're all done,' David Bailey said, a

couple of hours later. 'I'll get back and develop the films after lunch, and you're welcome to come and watch. I always try to deliver the proofs as soon as possible before any of 'em pop off. You never know how long some of 'em are going to last.'

Alex didn't get his meaning for a minute, and then she did. His words were crude, but she couldn't deny that some of the sicklier ones didn't look as if they would last another day.

She smiled more warmly at the circle of them in the sunny day-room, most of them nodding away in their armchairs after the excitement of the photography session. And thinking how awful it must be to wake up every morning and wonder whose was going to be the next empty chair...

'Miss Best,' she heard Johnson's voice. 'There's coffee for you and Mr Bailey in my office when you're ready.'

David chuckled. 'He probably thinks I'm monopolizing you. He doesn't like me much, because the old dears always fawn over me when I come. Still, it gives them something to think about other than death, doesn't it?'

'How often do you come here then?'

'Christmas, Summer – and any birthdays and anniversaries that they request. I supply folders for them to send the photos to their relatives if they want them. They usually do.

It reminds those outside that they're still alive.'

'And they pay you, of course.'

'I'm not in it for my health, love. And you only have to look at them to know they can afford it. I enjoy having a jaw with 'em, though,' he added, belying his first words.

'Did you ever meet Trevor Unwin?' she said, as they left the day room for Johnson's office. 'You know, the one who–'

'Oh, I know who he was all right. I did meet him here once,' David said. 'Creepy kind of feller. Didn't surprise me at all to learn that he'd topped himself.'

'Really? Why do you say that?' Alex said.

David shrugged. 'He didn't have the bottle to carry out a murder without either being goaded into it, or being very well paid to do it. It stood to reason that the worry of what he'd done would get to him eventually. He wasn't a natural killer.'

'That's interesting. You're quite a philosopher on the quiet, aren't you, David?'

He gave a hooting laugh. 'Hell's bells, I've been called many things, but never one of them before!'

'Listen, when we've had coffee, how about lunch in a local pub? My treat.'

'Sure, why not? I always fancied being a kept man,' he said lazily, his eyes twinkling. 'And then we'll go to my dark room and see what develops.'

'Oh God, not that old chestnut,' Alex groaned. 'And don't let it go to your head. I want to talk business.'

They got back to David's cottage in the early afternoon, with the smell of beer on his lips, and the taste of curry on hers. Alex had resisted drinking at lunchtime, needing to keep her head clear and her fingers crossed for anything that might show up on the shots she had taken in Battery Mews.

She had always enjoyed watching the magic of developing and printing, and had once thought of dabbling in it herself. It would make a lot of sense, instead of sending her pics away to be developed, and risking some keen-eyed assistant sensing that there might be a scoop here...

She instinctively trusted David Bailey, but she wasn't going to pass over her own film until they had done the morning shots from the retirement home. Once his films were through the developing stage they were quickly dried, so that he could print off a set of proofs, and then enlarge the ones he intended showing to the residents.

Like all photographers, he had taken plenty of them, and they spent an absorbing couple of hours before he was satisfied with the selection he had to show his sitters the following morning.

'We'll take a break for a cup of tea, if you

like,' he said finally, straightening his back. 'I've got some chocolate biccies somewhere, I think.'

'David, you're a man after my own heart,' Alex said with a grin. She felt quite safe saying it, sure it was *all* he was after. By now she knew that he was a self-employed market gardener and had been a widower for many years.

But now he was doggedly single and proud of it, content enough with his life to do no more than chat up the elderly ladies he came into contact with in his side-line.

'You never did tell me what you're doing at Happy Days, Alex,' he remarked over the shared sensual intimacy of dunking biscuits in their tea until the chocolate began to melt. 'Do you have someone who's going to live there?'

She shook her head. She trusted him, but she wasn't prepared to tell him any more than she had to. And only Graham Johnson at the retirement home knew her true profession.

'I met Mr Johnson a while ago, and he was kind enough to say that if ever I needed a little break, I should call in. I'm a business consultant, and sometimes you just have to get away from the rat-race. Need I say more?'

David put his hand over hers in a mute gesture of understanding, when in reality she had told him nothing.

'So what's this little favour you think I can do for you, then? You only have to ask, and if I can oblige, I will.'

As he squeezed her hand, for a weird second the image of Gary Hollis was strong in Alex's head. If Gary had said those words they would have been loaded with innuendo, and there wouldn't have been any doubt as to whether he could, or would, oblige...

She blinked, wondering what the hell she was thinking of, when there were far more important matters to deal right now than Gary's ever-rampant libido.

'I've got a film to be developed, and I need some enlargements made of the prints. I know it's a bit of a cheek when we've only just met, and I'll pay you, of course–'

'No, you won't. It'll be a pleasure, and your company's all the payment I need.'

He was a love, she thought. He didn't question her, though he might well be more curious when he saw how many shots she had taken of a man crossing a road at night...

'Gawd!' David frowned through his magnifying glass at the dark negatives. 'Not the best shots in the world, are they? Who is he, your boyfriend out on the razzle or something?'

He chuckled as he spoke, as if he had said something terribly daring.

'Hardly,' Alex said. 'I'd promised to get a series of London street scenes for a friend who used to live around that way. The man took so long crossing the street, that I think he must have been drunk. It seemed a good idea to keep him in the shots to give them some perspective,' she invented wildly.

She should have thought it through. Why would anybody believe such a stupid story? Unless they were completely artless, and had no inkling about the existence of a shadier world than that of market gardening and taking photos of gentle old ladies...?

'It can often prove profitable,' David agreed. 'A good photographer always takes more shots than he needs, and I daresay you got a little curious about the chap. He needed to move quicker when that car came around the corner, though.'

'Car?' Alex said, as if she had never seen it before.

But there it was, of course. Big, black and beautiful if you could call an instrument of death beautiful – engulfing the scene and Harold Dawes with it, seconds before the dazzling headlights had split the darkness and mowed him down.

And she was starting to think in pure Raymond Chandlerese now... For a moment she wished desperately that she had kept her camera clicking, to catch the moment of death ... and just as instantly, with a growing feeling of nausea in her stomach, she thanked God that she hadn't. Especially when it would have shocked the gentle man with her now.

Just looking at the negatives, she was reliving it all over again. Her thoughts went off at an unwelcome tangent. Wasn't witnessing a murder – and not informing on it – tantamount to diverting the course of justice? A murderer had to be caught before he killed again. And who would he kill?

'Are you all right, Alex? You don't look so good.'

She heard David's anxious voice as if it was coming through a thick layer of fog. She struggled to ignore the horror of her thoughts, and nodded quickly at his troubled face in the dim red light of the dark room.

'I'm not sure I should have had that curry,' she said huskily. 'And I think perhaps the smell of the chemicals in here has got down my chest. I'm OK, honestly, so how soon can you do me some enlargements?'

She didn't want to appear too anxious, but by now she was longing to get some prints in her hands and to get out of there and study them alone. She didn't want David poring over them, and starting to wonder just why she was so keen to have so many pictures of a man in the middle of the road with a car threatening to run him over.

Especially if the crime was going to be reported on TV or in the press later on, and he started to put two and two together. She doubted that he would think she had actually been connected in any way, but he might just wonder what the hell she had been doing there, and start remembering her feeble story.

He might even contact the local police or newspaper, thinking it was his duty to do so, and anticipating his own moment of glory... He might never have welcomed it, but when the chips were down, nobody was averse to getting their share.

'David, I need to get back to London soon, so if you could just do me those enlargements, I'd be very glad,' Alex said. 'One of each neg will be fine, then I can send the best ones to my friend.'

'Will do,' he said cheerfully, and she blessed his sweet innocence that saw nothing peculiar in such a bizarre tale.

There *were* good people in the world, and he was definitely one of them.

She didn't even stop to look at the photos properly when he had finished his work, and thankfully, neither did he. She just pushed them into a large envelope and exclaimed that she had no idea it had got so late, and she would have to go. He didn't try to stop her, just gave her an awkward kiss on her cheek as she got back into her car.

'Any time you want any more work done, I'm your man.'

'Thanks. I'll remember that, David!'

She drove away and got back to Happy Days just as the residents were having their late afternoon tea and slice of cake. Graham Johnson was fussily in attendance, and she could hardly go straight to her room without appearing stand-offish. She felt obliged to join them, and to listen to the various female comments about that lovely David Bailey.

Some of them were quite girlish and twittery, thought Alex. It endeared her to him even more, that he could bring such a ray of sunshine into their old lives. Just like that old Morecambe and Wise theme song ... *Bring me sunshine ... in your smile...*

She knew what she was doing, of course. Thinking of anything, no matter how inane, or how futile, to stop her thinking about last night. But that was exactly what she would be forced to do, the minute she got out the enlargements and studied them properly.

'Are you a professional young woman?' she heard one of the elderly gents bark at her.

'Oh. Yes. I'm a business consultant,' she said, glibly repeating what she had said to David.

'Thought so. You've got that air about you.'

'Is that good?' she asked him with a smile.

'Mebbe. As long as you don't get too tough. I can't abide tough women. They should know their place, and not go about burning their bra*zeers or* waving banners. One of 'em even threw herself under the king's horse. Damn stupid gel.'

Graham Johnson floated near enough to hear him.

'Now, now, you're getting mixed up again, Stephen, and Miss Best doesn't want to be bothered with your nonsense.'

He turned to Alex and spoke in an aside.

'Sometimes he can't remember which decade he's in, so don't let him get you involved in a long conversation.'

'Thanks. I'll remember that,' she said, only just working out the meaning of a bra*zeer*...

But she couldn't help feeling desperately sorry for the wizened old man all the same, and prayed that she would never get into the same state herself.

'How long do you plan on staying with us?' Johnson went on. 'It's no trouble, you understand, but we may be needing the room quite soon–'

'Of course. I shall be leaving tomorrow morning, Mr Johnson,' Alex said. 'And naturally, you must bill me for the room. I wouldn't have come here if that wasn't understood.'

And from his satisfied smile as he

wandered away from her, she knew she'd understood him very well.

Once in her room she opened the envelope with a mixture of dread and anticipation. Her blood was pumping, and she was conscious of the sound of her heartbeats as she flipped through the first pictures, and got to the ones she really wanted to see.

The ones with the car in the background. The big black Jaguar car that she was certain belonged to Moira's lover. The killer. Mister Big.

She didn't want to look at Harold Dawes' figure in the foreground. Remembering how he had swayed and lurched, and the way he had half-turned as he sensed the oncoming car. Alex couldn't avoid picturing it all over again, only now it was happening in a series of her own pics as if it was one of those slow motion TV action replays.

In her head she could still hear Dawes' screams in the instant that he realized what was happening. She could hear the dull impact as the relentless force of metal and steel struck the body. She could recall her own terrified reaction as she hurled her camera to the floor of the hire car and doubled over on the passenger seat so that she wouldn't be seen as the Jaguar tore past her.

Her hands were sweating now, and she

cursed herself for her weakness. It was a bloody wonder the camera had survived too, but thank God it had ... because here in her hands was everything she had wanted to see.

She had finished filming seconds before the car's headlights had lit up the street. But there were street lights at each end of the Mews, positioned in such a way that part of the car's number plate was illuminated. Not all, but part of it ... and if the gods were still smiling on her, it would be enough to identify the owner.

Providing she had the balls to ask DCI Nick Frobisher to find out who it belonged to. Because once she did that, she knew her part in it would be all over. She would have to come clean. And maybe it was time. It was far and away past the time for going it alone, she thought with a shiver.

She had switched off her mobile the minute she left London. It seemed like centuries ago, but she hadn't wanted any-one to contact her, wanting to bury her head in the sand like an ostrich, and have nothing to do with killers and crimes ... but she could no longer pretend that this had nothing to do with her, and after the evening meal she went to her room and switched her mobile on again.

She tried to think logically. As far as she knew, it hadn't been MB who had stalked her, or sent her the stupid things through the post – or telephoned her and rifled her office and the flat. If her guess was correct, he was a person who kept out of the way and delegated, and it would have been Harold Dawes who had done all those things.

Knowing how she had so often snubbed him in his major guise on the cruise ship, he would have taken a malicious pleasure in scaring her. Some guys got off on it ... and MB may not even know who she was, or about her connection with the Wolstenholme women.

Trying to keep her nerves under control, Alex knew it was a reasonable supposition. But she couldn't be absolutely certain that Dawes hadn't passed on all the information about her. And she had no wish to be next on his list.

The sound of her mobile phone made her heart leap. She snatched it up and mouthed her name into it.

'Where the hell have you been, Alex? I've been trying to get hold of you for hours,' Nick bawled at her. 'You won't have heard the news, because we're putting a press block on it for the present, but you'd better know what's happened.'

She closed her eyes, sitting heavily on the bed with the photos spilled out all around her. The incriminating photos that could trap a murderer.

'Nick, I think I know—' she choked.

'It's that bastard Dawes, the one who passed himself off as a major, remember? Late last night he was a DOA hit and run stiff, and you wouldn't believe the stuff he had stashed at his bed-sit. There's enough passports and changes of identity to fill a book, and I reckon he's been behind a thriving little blackmail scam. You know the kind of thing. Masses of magazines and newspapers with half the headlines cut out, and an old typewriter and pots of paste, all ready for sending out threatening letters to his victims. And guess what else? From the evidence found, he's definitely connected to the Worthing women, and it's highly likely he was responsible for that second killing. Forensics are on to it now—'

'Nick, will you *stop!*' Alex screamed. 'I can't take any more of this!'

There was a slight pause, and then he snapped at her:

'What the hell's got into you? Did you already know anything about this, Alex? If you do, you know bloody well it's your duty to contact the incident room in Worthing—'

'*Christ*, Nick! Can't you forget about duty for one Goddamned minute? I don't know what to do—' she said, her voice suddenly faltering.

'I'll be right round,' he said, and the line went dead.

She stared at the phone stupidly for a moment. But he couldn't be right round, because he didn't know where she was.

He had simply assumed she was in her flat. Instead of which, she was miles from London, in a place he didn't know about, because she had never mentioned Happy Days Retirement Home. There was a hell of a lot she hadn't told him about.

Alex licked her dry lips. She should call him right back. She should get back on the road and head for home. But there was still a chance, however small – or maybe horrendously large that MB *did* know who she was and where she lived.

She daren't risk going back there yet. The flat that had always been her haven was now a dangerous place. She was staying put for tonight, but after that ... she tried to think where she could go that was safe.

She didn't know where Gary lived, and anyway, there was no point in involving him, even though he had proved once before that he had a logical brain when it came to sorting her out. There was Mrs Dooley's guest house in Worthing, but she dismissed the thought of going back there.

Doreen and May, Moira's weird friends, would almost certainly offer her a roof, but she had no idea where they lived, and the thought of being subjected to more of their omens and astrological charts, would be enough to drive her completely around the bend.

An anonymous B & B was the obvious answer. Or there was Moira's place. It would be standing empty now, and the police would surely have finished with it.

According to Doreen and May – whom she could only think of in duplicate terms like a comedy act now it would eventually be sold at auction and the proceeds distributed to the charities the late owners had named. Presumably none of it could happen until after the inquest and the Will was made public – and legal procedures could take months to be completed. But it would be madness to go to Moira's house.

She tried to think rationally. The Worthing police would only be concerned with who had strangled and drowned Moira Wolstenholme. The inquiry would be continuing, but it was local.

Normally, an anonymous hit and run incident in London would have had nothing to do with them, and it should have been a total coincidence if the victim turned out to be connected with a Worthing murder investigation. But now Nick had connected the major with it all. and forensics were on to it.

Her mobile rang again, and she flinched, almost too scared to answer it. If Nick continued probing, she wasn't sure how long her nerves would last out before she blabbed everything. But wasn't that what she intended doing, anyway? She was in a state of total confusion, not knowing what to do next, and she snapped into the phone.

'I've got a couple of jobs near Chichester tomorrow, babe,' she heard Gary Hollis's sexy voice say. 'How do you fancy a trip to the south coast and staying overnight for old times' sake? I could pick you up in the morning–'

'Gary, I'm not at the flat,' she broke in, choked.

She thought rapidly, all she knew of the town was that it had a railway station and that it was well away from London.

'Getting away sounds good to me right now, though. How about if I meet you in Chichester at one o'clock by the station, and we'll take it from there? I'm not so sure about the overnight, so don't count on it.'

But it was just what she needed. A place to go. A friend. Some definite direction in her life to give her time to think. And the uncomplicated company of Gary Hollis.

She smiled thinly. Uncomplicated was the word. All Gary ever wanted was to get her into bed.

But the thought of tomorrow made the night less terrifying, and she managed to get some sleep without imagining that MB was about to burst in on her with a submachine gun at any minute. *And she had been watching too many late-night horror movies lately,* she told herself severely.

Alex planned to check out of Happy Days soon after breakfast the next morning, and head west. She would reach Chichester and the surrounding countryside long before one o'clock, and she couldn't get away from Beckingham fast enough. But she still had one more thing to do before she left, and oddly enough, Gary had given her the idea.

She called a rapid courier service in Worthing and made her request, and a middle-aged man sitting incongruously on his motorbike arrived at Happy Days a short while later. She met him at the gate, handed him a large brown envelope and paid the fee for express delivery.

And then she breathed a sigh of relief as she saw him leave, knowing that within an hour or so, DCI Frobisher would have the incriminating photographs in his hand, with her request to check out the car number plate. He would know at once that it was Battery Mews, and the identity of the man in front of the car.

It hardly mattered whether or not Nick quizzed the courier rider about where he had picked up the package, because she would be long gone from Beckingham and Happy Days before he could check up on her.

Feeling as if she was still on a razor's edge, she felt a touch better to know that she hadn't entirely obstructed the course of justice, while keeping herself out of it as much as possible. But it was vital that the police tracked down the car owner of the hit and run attack – and more than vital for Nick to trace him. He would know the significance of it all, as well as the danger to herself. And he would surely understand why she had gone to ground.

It wasn't what she had gone into this game for, Alex thought miserably, but it was no longer a game, anyway. It was deadly serious – and she could be the one to end up dead.

She reached Chichester after taking several wrong turnings, knowing that she wasn't giving her full attention to the road. It wasn't the best time to be driving, anyway, with her nerves in shreds. But once there, she parked her car and browsed around the town for a while, taking in the local shops and cafes, checking out the theatre to see what was on, wasting time drinking umpteen cups of coffee and deciding whether to go for a fresh-baked apple turnover or a jam doughnut or a chocolate eclair, and ending up with one of each, and to hell with it. She needed sustenance.

Gary roared up on his Harley Davidson in the station car park shortly before one o'clock, and she felt almost wild with relief to see him. She hugged him more tightly than he had expected, and she didn't miss the instant gleam in his eyes.

'Don't get excited,' she muttered. 'I'm not sure if I'm staying overnight yet.'

She ignored the little voice inside her head that asked where the hell she was going to go if she didn't stay here.

'We'll get around to that later, babe,' he said easily, as if he couldn't imagine for a minute that she was going to turn him down after agreeing this far.

And neither could she. What was the point?

'Have you done your deliveries?' she asked next.

'Yeah, rushed them through so we could have the afternoon to ourselves. I know a nice little pub on the way to the coast, if you're peckish. They do bed and breakfast too—'

'Don't push me,' Alex grinned. 'But I'm not leaving my car here, so I'd better follow you, and I'll leave it at the pub after lunch while we take a ride on the bike.'

She didn't exactly mention booking in for the night at the same time, but they both knew it was what she meant.

'So what's on your mind?' he asked, when they had ordered their ploughman's lunches at the quaint country pub.

'What do you mean?'

'Come on, sweetheart, I know you well enough to know when you're on a case and it's not going well.'

'You sound just like somebody in an American gangster movie,' she said crossly.

'And you'd never have agreed to join me so quickly if you didn't need a shoulder. So tell me.'

She bit into her hunk of bread that was oozing with butter now, and the sensual aromas of hot coffee, Cheddar cheese and pickle teased her nostrils.

But she wasn't ready for telling anything yet. While it was still in her head and nobody else's, it didn't have to be real. It was still all in fantasy-land ... she wished.

'I had to get away, that's all. Things have got rather messy, and I needed some space to see things clearly.'

God, she sounded as loony as Moira's friends now, instead of the feisty private eye she was supposed to be.

'And have you seen it clearly now?' Gary persisted.

'No. Not quite. Not yet. But I'm working on it.'

He gave a heavy sigh. 'Look, babe, if you want to confide in me, fine. If not, then forget it and let's just concentrate on spending a few hours with the simple life.'

'You're right. If you can't do anything

about it, why worry?' she said brightly.

And despite his city smart ID, Gary always knew how to enjoy the simple life, whether it was playing the fruit machines at a tacky seaside entertainment venue, or walking along the sands at the water's edge with their shoes off and their jeans rolled up, or skimming pebbles into the sea. And gradually Alex's ferocious tension began to ease.

It tightened again as soon as they were on their way back to the pub, and she saw the terse evening headlines on a stand outside a local newsagent's shop. Her stomach churned sickeningly as she read the gigantic words.

WAS LAMBETH HIT AND RUN VICTIM MURDER TARGET?

'This wasn't anything do with your case, was it?' Gary said with a grin. And then he saw her white face. *'Christ*, Alex, don't tell me it was!'

'Let's get back to the pub,' she said, her teeth beginning to chatter. She badly needed the security of four walls around her again. But not her own.

Four anonymous walls, where no one knew her but Gary. She had learned long ago that she could trust him, and she made no more objection when he had checked them into a double room for the night and took her in his arms.

'How bad is it?' he demanded.

'How bad do you want it? One murder or three, it's still murder, isn't it?'

He gaped at her, his tuneless whistle dying on his lips as he saw the nameless fear in her eyes.

'Three?'

'Three. And I was somehow caught up in every one of them. God knows I didn't mean to be, and I wasn't meant to be–'

Not unless there had been some heavenly, ethereal plan in Madame Leanora's astrological chart, that said Alexandra Best, private investigator, was destined to be on the same cruise ship as herself, and that all the events that followed were pre-ordained...

'Alex, are you OK?'

Gary's voice was harsh in her ears, and she realized he had pushed her heavily on to the bed. A damn good job he had, she thought, and without his usual intent too. Because if he hadn't pushed her there, she would surely have fallen.

'Do you believe in omens and second sight and all that rubbish?' She ignored his question, and asked him the same thing she had asked Nick Frobisher a lifetime ago.

'Christ, no. You're not going weirdo on me, are you, babe?' he said uneasily. 'I never took you for a spook.'

'I'm not,' Alex said, with a shaky laugh. 'Not me. Just everybody I seem to have been in contact with recently.'

'Well, you can count me out of that for a start. So are you going to tell me what this is all about? Because if not, I can think of far better things to do to pass the time.'

Her thoughts went beyond anything he was saying. She couldn't seem to concentrate on two things at the same time any more. She also needed to call Nick. She had no choice now.

She had to know if he had got the photos, and if he had acted on them, or if the newspaper headlines were merely guesswork.

Or if some other witness had come forward to give some lurid story of how they had seen Harold Dawes lurching across Battery Mews, and that a big black car had run him down. And by the way, there was a small green car parked at the end of the Mews too, and it had been there for some time.

She felt Gary's lips nuzzling her ear. His leathers crackled with animal strength, accentuating his maleness, and his arms were tight around her. He was a walking advert for testosterone, she thought weakly, as she had thought so many times before. And he wanted her. And she wasn't made of wood.

'I will tell you, Gary,' she mumbled. 'Later.'

A long while later, they surfaced from the joyful, chaotic seduction of the double bed. They shared a sensual shower before returning to bed, where they lay entwined in a comfortably intimate stupor until a different kind of need made them think of food.

'I shall expect the works after that,' Alex told him. 'Steak and chips and all the trimmings the place can muster.'

'Sex always did make you hungry, didn't it, doll?' Gary said with a wicked laugh. 'And I thought you'd already had the works. But if you want more—'

'Oh yeah? Superman, are you?'

'Try me,' he taunted, but she pushed him away, because the memory of why she was here was already overtaking the hedonistic pleasures of the last couple of hours. And she couldn't ignore it much longer.

Gary sensed her change of mood, and leaned up on his elbow to look down at her.

'So tell me about these three murders, and what's got you so rattled,' he said, one finger idly circling her nipple.

She pushed his hand away. The mood had definitely gone, and she felt chilled. She reached for the duvet and pulled it over both of them with a shudder.

'What's got me rattled, as you call it, is that I think I may be next in line.'

He didn't twig for a moment, and then he

sat up straight, and his voice had a much harder edge to it than usual.

'What the frigging hell have you got yourself into this time, Alex?'

It was far too complicated to tell him all of it in detail, so she ran through the essentials. About meeting Leanora and her prophesies; and Moira's arrival at her office; and the major's appearance at Leanora's funeral; and the strange friends who made her cringe; her own anonymous threats; and then Moira's death; David Bailey who had been a friend; and the major's hit and run accident that was no accident at all, but cold-blooded murder; and who she now knew was a con man called Harold Dawes and not a major at all...

'Slow down, for God's sake. I can't take it all in,' Gary snapped. 'I know one thing, though. You should give up this bloody job, Alex. I told you that before, didn't I?'

'You did, and I can't. Not now, anyway. Not until I see this through, and they find Mister Big.'

He eyed her as if she was truly crazy now.

'Mister Big? Bloody hell, Alex, how many detective novels have you been reading lately?'

'I swear to you, Gary, there's somebody pretty big behind all this, and as yet I don't know who it is. But until he's behind bars, I won't feel safe. I know too much.'

Her mouth was dry again, wondering how a simple request from a woman client to check out who had been stalking her, could have led to this.

'So what are you going to do now?'

'What I should have done a long time ago. I'm calling Nick. He'll have got the photos I sent him by now, and with any luck he'll have traced the car's owner. I have to know who it is.'

She switched on her mobile and dialled his office number before she could change her mind. To her fury, she got his answering service. She rang her own answering machine at the flat to check on any messages left for her, in the hope that he would have contacted her during the day.

The flat mechanical voice told her that there were two messages. She waited for the click and then a familiar voice cut in, filled with urgency.

'Alex, it's Nick. I've got the envelope. The possibility is too big to discuss on the phone. Wherever you are, call me as soon as you're back at the flat and I'll meet you there. And take care.'

The second message was brief, spoken in a cultured male voice she had never heard before. There were only five words. The warning it contained was similar to Nick's, but said with far more menace.

'Watch your back, Miss Best.'

Chapter 13

'I have to go home,' she stuttered. 'I have to see Nick as soon as possible. I'm sorry, Gary.'

'What about tonight?'

'To hell with tonight. This is more important. Look, I'll pay for the room–'

'No, you bloody won't. What's going on? What were those messages?'

'Nick's got some information I need.'

'Bollocks. Since when were you so bloody keen to work hand in glove with the police? Or should that be hand in crotch with that nerd–'

'*Leave* it, Gary,' she snapped. 'I have to go.'

'No, you don't.'

He grabbed her wrist as she picked up her bag and began stuffing her things inside it. He had a vicious grip, and the pain shot through her flesh as he twisted it, but she was damned if she was going to let him know it.

'You're not messing me about, are you, doll?'

'Why should I be? We both knew this was never going to be a permanent arrangement. You got in touch with me after God knows how long, and expected me to come running. Well, screw you, Gary. Now stop being so childish and let me *go!*'

'Screw *you* then.'

He spoke without innuendo for once, letting her go savagely. She rubbed her wrist where the skin was reddening. She had forgotten how petulant and aggressive he could be.

He was great in small doses, and that was all. The fact of the matter was, she didn't even care. And it was a hell of an indictment on both of them if they were so shallow. But she didn't have the time to think about that now.

She turned back to where he was standing with arms folded in the middle of the room. The words immovable statue, seemed fairly appropriate.

'I'll call you sometime, Gary. OK?'

He shrugged and turned his back on her.

'Suit yourself. I may just be around.'

She resisted slamming the door behind her as she ran down the stairs and out to her car. He was like a flaming five-year-old when he didn't get his own way, she raged. But she knew that.

Just as she knew that her anger was keeping her excitement under control from anticipating what Nick had to tell her. And more importantly, squashing her fear about the threat in the second message on her answer machine.

She knew she should upgrade her mobile phone to one that had text on it, then she could access messages without having to listen to a voice and be scared half to death.

She was behind the times ... and she knew that some of Nick's people mocked her for not being connected to the Internet. 'Amateur detective' was how they thought of her. Well, screw them too.

Once on the road to London Alex left a message for Nick to say she would be home late that evening.

She couldn't give him any specific time, but she said she needed to see him, however late it got. His hours were irregular, anyway, and she knew he would turn up when he could. The summer traffic heading away from the coast was heavier than expected, and she had no idea how long the journey would take.

And hopefully, this whole thing could then come to an end. She was sick of the Wolstenholmes and anything to do with them. She wished she had never set foot on a certain cruise ship and opted for a weekend in Morecambe instead. She grimaced at the thought. Nothing against you, Morecambe, she added silently, but a sedate boarding house would have been ...

well, probably dead boring and full of sen cits.

She let herself inside her flat cautiously, and stood quite still for a few moments to pick up any kind of alien atmosphere, but all seemed as before except for the bundle of mail on the carpet. She picked it up quickly, and flipped through it. Mostly junk as usual. Except for the padded envelope with a Worthing postmark.

Her heart beating fast, she slit it open, and took out a smaller padded envelope inside. No expense spared, obviously. This one was also addressed to her, though it was unstamped, and her heart jumped as she recognized Moira Wolstenholme's firm handwriting. There was a small note stuck to the outside of the envelope.

'Now that the police have finished with Moira's house, May and I have been authorized to sort out the rest,' Doreen had written. 'It's a far from happy task, but someone has to do it and better someone who was a friend, than anyone else. I'm sure you would agree. You always had such a kindly aura about you, dear. Anyway, the enclosed envelope was addressed to you, so we knew you were meant to have it.'

Full marks for deduction, thought Alex, ignoring the comment about her kindly aura. The way she felt about the anonymous caller on her answer machine had her feeling anything but kindly.

Her hands were shaking as she ripped open the second envelope, hoping like mad that it wasn't going to contain more money. If it did, there would be a hell of a lot, or maybe it was something of value. Jewellery or some personal token of thanks for her services. Something that had belonged to Moira or her mother ... God, she hoped not. She didn't deserve it, since she still didn't feel she had actually done what she had been hired to do ... and she certainly didn't *want* it.

The envelope contained a video cassette. Moira had stuck a post-it note on it that simply said 'Play Me'.

Alex would have given anything not to have to play it, even though she guessed it probably held the key to the whole mystery. But a video sent after someone's death could only mean one thing. There was something nasty about to come out of the woodwork, or in this case, the video machine.

But if she wanted to know the truth, then she had no option. She pushed the cassette into her machine and switched it on. It took a few minutes for the TV to warm up and for the video to begin. As she saw Moira's face come into focus at the front of the screen, it was also obviously a home movie.

Oh God, was it going to be confession

time now? Had Moira persuaded her mother that it was time to come clean and tell the world all about their scams? There were plenty of crims who couldn't resist boasting about the way they had fooled people, and this cassette had evidently been preserved for posting until after Moira and her mother were dead.

Alex gasped as the scene settled down and came into steadier focus. The person holding the camera had either adjusted it or put it on a tripod, and there were two people on screen now. A man and a woman in bed, and they were naked.

One of them was Moira, and although the man was instantly familiar as a public figure, Alex couldn't pin-point him by name for a few seconds. Once she did, she felt a huge shock of disbelief. She had assumed Moira's lover to be someone of importance, but she would never have guessed ... who would? These people were supposed to be above the human failings of ordinary mortals.

All her instincts reacted against watching the video as it progressed, especially when the action moved away from the man's face as the person filming ensured that the viewer would be drawn to the most revolting and degrading sexual acts.

Had it been Leanora who had filmed all this filth? Alex found it almost impossible to connect the insignificant, dun-coloured woman on the cruise ship with a woman who would film her daughter in the tortuous positions the two people were getting themselves into now.

But it had to be her. It was all part of the blackmailing scam. Mother and daughter had to be in it together.

And it proved how the most seemingly innocent people could create illusions of respectability. Nothing was ever what it seemed. She had been told to always remember that.

Watching with disgust now, she saw how the man was being spread-eagled and manacled to the bed. There was a look of lecherous bliss on his face while the woman's enormous buttocks were raised to the ceiling, as she leaned over him and...

'Good God, Moira,' Alex whispered. 'Is this what it was all about? Had you and Leanora already sent him a copy of this filth too to get even more money out of him? No wonder she got stabbed and you ended up in the bloody swimming-pool.'

Her thoughts spun crazily. All this time she had thought the Wolstenholme women were blackmailing Moira's well-heeled lover on something illegal that Leanora might have had wormed out of him during her psychic readings. People usually gave away far more than they thought they did, and led the mystic into giving them apparently startling revelations.

But Alex had never thought of this. It didn't make sense that the cassette had been addressed and ready to send to her, either. Unless Leanora's psychic nonsense – which didn't seem so crazy and bizarre at this moment – had rubbed off on Moira, and persuaded her to take precautions.

So that in case anything unexpected happened to her, and she ended up as dead as her mother, they knew they could trust Alex to see that this pervert would be caught...

She switched off the video with shaking hands, unable to bear any more of it.

Nick had always told her to think laterally. And when she recalled the leering face of the man in the video, rather than any other part of his anatomy that had been exposed in all its disgusting and ageing glory, Alex forced herself to wonder why such a man would ever have got in touch with a clairvoyant in the first place.

But he wouldn't, of course. A man in his position – professionally speaking – would have had no truck with such stuff. In his business he had to deal with scientific facts, not ethereal mumbo-jumbo. So it figured that he had met Moira first, and she had introduced him to her mother's world.

He may not even have been involved as a

client at all. His name may simply have been included in Leanora's notebook as one of their blackmailing successes. Or just a possible. God, what a fool she had been not to think of it before.

She had never thought of Moira as a raving nympho, but with the video cassette still far too vivid in her mind, the word succubus came all too readily to her. She quickly pushed it out again and tried to think logically. And as laterally as Nick would. It also meant thinking backwards.

Maybe her mother's chance meeting with private eye Alex Best on a cruise ship had inspired Moira to think up this elaborate scheme to involve her. Moira had said she rarely came to London, but she had certainly seemed to know her way around. So maybe everything Moira had ever told her was a lie.

She had wanted her lover caught and put away, since he had possibly begun threatening to expose their blackmailing scam, but she had been loath to actually name him.

But once Alex had seen his face and knew his name, Moira must have known she would have to go to the police. So Moira had wanted him caught, but not through her own efforts. She had used Alex as the scapegoat. Maybe the dead flowers, and the anonymous phone calls said in that weird husky voice, had come from Moira too, and not Mister Big.

Except for that last one on the answer machine, Alex reminded herself. Moira was dead, so that couldn't have been her voice – and Alex refused to give headroom to a disembodied voice coming through the ether. She wasn't going down that road, thanks very much. But the only thing the Wolstenholmes couldn't have foreseen was that he would turn out to be a murderer. So Leanora hadn't been *that* clever a clairvoyant, Alex thought, with a ridiculous sense of satisfaction.

When she thought about the lewd video again, Alex's nickname for him had pathetic overtones in the circumstances, and anyway, she didn't need his nickname now. She knew who he was. His hated, pompous face was often prominent in the newspapers – and she wished it was all she had seen.

But there was no going back on it now. He would have to be exposed for the filth that he was. She winced at the word, but there was no other she could think of. Exposed he was, and exposed he would have to be, if only to show the world that even the most eminent and respectable of men could have a darker side to them.

For a moment she imagined the newspaper headlines once the shit hit the fan. They would be huge. Everything would have to come out. Not just that he was a hit and run murderer in a backstreet London mews, but also the mastermind behind the murders of a Worthing woman and her daughter.

And Alex would have to be involved, no matter how much she hated the thought of giving evidence. She always tried to steer clear of that kind of publicity. It didn't help her profession for everyone to know who she was, even when it proved her astuteness. In this instance, she didn't feel very bloody clever, just used.

A line from a crime novel flashed into her mind. *The private eye worked best who worked alone.* She fervently agreed. Once everyone knew who she was, people might well be wary of hiring her services. It might work the other way, but she knew she would be more than willing for the police to have all the glory in this case.

By now, Nick would know as much as she did, anyway. Well, nearly. He wouldn't have seen the video evidence she had here. But his message implied that he had traced the owner of the black Jaguar. He may already have sent his people to the man's palatial home by now, to arrest him on suspicion of murder. And the nightmare would be over.

The sound of her buzzer made her jump. She mouthed into it and the building superintendent droned from below.

'You've got a visitor, Miss Best. Shall I

send him up?'

'Yes, please,' she almost gasped, risking a small smile at the super's usual sense of reverence at her friendship with DCI Frobisher.

Thank God he was here. She had never needed him more. And once she knew that they had nailed this bastard, she could get on with the rest of her life. It no longer seemed like a pretentious line. Just a relieved one.

And the prospect of taking on future cases such as an everyday case of fraud, or tracking down a runaway teenager or two, seemed like childs' play in more ways than one.

She left her door on the latch, knowing that Nick would be up in the lift at any minute. She bent down to rewind the video cassette, meaning to hand it right over to him and never wanting to see it again. Porno movies? You could keep them!

And if that was getting soft and squeamish, so be it. It was better than being so tough that she had nothing feminine left about her. That wasn't part of the deal.

'I told you to watch your back, Miss Best.'

She heard the cultured voice at the same moment that she heard her door click shut. She turned quickly, but not quickly enough. The man was right behind her, crossing the room with amazing speed and agility for such a muscly, well-built man.

And the only thing she could think about was thanking God that she didn't still have the video running. But now that he knew he was virtually caught, he would probably have enjoyed seeing it. He would have felt proud of his prowess. He may have forced her to watch it with him, or even tried to make her re-enact what he had done with Moira ... she almost retched at the thought of that ugly, rampant flesh...

'What do you want? Who are you?' she said in a cracked voice.

He gave a throaty laugh that chilled her.

'Oh, I think you know very well who I am, Miss Best. And what I want.'

She prayed desperately that Nick would come soon, and took refuge in bravado.

'I haven't a clue what you want with me,' she snapped.

'Really. Then we'll forget my female connections for the moment and weigh up the most recent evidence. You hired a car a few days ago. A green car. You drove it to Battery Mews.'

Alex found it difficult to speak for a minute. Her pulse was beating wildly in her throat. Wildly and painfully.

'I don't know what you're talking about. I have my own car,' she croaked at last.

'I know you have. So let's just think why a

private investigator would want to hire a car, shall we?'

He was in prime prosecuting mode now. She realized that his flabby mouth was grinning, and he had clearly decided to play games with her. She thought of that mouth slavering over Moira, and shuddered the image away. Whatever Moira had done, she and her mother had done it for exploitation and money, while this man's deeds were evil, and calculatingly murderous. But she had to forget her disgust and keep him talking as long as possible. Until Nick got here.

'So you know I'm a private investigator, do you?'

He gave an aggrieved sigh. 'Don't patronize me, Miss Best. In my profession it's pathetically easy to find out such basic facts.'

'Your profession!' Alex almost spat out the words. 'You should be ashamed to even say the word, after the way you've abused it. People trust you and you shit on them.'

His eyes flashed dangerously, and she stepped back a pace until she was against the hard surface of the sideboard. To her horror she knocked the envelope with Moira's handwriting on it to the floor, but he didn't notice it. She could see the veins pumping in his neck, and wished desperately that he'd have a fatal heart attack and save everybody the trouble.

'So just what did you see at Battery Mews, Miss Best?'

'Nothing, because I wasn't there. I don't know where the hell it is. You've got the wrong person.'

He gave another elaborate sigh. 'I do hate it when people lie to me, and so many of them do. I see it all the time in my court, and my heart goes out to them, because I understand that no one wants to be there at all. But they have to be punished, of course. They have to serve their sentences, even if it means they never know freedom again.'

'And you enjoy that, don't you? You enjoy acting like God, and sentencing people to years and years of imprisonment, even if they don't deserve it. You get off on it, I suppose?'

She tried to keep up the air of bravado, but she was increasingly aware of how vulnerable she was, alone in her flat with a murderer. And where the hell was Nick?

'Oh yes,' her captor said dreamily. 'I enjoy that. Though I do wish you young people would use the Queen's English instead of these ridiculous expressions. I thought better of you, Miss Best. *Get off* on it, indeed, when what you really mean is–'

'We both know what it means, Lord Ingleby,' she snapped.

God, he was sick. As she used his name for

the first time, she saw his florid face darken even more, and who knew what was happening down below? She felt like vomiting at the thought, still with that damning video in her mind.

She must have made an expression of disgust, because his face froze again. It was like a mask now, and something like a blowtorch of fear shot through Alex.

'So what are we going to do about you, little lady?' he said, his voice suddenly soft with menace.

He moved slowly towards her, and to Alex's dilated eyes, he seemed to fill the entire space in the room, and she shrank back even more. He was a murderer, and he wouldn't hesitate to add her to his list of victims.

'Look, Lord Ingleby–'

'Yes, you know who I am,' he snarled, his manner changing with the speed of light. 'And much good it will do you, slut. You're all the same–'

'I'm not the only one who knows about you! The police are on to you, and they've got plenty of evidence about you and Harold Dawes, and about Moira and her mother and the way you manipulated people to do what you wanted, including that poor Trevor Unwin–'

'Ah yes, Moira,' he said, his ferrety eyes glittering, and ignoring all the rest. 'It was a pity she had to go. She was very amenable to my needs. But then she and her mother became greedy, and I had my reputation to think about. They were threatening to ruin me, and I couldn't allow that.'

'So you killed her, just as you killed her mother.'

'I didn't kill either of them, Miss Best. You should get your facts correct before you risk a libel action.'

'Really? And are you going to take me to court?' Alex said, her lips chattering as she saw him take a thin cord out of his pocket and twist it in his hands almost lovingly.

'That won't be necessary.'

She tensed herself as he came near, his arms raised in readiness for twining the cord around her neck. It was going to happen, and if Nick didn't arrive soon, there was nothing she could do to stop it.

But from somewhere in the depths of her terror Alex remembered her long-ago course of karate. She hadn't used it for a very long time, and she knew she would be rusty now, but she was young and strong, and he was bulky and out of condition, as she well knew from his video.

As he neared her, she jabbed two rigid fingers straight into his neck, and as he grunted she punched her other fist into his groin with all her strength and heard him howl with pain as he doubled up.

She was still wearing her driving shoes, and she gave him a vicious kick on the shin. He didn't seem to know which tender part of him to grab first.

But he wasn't done with her yet, and he crawled on all fours towards her, cornering her.

'*Bitch*,' he yelled, losing all semblance of lordly gentility. 'You stinking, mother-fucking bitch! You're like all the rest of them, only good for one thing. And I'll have you yet, one way or another.'

Alex doubted that he'd be able to do anything at all with his genitals after she had fisted him, but she realised he was stronger than she would have believed.

And she was still alone with him, and he still had that cord dangling in his hand. Almost wetting herself with fear, in desperation she grabbed a heavy china vase from the sideboard and flung it at his head. It splintered at once, and a trail of blood trickled down his cheek.

He shook his head, momentarily dazed, but nothing seemed to stop him. She heard her own sobs, deep inside her, and then she was screaming at him.

'You'll never get away with it, you bastard. Every newspaper in the country will hear about a high court judge who was nothing more than a filthy pervert—'

Her legs seemed to have turned to water.

It wasn't just a fictional phrase then, she thought hysterically. It actually did feel like that. And then she felt swift humiliation as she knew what the hot wetness between her legs really was. He had reduced her to this, she sobbed, and she slid down against the wall as he crawled towards her.

He had the twisted cord in his hands now, and she knew she would be unable to stop him. It was fade-out time ... and the sobs became a thick whimpering in her throat, like that of a cornered animal.

They both heard the violent kicks on her door at the same time, and then it burst open, and her entire glazed vision was suddenly filled with people in uniform, rushing inside the flat and hauling the bastard to his feet and away from her.

Outside in the hallway, the building superintendent was goggle-eyed and scared. Neighbours were craning their necks to see what was going on, and being hustled away. And one man was striding towards her and holding her tight, as if he would never let her go...

'*Nick*,' she sobbed hysterically. 'Oh God, Nick, I thought you were never going to get here – you don't know – oh, you don't know–'

'Hush, sweetheart, it's all over.' His voice was harsh against her hair. 'As soon as we traced the bastard's car number from your photos, the rest of it followed. The Worthing police had done a good job, and forensics supplied the last bit of evidence to nail him. He'll spend the rest of his natural behind bars.'

'I'd do more than that to him,' she sobbed. 'I'd string him up by his—'

'I'll bet you would,' Nick said, the smallest hint of a smile in his voice now. 'That's why I thank God you're on my side, darling.'

She said nothing for a moment. She was still held tightly in his arms, vaguely realizing that everyone else was leaving, and that her door was being dragged shut. Presumably there were other people to deal with matters from now on, while Nick had elected to stay behind and take her statement.

It would have to be done, of course, she thought, trying desperately to pull herself back to reality and remember that she was still a professional with a job to conclude. And hoping that she never got another one like this one.

'You'll want to know about everything that's been happening,' she mumbled. 'I've held out on you for too long, Nick, and I'm sorry about that, but my client—'

'Your client was a high-class call girl, Alex,' he told her calmly.

She gasped, and jerked away from him to stare into his face.

'Moira? You don't mean Moira?' she said stupidly, because of course he did, since she was her current client.

'That's how she got to know Lord Ingleby in the first place, and her sweet little old mother was a madam in more than one sense of the word. She took everybody in, and between them they had a high old blackmailing scam going. But they reached too far when they tried getting extortionate sums out of a high court judge. He had far too many contacts to be worried by them at first, and plenty of money to hire his minions to do his dirty work for him.'

'Until he decided to run down Harold Dawes himself,' she said, shivering at the memory.

'Harold Dawes made the fatal mistake of letting Ingleby know of his drinking habits. He discovered that Dawes started bragging about all the money for drink that was available whenever he wanted it and hinting at his sources. That was when Ingleby decided he had to go.'

Alex shuddered. 'I can hardly believe it. They all led double lives. If you had seen Leanora on the cruise, and the major too – Harold Dawes. I mean. You'd never have believed either of them could be so evil. Nor Moira. I trusted her completely, and I should have known better. You always warned me that people are not always what they seem, didn't you?' she said bitterly.

'They rarely are, sweetheart.'

'The one I really feel sorry for is Trevor Unwin.'

'Good God, why feel sorry for that low-life? He stabbed your Madame L. to death, and a right hatchet job he made of it. It couldn't have been pleasant.'

'I doubt that any murder victim finds it pleasant! But if there's any justification in it at all, I happen to know he did it for the sake of his mother, to give her some comfort in a genteel nursing home for the rest of her days.'

As he looked at her sceptically, she risked a small smile, surprised to find that her lips could still move in an upward direction at all.

'There's a hell of a lot you don't know, Nick, and it will be a huge relief now to tell you all of it. But I think it ought to wait a little while longer. I really need to take a shower and get into some different clothes.'

'I think that would be a good idea. I wondered where the smell was coming from. It's not your usual fragrance, darling.'

Oh God, he knew that too.

But if she thought he was losing interest in her because she had done the unforgiveable and peed herself, she knew it didn't matter a damn as his arms folded around her again, and his voice was rough with real affection as he spoke against her cheek.

'Do you think any of it bothers me, Alex? Just to know you're safe is all that matters. And rather than a shower, you'd do better to soak in a warm bath to get rid of tension. Stay right where you are and I'll run it for you,' he ordered.

She did as she was told. She had no strength to do otherwise. But the sense of relief was so overwhelming that by the time she had stripped off her clothes and stepped into the warm bath Nick had filled for her, she washed quickly, and then she simply sat in the soapy water with her knees up to her chin and her arms wrapped tightly around them, and wept.

'Right, so now that's all done, let's have you out of there,' she heard him say briskly a few minutes later.

He held out a bath towel, wrapped her inside it and began gently patting her dry. There wasn't a single overtone of sexuality in the action, and she blessed him for it.

Now wasn't the time for love. But she did love him. She had always loved him – and she knew that in her highly emotional state she could be in danger of mixing love and gratitude. She owed him her life, but her emotions were too acute right now to sort out her true feelings, and she knew he wouldn't press it. But she had to say something.

'Nick, you know how grateful I am – and I know how bloody feeble that sounds. But you must be aware how overwhelmed I'm feeling – and that if you hadn't arrived when you did–'

'I know. Like the cavalry coming over the hill, as usual. Of course I know how you're feeling, so you needn't try to explain. Just relax, Alex. And I'm not leaving you alone tonight, so if you've got any objections to that, say so now and I'll arrange for a WPC to stay with you.'

She managed a second smile. Things were looking up.

'Are you kidding? Since when did I ever prefer a WPC to my own special bodyguard? And please don't say anything about it being a pretty special body to guard,' she pleaded.

'Good,' he said. 'Then coffee's next on the agenda, and something to eat. I can manage an omelette, though I'm not much good at making anything else. I don't know about you, but using up all that adrenaline makes me ravenous.'

'I'm hungry too,' Alex said, realizing that she was. It seemed hours since she had eaten anything, and she had missed out on dinner with Gary in what seemed like another lifetime.

'You see to the coffee and I'll make the omelette,' she said. 'It's my kitchen, remember?'

'Yes, ma'am. I never pretended to be good husband material, anyway.'

'Oh, I wouldn't say that,' Alex told him. 'You'll make some girl a great husband one of these days.'

'Is that a proposal?'

'No. Just a bit of psychic prediction. You forget I've had a basinful of it in the last few months.'

She gave a small shiver, but already she was starting to get things into perspective. She was here and she was alive, and the case was as good as over. At least the man at the root of it was going to be brought to justice, and it seemed a sweet twist of fate that a high court judge was finally going to get a taste of his own medicine.

This particular one was notorious for doling out unnecessarily vicious and heavy sentences, which was why anyone coming into his court was always extra fearful of their fate. And his cases always got lurid prominence in the press by reporters only too willing to show their contempt for his methods. They were certainly going to have a field day now, and she was *glad*.

'Laying ghosts, Alex?' Nick said quietly, and she realized she had been staring into space for the last few minutes. The smell of percolating coffee began to waft into her nostrils, hot and sensual, and also blessedly normal.

'Just a few,' she admitted. 'Ingleby was the real villain, but those two women—' she shook her head slowly. 'I never thought I could be so taken in by anyone. But it seems I've still got a lot to learn about people.'

'It happens to all of us. It's always them against us. Haven't you discovered that yet? The crims think they can get away with it, and even the good guys will screw us any way they can. Let it go, darling. Tomorrow's another day.'

She started to laugh. 'That was *almost* straight out of *Gone With the Wind*, Nick.'

'Was it?' he grinned. 'I wasn't feeling particularly romantic, but I can always be persuaded. Maybe we could take out the video and watch it together.'

Her laughter faded. 'Maybe. But let's leave that for another day too. There's another video you need to watch first, and I think I'll leave you to it while I make the omelette.'

She couldn't bear to watch it again. Especially not with him. He was a decent man who often had a rotten job to do, and she had always known that porno movies were definitely not for her. She didn't think he would relish them, either.

She had drunk a much-needed mug of black coffee and was still breaking eggs into a bowl and whisking them half-heartedly when he came into the kitchen a short while later.

'I've seen enough,' he said in a clipped voice. 'And you can forget any sense of outrage on the Wolstenholmes' behalf, Alex. Any woman who can film her daughter like that isn't worth a rag, and nor is the daughter who was willing to be filmed. They're both as perverted as Ingleby.'

'I know,' Alex said.

'So now can we put it all behind us and *eat?*'

As he spoke, Alex felt her stomach rumble. Her father used to tease her, saying that the day she refused food would be the day she gave up living. And this wasn't the day. This definitely wasn't the day. This was the first day of the rest of her life. And if she didn't stop thinking in these bloody cringe-making clichés, she was going to turn into a smirking Stepford wife. She spoke quickly.

'I've got some frozen chips in the freezer. Fancy them to go with the omelette? They'll only take five minutes in the microwave, and they'll be ready by the time I've finished with these eggs.'

'Then what are you waiting for, woman?' Nick said.

Without warning she gave an enormous yawn. She was so tired she could hardly see straight, but she knew she needed food before anything else. And then she needed her bed, more than she had ever needed it before.

'Sleep with me, Nick,' she said abruptly.

'Hey, I intend to,' he said, and then he paused. 'Was there any doubt about that?'

'Well, there was always the sofa. But I mean *sleep* with me and nothing else. I need to feel your arms around me, and to wake up tomorrow knowing that you're still there. I need to feel safe.'

'And you think that will happen with me?' he teased her with a touch of the old arrogance in his voice. 'You trust me that much?'

'I do,' she said solemnly. 'For tonight, anyway. And as you said, tomorrow's another day.'

'Is that another prediction?'

'Maybe. Or a promise. But don't count on it. I'm not into seeing into the future.'

But she was smiling as she said it.

The publishers hope that this book has given you enjoyable reading. Large Print Books are especially designed to be as easy to see and hold as possible. If you wish a complete list of our books please ask at your local library or write directly to:

Magna Large Print Books
Magna House, Long Preston,
Skipton, North Yorkshire.
BD23 4ND

This Large Print Book, for people
who cannot read normal print,
is published under the auspices of

THE ULVERSCROFT FOUNDATION